Clare Jay's short stories and p... appeared in anthologies. She has and tutors the subject at unive... 'Dreaming into writing' workshops at international conferences and has lived in five European countries and travelled extensively in South-East Asia. *Breathing in Colour* is her first novel.

Visit Clare at: www.clarejay.com

Breathing
in
Colour

Clare Jay

PIATKUS

First published in Great Britain as a paperback original in 2009
by Piatkus Books

A CIP catalogue record for this book
is available from the British Library.

ISBN 978-0-7499-2978-7

Typeset in Times by Action Publishing Technology Ltd, Gloucester
Printed and bound in Great Britain by Clays Ltd, St Ives plc

Papers used by Piatkus Books are natural, renewable and recyclable
products made from wood grown in sustainable forests and certified
in accordance with the rules of the Forest Stewardship Council.

Mixed Sources
Product group from well-managed
forests and other controlled sources
www.fsc.org Cert no. SGS-COC-004081
© 1996 Forest Stewardship Council

Piatkus Books
An imprint of
Little, Brown Book Group
100 Victoria Embankment
London EC4Y 0DY

An Hachette Livre UK Company
www.hachettelivre.co.uk

www.piatkus.co.uk

For my family and friends
and for Markus, who walks with me through the world
and knows its beauty

Acknowledgements

Many people have supported me in the writing of *Breathing in Colour*, which was originally written as part of the Creative Writing PhD which I completed in 2007 at the University of Leeds. The thesis title was 'The Role of Lucid Dreaming in the Process of Creative Writing', and my appreciation goes to my earliest readers and advisors: Dr Sita Popat, Dr Harriet Tarlo, Dr Steve Keane, Rob Watson, Dr David Steel, Dr Jenny Newman, Dr Terry Gifford.

I am indebted to the International Association for the Study of Dreams (IASD); they have published my research, presented me with awards, exhibited my lucid dream collages, and invited me to give paper presentations and my 'Dreaming into Creative Writing' workshops at their annual conferences. Special thanks to Dr Beverly D'Urso, Jean Campbell, Robert Waggoner, Richard Russo, Dr Ed Kellogg. My sincere thanks goes to all those who have generously shared the imagery, sensations, and emotions of their lucid dreams with me.

Warmest thanks to my agent, Jane Conway-Gordon, my editor, Emma Beswetherick, and the team at Piatkus, all of whom worked so hard to get this book out on the shelves and looking fabulous. Clio Gray from HISSAC, Merric

Davidson from *The New Writer*, and Dr Jan Fortune-Wood of Cinnamon Press gave me encouragement when my short stories and poetry won prizes in their competitions. The Open University has been highly supportive of my writing.

Love and thanks to my treasured friends in Totnes, London, Germany, France, Portugal, Spain, Italy, and the States, who help to make life beautiful. You know who you are! A huge thank you goes to my mother Penny, who has passed on to me her fascination for languages and literature, and my father Martyn, who has passed on the travel bug. My sister and brothers, Diana, Roger, and Bryan, encourage me with their belief that I can do anything I set out to do in life – a belief which I also hold about them. Finally, I would like to thank my husband, Markus: he is my first reader, my valued critic, and my love.

Chapter One

The night she learned of her daughter's disappearance, Alida's head was full of the past.

Sleep had eluded her for hours, and although she was still in her bedroom, she was sitting on the swivel chair at her desk in front of the bay window, her hair falling forwards in loose, dark spirals as she looked at the object she held in her hands. Her slender knees were drawn up to her chest and she had pulled on her oldest cardigan, which was made of raw silk fibres knotted together in shades of red. Years ago, she had slipped it on to keep her warm while she breastfed. Wearing it reminded her of simpler times. The bedroom was filled with amber shadows from the bedside lamp, and through a crack in the curtains the sky was beginning to lighten. Three floors down, the occasional car rumbled past as London began to stir.

In her hands, Alida was holding a four-inch long treasure chest originally made of cardboard, but unidentifiable as such due to the profusion of sequins glued to every surface, gold, silver, green, so that even after more than a dozen years, the little box shimmered. Mia had presented her with it one Mother's Day before she turned six, before their world changed beyond recognition.

Alida recalled Mia's stripy scarf trailing to the ground, her smile almost too wide for her small face as she ran towards her across the playground and thrust the treasure chest – still sticky in places – into her hands.

'These are the stars we catch before I go to sleep,' Mia had announced, her eyes ablaze with pride as she pointed at the sequins. 'When the pink ones sparkle, they fizz in my mouth like sherbet.'

Her talented, multi-sensory daughter. Whenever a sequin dropped off, Alida would stick it back on with Superglue so that now the chest had a smooth, tight carapace, broken by the protrusion of sequin edges when she ran her finger over it. The chest, more Superglue now than cardboard, had become a permanent feature on Alida's desk. More than any other object, it evoked the happiest moments of her life; the time when she, Ian and Mia had formed a tight circle of love and anything had seemed possible.

As usual, Alida tried to shift her thoughts away from the event that had destroyed their happy balance. Closing her eyes, she tipped her head back to ease her neck muscles. In her mind's eye, she saw an image of a man with a silver disc in place of a head standing in a yellow desert. The sun flashed off the disc. It was something she had dreamed earlier that night; one of the many disconnected but highly real dreams she'd had before emerging from sleep altogether. The disc-headed man had been holding Mia's treasure chest in one of his hands, she remembered now. And in the open palm of his other hand had lain a baby with curled fists and carved, still features. He had stretched both arms out to Alida in invitation, as if asking her to make a choice.

The telephone shrilled; a shocking sound in the silence which caused Alida to swivel quickly around in her chair to stare at it. Instantly, she thought of Mia. She had only telephoned once in all the many weeks that she'd been travelling in India, but Alida was ever hopeful. Perhaps Mia had mixed up the time difference and that's why she was calling so very early.

2

Or perhaps she was in some kind of trouble.

Putting the treasure chest hastily back on her desk, Alida jumped to her feet and scrambled across the bed. She picked up the phone on her bedside table on the second ring.

'Hello?'

At first, the only word she even half understood was 'madam'. Her first confused thought was that if the disc-headed man had a mouth to open, he too would speak in this exotic jumble of sounds and call her madam in a voice as rich as treacle. But as the plastic casing of her phone pressed coolly against her cheek, the caller's words separated from the accent which wound around them and hung in the air like a threat.

Alida jerked her body upright.

'Who are you?' she demanded. 'What's happened?'

Now the man's voice scraped through her ears like gravel. As Alida listened, the hand holding the telephone tightened until the knuckles strained at the skin.

'India, you say?'

Her voice was high and anxious. 'Yes, Mia Salter is my daughter, but what . . .? Her passport? Gone missing? I'm sorry, you'll have to speak more clearly, there's such a bad echo. Which is missing, the passport or my daughter? Oh my God. Eight days? No, no, she hasn't contacted me . . . The morgue? What are you suggesting? Are you trying to tell me you think my daughter is dead? . . . Dead, I said . . . My God, do you really think she. . . A pen, yes. Wait, let me just . . . OK, ready. Case file number . . . got it. Madurai, southern India . . . Guru? That's the name of the hotel? Hotel Guru. Room seven. I'll take the next possible plane . . . Yes, I realise that, but she could be hurt, she might need help, she might be lying senseless in a ditch somewhere . . . I *am* calm, but how would you feel if it were your daughter? . . . I said how would you . . . I understand. I'll be there as soon as I can. I'll find her.'

Alida's hands were shaking too badly for her to slot the cordless telephone back onto its stand. Instead she slid it onto the bedside table and stared frozen-eyed into the orange glow of her nightlight. Her mind flashed with accident scenes: concertinaed train carriages, turned-over buses. Bloodied tarmac. In the warm light, the worry grooves on Alida's narrow face were softened and her eyes, deep and dark, were Mia's.

'Daughter is lost,' the Indian policeman had said with a shrug in his voice as if advising her not to waste her airfare. 'Find her cannot guarantee.'

Alida could taste bile at the back of her throat. The bedroom around her seemed vast; she felt shrunken. 'Not again,' she whispered.

'Many foreigners go missing,' the policeman had said. 'Often we find them well and alive. But accidents also are possible. Then unhappily we find them in the morgue.' In the aching space behind her eyelids, Alida could feel the memories escalating into grief and rage as they had done before.

Her bedroom was steeped in expectant silence. 'I'm not going to cry,' she muttered. 'It can't be too late.'

The curtains were momentarily parted as a waft of air tumbled in from the night and rolled across the wooden floor. Its coolness enveloped Alida like a shroud as she sat on the bed, so that she curled her toes up and shivered.

I'm going to India, she thought, and in one smooth motion she gathered her limbs and leaped from the bed.

Still trembling, blinking away the stars floating in her vision, Alida stood barefoot on the floor and tried to think rationally. She switched on the main light and flung open her wardrobe. A life-sized baby doll slid onto the polished wooden floorboards. She picked it up by its soft belly and crammed it back into her workbag, leaving ten plastic toes and a bald head visible above the leather rim. Pushed against the back of the wardrobe was the old-fashioned brown suitcase which had once belonged to her father. When the case was lying open on the bed, Alida realised she didn't know where to begin. What would she need in India? On the duvet, she made a comforting pile of make-up and shampoo. She picked out a pair of low-heeled sandals. Then she saw the framed head-and-shoulders photograph of Mia which she kept on her bedside table. As she picked up the delicate silver frame, she had a disconcerting image of herself traipsing through the streets of India, showing people the picture and explaining that this was her lost daughter.

In the photograph, Mia was standing under a tree in Hyde Park on a blue January morning. The wind had loosened her corkscrew curls of dark hair so that individual strands snaked around her face, which was rosy with cold. Mia had a theory that on windy days she and her mother both ended up looking like Medusas, their hair whipped into a halo of snakes. Her eyes, caught in the wintry sunshine, were dark gold beneath strong, curved eyebrows and her wide mouth rocked with laughter as she breathed out a big white cloud of cold air. That day, the tensions which spiked the two of them apart had momentarily subsided, and they had fallen into step like experienced dance partners. 'Take a picture of my cloudy white breath flying away from me on the wind,' Mia had said. Alida had taken several, with Mia laughing as she tried to make different shaped clouds. The picture had been taken eighteen months ago, when she had just turned seventeen. Alida tipped it gently into her handbag.

She had to tell Mia's father. His most recent address wouldn't be written inside Mia's passport, which was where the police must have found her own contact details. Would it be acceptable, she wondered, if she just emailed him from India with the news? Sighing, she retrieved the telephone from the edge of her bedside table.

'What?' complained a husky female voice after three rings.

5

'Maggie, it's Alida. I need to speak to Ian.' She could hear the wobble in her voice, and frowned.

'At half five in the morning?' But she was already handing the telephone over. Alida pictured Ian's crumpled, unshaved face, his dirty-blond hair flopping over his eyebrows and the bright blue of his eyes blinking awake.

''Lida. Something wrong?'

'It's Mia.' Alida bit her lip, her feet freezing on the floor. 'I got a call. She's in India.' To her dismay, her voice tripped up on the word India and tears started to slide from her eyes.

'I know she is,' said Ian impatiently. 'It's been three months now, hasn't it?' His voice was ragged around the edges, as if he'd had too much to drink the previous night. 'What did she say?'

'Nothing, I didn't speak to her.' Alida coughed to get the lump out of her throat. 'It was a policeman.' Teardrops were rolling off her cheeks and landing in hot splashes on her vest top.

'What?' Now Ian's voice was sharp with concern. 'What the hell did he say?'

'He... Mia's lost.'

'Lost? Alida, *stop* crying for one second and give me the details.'

'I'm sorry, I'm just ... She didn't pay her hotel room for a week and the police found her passport but nobody's seen her and I don't even know if they're looking properly because he said there were no guarantees and just talked about morgues, although sometimes they do find foreigners alive and well, he said, but when he said the word "morgue" something burst inside me because I could see her, I could see—'

'You're completely incoherent. I'm coming over.'

The line went dead.

Alida laid the telephone face down on the bed. She closed her eyes and saw Mia stretched out like a paper doll on the coroner's table. Images arched across her mind, as short-lived and as mesmerising as fireworks. Ian, hurling a Moroccan vase across the sitting room of the house they had once shared, his eyes slits of fury as it shattered against the wall. A beautiful baby with curling eyelashes and chafed red skin on her chest. Mia huddled naked on a stone floor while her kidnappers debated whether to rape her again or slit her throat. Then she saw the disc-headed man from her dream. He was standing up again in the desert, his fists closed this time. He was only there for a second, but he was very real. His skin gleamed brown in the sunlight. When he vanished, Alida opened her eyes and forced herself to think. Ian's job as a computer systems analyst took him to North London four out of five days a week, but he lived nearby. He would be there in fifteen minutes, filling her flat with the smell of his over-sweet aftershave and issuing orders. She walked into her dolphin-tiled bathroom and splashed cold water over her face. When she returned to the bedroom she dialled Ian's mobile number.

'Don't bother coming round,' she told him calmly, sitting down on the bed.

'Why not?'

'I'd rather just speak to you on the phone,' she said, lifting her chilly feet from the floor and drawing her knees up to her chest.

'I'm practically on my way out of the door already,' he protested.

Alida stifled a sigh. 'I don't want you to come round.'

Ian's voice hardened. 'Look, our daughter is in Christ knows what trouble, and I'm coming over to discuss it with you. Like it or not.'

'No, Ian,' she said firmly, drawing the edges of her cardigan over her toes. Tough gold crackles of embroidery thread spiked through the weave and she twisted them together between forefinger and thumb. 'I have a lot to organise. I'm going to India to look for her, you see.'

There was a pause.

'You're *what*?'

'I'm going to find her.'

'The idea of you in India is laughable. What would someone like you be able to do for anyone in a country like that?'

'What's that supposed to mean?' Her tone was dismissive, but she was hurt.

'It means, Alida, that you're the kind of woman who refuses to go camping because she's worried about insects coming into the bloody tent. If you can't even sleep in a tent, how do you think you'll survive on your own in a place like that? You're just not up to it.'

Alida's free hand gripped the edge of the bed. It pained her that even during such a conversation as this – the conversation no parent ever wants to have – they still found it hard to be civil: Ian undermining her at the first opportunity, her biting back retorts which would lead to a row. Not for the first time, she reflected that there was an unbearable intimacy to sharing a tragedy with another person. Together, she and Ian had discovered that life could give with one hand then snatch away with the other, leaving them limbless, blank with despair. Even now, the two of them couldn't look at each other without glimpsing, with dread, the private pain ingrained in the other's face. They protected themselves by keeping their contact with each other minimal and bordering on animosity.

'You won't go,' Ian said into her silence, 'so I won't waste my breath talking about it.' Then, as if he realised he'd been too harsh, a conciliatory note crept into his voice and it took on the warm rumble that Alida had once loved. 'Look, 'Lida, if you really don't want me coming to the flat, then just give me all the details again. Tell me everything that policeman said. Every word of it.'

When they had finished, Alida sat staring at the bedroom

door. Talking with Ian had made Mia's disappearance real. He was going to make some calls, he said, to the British Embassy and to the police station in Madurai, to get the ball rolling. If need be, he would fly out there himself. Neither of them had referred again to Alida's statement that she was going to look for Mia. She got up and went to her desk, which was awash with papers. Scribbled notes and word clusters lay side by side with A4 transparencies featuring genital warts. Alida juggled jobs ranging from proof-reading to working as an English teacher in a language centre, and she had been lecturing teenagers and pre-teens on the risks of unprotected sex for seven years in London schools. The programmable baby dolls she took along to the sex education classes always created interest, and having had Mia when she was only nineteen, Alida was well equipped to discuss the issues involved with early motherhood. She opened the top drawer and scooped up her passport and emergency credit card. Today was 19 July 2008, and her passport was valid for two more years.

Alida connected to the internet and found an open return flight from Heathrow to Madurai with Gulf Air and then Indian Airlines, stopping in Dubai and Bombay. It cost seven hundred pounds, which she would have to dig out of her savings account next month to pay off the credit card bill. The journey would take eighteen and a half hours, and she was flying at five that afternoon. Heathrow was an easy tube ride from South Kensington, but she would book a taxi to the station. She was about to stand up when her stomach twisted in panic. A visa, she thought. I'll need a bloody visa. She Googled 'Indian embassy visa' and found the High Commission of India website. *Passport photos*, she scribbled. *Visa fee*. She could pick one up from India House that morning.

By the time nine o'clock came along, Alida was fully packed. She sat cross-legged on the bed next to her suit-case, wrapping up the details of her life. At this moment

9

she didn't care about proof-reading deadlines or piles of bills mounting on her doorstep, but her mind was rushing ahead in full organisation mode, and she gave it free rein. She couldn't bear the idea of sitting and doing nothing – every action had to have meaning, had to constitute a step in the direction of finding Mia. She cancelled her classes and lectures for the next month. She left messages on her friends' answerphones explaining the situation and asking them to email her. She organised a direct debit with her electricity and telephone companies.

Finally, she broke the news to her mother and listened to her crying down the phone.

'Do you remember,' said her mother eventually, 'the day after her second birthday, when she removed her dirty nappy by herself and clouted poor Ian around the head with it as he lay in the grass trying to sunbathe?'

'She's not dead,' Alida said more brutally than she intended. 'Not dead, only lost. Temporarily misplaced. Please don't talk about her as if she were dead and all we have left are memories.'

'What'll I do if you don't come back either?' Her mother was quietly desperate. 'Get on a flight out there and get lost myself?' Alida nestled the phone closer to her ear and closed her eyes briefly in sympathy because she knew how hard it was to speak your greatest fears aloud. 'What's the good of us all following each other like sheep over a precipice?' she continued, and Alida knew she would be gripping the phone hard with her bejewelled fingers, leaning forwards on the sofa, her brown eyes sharp with the pain of this news. 'Let the police do their job. You won't know where to start. Do you realise how many people live in that country?'

She went on in the same vein for fifteen minutes, prodding at her fears until she had shaped them into something she could bear to look at. Alida listened patiently. In contrast with Ian's instant dismissal of her travel plans, her mother accepted her departure. She understood about the memories.

When Alida eventually allowed herself the time for a shower, the strong beat of the water revived her, stinging her nipples to hardness. She closed her eyes and let water stream over her face. She was counting, working something out. A few tears escaped from her eyes and were washed away. By the time she stepped steaming from the shower, Alida had finished her calculation.

She had not seen Mia for eighty-nine days and seventeen hours.

Chapter Two

Thursday, 15 May 2008

This is quite a daring thing I'm doing – travelling alone aged eighteen and a half through a country so full that it reminds me of my first time in the sea as a three-year-old in a floppy sunhat and my Pink Panther swimming costume. I waded in up to my waist holding my father's hand, and I gasped and gasped at the cold salt pushing into and around me, the gelatinous seaweed sliming up through my toes, the sunlight splashing so brightly on the tips of the waves that I heard musical notes as I watched. My father asked if I was enjoying myself and I couldn't respond. The velveteen foam, the thorny cries of the gulls, the cold potato grasp of his hand: these things took up all the spaces of my mind. Entering the sea was all-round sensory submersion and it turned me into a walking jelly. Being here is the same. I feel that no part of me can close itself off from India; it enters me from all around and, wholly submerged, I float in it, drown in it, sleep and dream and cry in it.

I've been here for three and a half weeks, and for the past ten days I've been having astonishing dreams. The dreams are full of the past. They show me in bright, alive images things that have been holding their breath in a corner of my mind for most of my life. The memories are different weights and shapes, and almost all of them scald me. I want to nail them to the page so that I can look at them without flinching. That's what this notebook is for.

Christmas 1995

Their voices slice up through my bed until the mattress is studded with pins which prickle my skin. She is half crying, half shouting. His chocolaty voice is trying to cram her words back into her mouth but they spill out in shards. I climb down onto the floor. Now the pins are in the carpet, puncturing the soles of my feet. I tiptoe painfully onto the landing. Here, it is much louder.

'. . . not in control any more. The whole thing could just fly apart, don't you get it?' she cries.

I kneel silently on the carpet and push my face between the banisters to hear better. The cool wood on my cheeks makes a comforting frame.

'You're collapsing into yourself, Alida. Who's that going to help?'

Her low, furious reply drills the air and turns it smoky grey. On my tongue, there's the faintest taste of ashes. I look down so that my eyes are almost closed, and swivel my gaze to the left. I can see the bottom of the sitting room door. It's half open, but they are beyond my vision.

'. . . no support. All you're interested in is getting our sex life back on track, as if that's the answer to everything.'

I edge further forwards and my ears burn against the wood.

'You can't shut yourself off from pleasure for the rest of your life.'

'Pleasure? Do you really think pleasure still exists for me in any way or form?'

My head pops through the banisters and the pressure eases off my ears. I can see further into the sitting room now. I can see the crackling green branches of the Christmas tree. The fairy lights are switched off. I can see the lower half of my mother as she sits in the armchair by the window. Her pale shins protrude from her dressing gown. Her hands are twisted into a bony sculpture which rests uneasily on her lap.

'Don't let what happened distance you from Mia.'

I listen intently, but I don't catch her murmured reply. There's a long pause. Too long. They must be getting tired. Any minute now they'll leave the sitting room and discover that I'm not in bed. I pull my head sharply back but the banisters grip it from either side. I push forwards, pull back. How could my head have grown bigger so fast? I pull until it hurts but still I can't get back through.

I'm here for good.

They'll have to feed me through the banisters, bring me a potty to wee in. Tears cut across my eyes and I consider calling down to them for help but my mother's voice wobbles through the door.

'... nonsense she comes out with, Ian. Recently she insisted that when the blackbirds sang in the garden, she could see golden bubbles coming out of their beaks. She's six years old and she talks as if she's taken LSD. If she weren't so caught up in her own little world, then perhaps—'

I scream, loud and wide. My scream tastes of vomity burps. It fractures the air in the hall.

They come running, orange and blue bounding up the stairs side by side.

'Stuck!' I screech, and blood slams through the veins in my head.

My father puts his hands on his hips and laughs in a shower of colour, but she pauses on the stairs with her hand at her throat. Her eyes are fixed on my face. She knows I heard her unfinished sentence. She knows I completed it in my mind and that it has already become part of me.

I continue to wail while my father soaps my ears to make them slippery and coaxes my head back through the

14

banisters. When my mother moves forwards to fold me into her arms, I don't let her touch me.

Spring 1996

I can be invisible.

I can disappear along the thin sigh of my breath, grow so quiet and still that I am not even sure I exist any more.

The gap between the double bed and the floor was just wide enough for me to slide into, shifting crablike until I reached the centre. My chest grazes the underside of the bed at the crest of every breath. I am a star-shaped spy, my fingers and heels making friends with the dust. How long have these soft balls of fluff lain here and what secrets have they heard my parents whisper?

Alida – that's what I call her nowadays, because the word 'Mummy' flays her face open like a slap – Alida is making the bed.

I drop my eyes sideways and watch her bare feet step nimbly as she tweaks and plumps. The cherry-red polish on her toenails is chipped. Her thoughts are far away from me, struggling through memories she cannot bear to remember or forget. She doesn't sense the tickle of my fingertips on the carpet. She doesn't hear the muffled booming of my heart.

Very soon I will be nothing more than a star-shaped scattering of fluff.

When I was a baby, my mother was a carousel of colours, the most dazzling thing I had ever seen. She smelled of milky vanilla love. She bounced and turned like the clown mobile above my cot. She spread warmth around me in orange layers and her hands comforted and played. If she vanished from sight for too long, I screwed up my fists and eyes and screamed myself purple. When she reappeared, relief would flood my nappy in a lava spurt of urine. She was everything to me, a giant with a giant's strength.

15

Now she is different. She has shrunk and her eyes don't laugh in streams of sparks. I want to be small again, but every day I grow bigger and she grows further away.

When he knelt by my bed to kiss me goodnight, Daddy said he might have to go away soon. His tie flopped onto my chest and I held it with both hands. It was slippery red and green stripes.

'Where away?' I asked. When he sighed, I tasted ashes on my tongue. I stared at him then, wide awake. Thin red threads trembled across the whites of his eyes. 'Don't go away,' I said. He laid his head on my chest and seemed to fall asleep. I clutched his tie and tried to count the hairs sprouting from his ear. His head was heavy and I didn't know what to do so I just said it again and again in a smashed glass voice.

'Don't go away.'

Chapter Three

The taxi was speeding through a stream of vehicles whose horns spanned several octaves. Alida was sitting tensely in the back with her fingers clamped tightly around the leather handle of her suitcase. Her brown eyes were darker than usual; the pupils wide due to her deep tiredness. She had pulled her shoulder-length brown hair into a loose ponytail and spiral tendrils sprang out around her scalp and clung damply to her cheeks and forehead. Her jade-green blouse flapped listlessly in the breeze coming through the open window, but despite this the heat didn't leave her skin. Her driver, a man in his forties with bony wrists and an extravagant moustache, seemed unaware that there were cyclists, carts, lorries and motorised rickshaws eddying around him. He sat low in his seat with his foot firmly on the accelerator and his eyes, Alida noted with alarm, were drooping closed. Was he about to fall asleep? She leaned forwards.

'Are you all right?' she demanded.

Without reducing his speed, he twisted his head around to look at her solemnly for a moment.

'No, please just—' She gestured helplessly at the windscreen. 'Just watch the road.'

He switched his gaze back to the road and she saw that his eyelids were open a fraction wider than before. That was something. She sat back in resignation and eased the window open. The handle was sticky. There was a smell pressing into her with hot, bullying fingers; she could taste it at the back of her throat. It wasn't unpleasant, just strange. She tried to isolate its individual elements but so many sprang to mind – rain clouds and exhaust fumes and cooked food and incense and heat and rotting fruit and other, unidentifiable things. The smell permeated the taxi upholstery, it came in with the breeze from the window, it was part of the very air. They were in the thick of Madurai rush-hour traffic and beyond the noise and the scrum she caught occasional glimpses of a slower world: vendors sitting on stools beside sacks of grain and pyramids of vegetables, a fat man who had set up a pavement trade as an ear cleaner, women in sequinned saris leaning over baskets of flowers. Alida rested her head on the window and tried to relax. Her grip on her suitcase didn't slacken.

The bag lay on a table in an airless room in the concrete heart of Madurai police station, an unattractive grey building with a battalion of shoe polishers squatting around its edges, as if smart shoes were needed in order to enter. The bag was fashioned from wide strips of turquoise and indigo material, and it bulged in the middle like a python that had swallowed an ostrich egg. Under the flat brown gaze of Officer Anand, Alida tugged at the zip. It was a strong steel zip and it travelled as smoothly as a surgeon's knife along the stomach of the bag, leaving a gaping split in its wake. Alida glimpsed a length of pink material and a wooden-handled hairbrush. Several long brown hairs were caught between the bristles and drifted away from the edges in meek spirals. She glanced at Anand, unwilling to dip her hand into the bag's entrails. He returned her gaze without so much as a flicker. Alida registered for the first time the faint scent that whispered up from the bag.

Tuberose.

'Daughter?' asked Anand, nodding towards the bag.

Everything was ludicrous: conversing in pidgin English

on the subject of daughters and bags through lips which were dry with disbelief, while memories of Mia spooled through her mind. Alida opened her mouth to laugh, but instead a tear skittered down over the film of perspiration on her right cheek.

In answer to Anand's question, she leaned forwards and zipped up the bag.

'Picture,' said Anand, and gestured to the right. Wrapped in dirty white linen and tied with string was a large rectangular shape.

'Is that Mia's too?'

'Yes, yes.'

'OK.' It must be a souvenir Mia had picked up along the way, a painting by a local artist, perhaps. Anand kindly helped her to carry it all through into the next room.

There were forms to fill in. Propped up at the wooden counter in a crowd of solemn-eyed Indian men, Alida scribbled and signed. Her suitcase – too bulky for this trip, she now realised – was standing beside her with the picture leaning against it. She had looped her handbag strap over her head so that it wouldn't slip off her shoulder. Mia's bag was clamped firmly between her ankles.

Outside the police station, dragging her luggage, she was confronted with a roar of life and sound which hung in the heat and dazed her. Hesitating on the pavement, she breathed in drains and exhaust fumes. A woman whose pink sari dripped off her angular shoulders and hips like liquid marzipan touched her arm. Her fingers were insistent through the thin material of Alida's blouse.

'*Baksheesh*,' she pleaded.

Alida glimpsed tired eyes and a garish nose stud which was attached by a chain to the woman's ear lobe. Then a jasmine garland dropped snakelike into her view. She followed its swinging tail around to her right and saw a stringy woman with smudges of kohl around her eyes.

'Thirty rupee,' said the woman.

Alida blinked. 'No, thank you.' Her forehead was slick with sweat. She scanned the hammering street for an empty taxi. Her peripheral vision was filled with jasmine flowers whose petals shook water droplets through the air, dispersing freshness.

'Good price,' said the jasmine-seller sulkily.

Alida looked into her face, which was covered in hairbreadth lines of fatigue, and the thought of being responsible for this woman's disappointment was too much. 'All right.' She leaned the picture against her leg and scrabbled in her trouser pocket. Her hand closed over the few coins she had been given when she had changed money at the airport. They felt greasy to the touch. She passed one of them to the marzipan sari woman and the rest to the seller, and her palm was filled with a fragrant rope of flowers.

A taxi drew up and a driver with gelled blue-black hair and a ready smile leaped out to help Alida with her bags. She handed them to him in relief.

'Hotel Raj, please.'

As the driver manoeuvred them into the traffic, Alida looked back. The jasmine seller was standing on the edge of the kerb, her eyes idly skimming Alida's taxi. Loop after loop of white flowers hung from her forearms and protruded from the sides of the bucket of water she carried. With her left hand, Alida gripped Mia's bag strap, and in her right hand, the jasmine garland lay crunchy and fresh. As she touched the flowers to her face and inhaled their sharp scent, the jasmine woman's dark eyes met hers for a brief instant before the taxi swung away.

When the porter had gone, Alida stood alone in her room in Hotel Raj and looked dully at the assembly of luggage on the polished teak floorboards. Exhaustion was spreading through her muscles in aching waves. The room was high-ceilinged and an ornate electric fan hung in the middle air. There was a wardrobe with mirrored doors and a sweeping double bed. The urge to drop onto the oceanic eiderdown and surrender to sleep was enormous. Alida touched a corner of the soft material and noticed the line of dirt under her fingernails.

The lady on the plane who had recommended Hotel Raj to her had advised her that it was important to adapt as quickly as possible to the change of time zone by aligning her meals and sleep cycle with that of India's. In India, it was late afternoon. Alida didn't want to know what time her body clock was running to. She had barely slept since hearing of Mia's disappearance over thirty hours before, and a humming sound came and went between her temples. Still, she needed to visit Hotel Guru, where Mia had stayed. The people who owned the hotel had met Mia, they had seen her getting along in this country. They could help her, she was sure of it.

There was no time to rest.

She splashed water over her face in the bathroom sink, and hurried out again.

Chapter Four

12 November 1995

It's my sixth birthday tomorrow and I am in my bed, sucking sobs under my thumb. I'm wearing my purple star pyjamas even though they don't reach down to my wrists and ankles any more. The cheerful rub of the material reminds me of how things used to be. Everything has changed and our whole house is hanging in black tatters. The taste of salt and ashes coats my throat and I try to swallow it away. My eyes are closed but inside my head they are wide open.

There's a noise: a rustling and shifting, something trying to get my attention. I sit up and find myself looking into a blue jewel of an eye. The eye is diamond-shaped and secrets are coiled inside it. I blink and see that it belongs to an elephant, a living, breathing elephant the size of my arms in a circle. Long trunk stroking through the grass on my duvet. Swan's wings feathering out across a back which is wrinkled with care.

I want to shout for my parents.

An elephant this magical could make everything all right again. I want to be sure it isn't a dream. But if it *is* a dream, if I move or make a sound, it might disappear and never come back. I breathe slowly. The elephant pulls up a sheaf of grass with a swish of its trunk and curls it into its dark triangular mouth. Its wings ripple as it chews. Its diamond eye watches me with a look of such beauty that my tears dry in thin lines on my cheeks. I think the elephant has always been here, I just never looked properly before. The air around it is cobwebby. Apart from me, it's the only real thing in my room. I want to reach out and hug it to my chest.

We look at each other for long, steady minutes. There's no need for words and their gaps which things slip through and get lost in. This winged elephant can see right into me and it doesn't blink or turn away. Every cell in my body goes limp and my mouth fills with the taste of milk and strawberries.

I float back against my pillows. The air flutters with swan feathers.

Summer 1996

Poppy's hair sings when she sweeps it off her face. She smells of blueberry bubble gum and Play-Doh. She says I have magic powers because I told her about the numbers having different colours and the bubbles that hop through the air when the birds sing. She can't see those things, but she agreed about my jumper being fire-engine red and said she could clearly see the specks of deeper blue in my bedroom carpet. I listened to her labelling the colours of my toys and books, but I still wasn't sure whether or not when we look at something we see it in the same way. You can't really trust words.

Poppy always has ideas for games. We have bike races down my bumpy garden and fall off on purpose at the end. We take our dolls for a swim in the paddling pool and create tidal waves so that we have to rescue them. We put earthworms together with daddy-long-legs spiders to see if they'll mate (they don't). Best of all, we play make-believe. Often, Poppy is a princess and I have to save her from garden trolls who are invisible to me but whom she can clearly see. She tells me what they're doing and I

23

swing my sword at them or lasso them with spells. When we get tired, we throw ourselves down in the grass and find faces in the clouds or hunt for four-leaved clovers or Poppy laughs herself silly pulling down on the tight curls which dangle around my face so they spring up like grasshoppers when she lets go. This morning Poppy gave me one of her long golden hairs to measure but instead I wound it tightly around my tongue so that it made spiral bulges. I stuck my new bulgy tongue out and rolled my eyes pretending to be a troll and we laughed until our stomachs ached with pleasure.

Grandma named Alida after an Italian singer, and Alida used to sing all the time, her voice damask pink and light as bubble wrap, but now all she does is shout with Daddy, so that it feels like pavement grit is being rubbed in my face and ears. When we heard them arguing inside just now, Poppy jumped up and slid the French windows shut with a magnificent bang. She dragged me down the garden by my hand and when we were out of sight she put her face very close to mine. I could see the tiny gaps between her eyelashes and a miniature me in the dark liquid of her pupils.

'Adults are morons,' she whispered angrily. 'We don't need them, Mia.'

Now we're sitting side by side making daisy-chain necklaces.

I love Poppy.

Winter 1996

Because I say odd things sometimes, Alida took me to see a big-bellied man with glasses shaped like train windows and a roasted-peanut smell. He showed me numbers and asked about the colours. I explained that number three was always turquoise and number eight was never anything but brown. He wrote down everything I said and I felt like a pop star giving an interview. I had to touch different materials and listen to certain words and tell him if they had a particular smell or taste for me, and when they did he got quite excited. He asked me what the name Samuel tasted of and when I said Wensleydale cheese he laughed and said that Samuel was his own name.

The best thing was that while he talked to me, Alida sat close by and looked at me. She really looked at me, as if she was seeing me in colour again for the first time in over a year. I kept looking across at her and she said, 'Don't look at me, darling, look at the doctor,' but she wasn't cross and there was something so kind in her eyes that it felt like warm water running all over my back.

The doctor played some music and asked me to describe how I felt. I told him about the golden bubbles that came with the peeping high notes and the green waves that the violin made. Because he seemed so interested, I even told him about the violet swirls I once saw around my body when Melissa played the flute in school assembly. He wasn't surprised but Alida was. She tried not to show it but I knew. Maybe she thought I should have told her about it, but it isn't always easy to talk to her.

He asked me whether I knew that not everyone can see or smell or taste in the way I can, and I said yes. I told him Poppy can see garden trolls that are invisible to me, and asked if he would like to talk to her too. He smiled so that his eyes disappeared into his cheeks and said he would prefer to talk to me. He told me that I experience the world in a very special way. He kept saying a word that sounded like synthesiser but wasn't. Alida wrote the word down on the back of her library card.

Later, I had to wait on my own in another room while the doctor spoke to Alida in private. I didn't like them talking on their own. If it's about me then I should be allowed to hear it. When Alida came out, I asked what the man had said about me and she told me he had said that she was lucky to have such a special seven-year-old. I

25

asked her why it had taken him ten minutes to say one sentence and she just laughed.

Afterwards, I had the best afternoon with Alida. She glowed in the way she used to, like sunshine through closed eyes. On the way to the zoo, we played a new game in the car which was the same as the games we played at the doctor's. She asked me what the name Alida felt like to me and I said cool glass columns and she went quiet for a minute.

'And what about the word "Mummy"?' she asked.

'It's apricot orange, my favourite colour,' I said, 'and it tastes of warm vanilla custard.'

Suddenly she indicated left and swerved over to the kerb. She stopped the car even though we were nowhere near the zoo yet and when I'd put the handbrake on (she always lets me do that), she turned to me and asked me to start calling her Mummy again, or at least Mum. I thought about it and said I would call her Mum.

'What does "Mum" taste of?' she asked.

'Warm vanilla custard,' I said, and she leaned over and hugged me.

Chapter Five

Hotel Guru was somnolent with the whirr of fans, and there were no human sounds. Damp stains bloomed in patterns of neglect above the reception. Alida found a poodle's head, the arms of a drowning person, and two elephants kissing. I'm so tired that I'm hallucinating, she thought. Her head swam gently on her neck and she shifted her gaze to her lap.

Just then, a ragged curtain was pushed aside and an emaciated man wearing sandals and a sarong slouched into the room with an apprehensive air. He was in his early fifties and had a moulting blond beard and watery blue eyes. His gaze moved briefly from her strappy sandals and linen trousers to her stylish blouse. He scratched his beard. 'You're not looking for a room here,' he stated. He had a faint American accent.

'I'm Alida Salter. Mia's mother.'

His eyes jumped in surprise. 'You got here quick.'

'Were you the one who reported her missing?'

'Yeah.' He watched her uneasily. 'Guess I shouldn't have waited so long.'

'You couldn't have known.' She noted the sag of his shoulders and the yellowish tinge of his skin. He looked ill.

'Warren,' he said, remembering his manners and extending a veiny hand.

Alida looked at him questioningly. Was that his first

27

name, or a surname? He had a limp handshake. Both of them were perspiring even though a fan was beating the hot air purposefully around their heads.

'Could I see the room she stayed in?' she asked, and felt weak at the prospect.

'Let me check that.' Warren leaned over and extracted a book from a drawer behind the counter. Its cover was pocked with tiny holes, as if someone had repeatedly stabbed it with a biro.

'It's room seven,' said Alida.

'Someone else in there now,' he reported apologetically. 'But we can go knock, see if they're in. Travellers tend to put their own padlocks on the door instead of using the ones we provide them with, so we may not be able to go in straight away. If I'd known you were coming . . .' He shrugged. His gaze lingered unconsciously on her lips and she looked away quickly. Men's eyes always dropped to Alida's mouth, which drew them with its sweetness; she had full lips with a natural curve at the corners so that even when she was at her most serious, she always looked approachable, as if the promise of a smile was never far away. The resolutely sweet shape of her lips had helped to prevent her face from hardening into bitterness in the years following the tragedy.

As she followed Warren up a dingy staircase, the questions she had prepared to ask him took flight and were lost in the creaking shadows. *Mia was here, she was here.* Alida's senses were attuned to every step she took, taking in the slight give of the wooden steps, the prickle of sweat under her arms, the odour of stale incense which hung in the air.

She walked up these steps. She smelled this smell.

The door to room seven was rotting away at the hinges. It was locked with a sturdy padlock which didn't belong to the hotel. Warren looked at Alida.

'We've got a rooftop café. If you want, you can sit up

there with a cold drink and try again in half an hour.'

'Will you join me and tell me everything you can remember about Mia's stay here?'

Warren hesitated. 'I'd be very happy to help in any way I can, but I'll tell you straight off that there's such a fast turnover of people in this place that I barely pay attention to most of them.' He fingered a tuft of his beard. 'As I've already explained to the police, I've been in and out of hospital for the past month and haven't kept track of business the way I normally would. A member of staff just noticed one day that the occupant of room seven hadn't paid for a week, and that's when we started to worry. When we got inside and realised she'd left her passport along with everything else, we called the police immediately.'

'So you might never have laid eyes on Mia?'

'As I say, with so many people passing through ...' Warren shook his head, then brightened. 'That said, we do have one regular guest at the moment, an Australian artist. Pretty well known on his home turf and in Indonesia, from what I can gather. He's been here almost two months now. Taos.'

'Sorry?'

'He's called Taos. Rhymes with house. I seem to remember him saying his parents named him after an art colony in New Mexico. Anyhow, you might be better off talking to him.' Warren turned away and motioned her to follow him. 'He spends most of his time in the café upstairs.'

A staircase even dingier than the first led to the roof. Stepping out into the sunlight, Alida felt as though she was emerging from a cave. Plants and flowers fringed the stone walls, and standing fans were strategically positioned around a cluster of tables with yellow parasols which leaned at rakish angles. A dozen travellers were sitting at the tables. One girl sitting on her own just to Alida's right

29

looked about Mia's age. A world-weary expression sat incongruously on her young face as she fiddled with her straw, dipping it in and out of a slender-necked bottle of Sprite. Like most of the other girls on the roof, she wore a vest top with a sarong and flip-flops, and her hair was covered with a bright triangle of material. The boys lounged in cotton trousers and their bare chests were decorated with tattoos or amulets strung on leather around their necks.

The wariness of the looks thrown in Alida's direction as she stepped onto the roof made her conscious of the jarring smartness of her own attire. The thin silk of her blouse was sticking uncomfortably to her skin but this didn't detract from its simple elegance, and her cream trousers were still outstandingly clean. *I look like someone's mother, come to pluck her wayward daughter from a party*.

Warren pointed her towards a table at the far end of the roof, where a tall, shaven-headed man wearing wrap-around orange sunglasses was sitting alone, walled in by plants and a fan. As they approached, Alida saw that he looked to be in his late twenties, and was writing what appeared to be a long letter. A4 sheets covered the table like unruly wallpaper, and were weighted down with empty glasses and ashtrays to stop them from floating away in the breeze.

Perhaps Taos felt himself being observed, or sensed the determined movement towards his space. When they were still a good few metres away, he raised his head, looked up into her face and straightened his back. There was an expectancy about the way he watched her approach, a certain tension which Alida couldn't put her finger on. She found herself wondering at the contrast he must see between the cool efficiency of her clothes and the state of her eyes. A glance in the wardrobe mirror at Hotel Raj had presented her with two dark tunnels ringed with fatigue.

'Taos,' said Warren affably as they reached his table. 'Alida Salter. She's looking for her daughter, the room-seven girl.'

30

'Mia,' said Alida. Her voice sounded crushed.

Taos inclined his head but said nothing. He had a strong nose, and the stubble on his face and scalp was blond. Alida had an impression of powerful, contained energy. There was an arresting quality to this face, half-hidden though it was by the sunglasses and the short gold filaments of stubble which caught in the sunlight, lending him an accidental sparkle. Printed on his grey T-shirt was a goddess wearing a skull necklace. Her wide black eyes stared triumphantly at Alida.

'I thought you might have talked to her while she was staying here,' added Warren.

'What if I did?' His hands were spread protectively over his papers. It was clear he did not appreciate being disturbed.

'Anything you can tell me about the way my daughter seemed or the things she talked about while she was here could be useful in helping me find her,' said Alida anxiously.

Taos shrugged. 'Fine.' He started to sweep the papers up. Alida glanced down at the sheet in front of her and instead of sentences, she saw a line drawing of a tiger falling from a cliff into a boiling sea. The tiger's head twisted to the side as it fell and its eyes were glowing orbs. Taos whisked the drawing away and Alida watched the shadowy outline of his eyes through his sunglasses as he stacked the papers together.

Warren fussed around, pulling up a seat for Alida. 'Are you hungry? Thirsty?' he asked as she sat down opposite Taos.

Alida hesitated. The smell of food wafted her way from the bowls of curried vegetables and steaming rice set on neighbouring tables. 'Actually, I'm starving.' She forced a smile.

'I'll bring you something decent,' he promised, and left.

Taos extracted a battered purple folder from a bag on the floor by his chair and concealed his sheaf of papers in

31

it. Something about the thin, sensual line of his lips reminded Alida of her first boyfriend, a graceless thirteen-year-old called Dean who had once asked her whether girls got a sexual thrill from inserting tampons.

'Think you'll find her?' asked Taos, startling her. His offhand tone was at odds with the intensity that emanated from his large frame. His Australian accent was light, his voice resonant.

'Yes,' said Alida simply.

'Think she wants to be found?'

'What sort of a question is that?' She couldn't see past his flylike sunglasses.

'It's the first question you should ask yourself before you go chasing around India looking for her.'

Alida tensed. 'What are you trying to tell me?'

'Nothing,' said Taos, rocking back in his seat and folding his arms. 'I just know that some people come to India to shrug certain things off, that's all. Their past, their families.'

'Is that what you've done? Left your poor mother wondering where the hell you are, not knowing if you're dead or alive?' Alida spoke evenly, but she could feel the muscles in her neck tighten with resentment.

Taos frowned but said nothing. He opened a silver tin and stared to fill a cigarette paper with spidery strands of tobacco.

'Listen,' said Alida, gripped by urgency. 'I don't care about your theories. I just want to find my daughter, and if you hide the slightest thing from me, the tiniest detail—'

'Are you threatening me?' The coldness in his voice cut her dead. He had stopped making his cigarette and was sitting very still.

Alida took a deep breath and slumped back in her chair. The man was impossible to talk to. She considered how best to deal with him.

'Try to imagine how I feel,' she said after a moment. 'I'm terrified for her safety. I have no way of knowing, you see.

Whether she's been kidnapped and sold to a brothel, or beaten to a pulp in a back street, or if she was the victim of a hit-and-run accident and is lying broken in a ditch.' She paused, and then had to close her mouth to stop herself from naming all the other fears which had been piling up in her mind since the phone call.

There was a short silence. Alida looked down at her hands, which, unlike Mia's, were small and fine-boned. Our hair, and our eyes, she thought. That's where the similarity stops.

'I once heard a story about a Kiwi who went missing in India,' said Taos.

Alida stiffened, unprepared for tales of doom. She raised her eyes slowly from her hands.

'For ten years he was lost without trace,' continued Taos, his voice as detached as a newsreader's. 'Then friends of his parents, who had never met the boy but knew about his case, went on holiday to India. One day they were in Bombay main train station and a beggar spoke to them. He was in a real state, but his English was astonishingly good. Only after they had left the station did it occur to them that he might be their friends' missing son. They told their friends of their suspicion and another family friend who lived in Bombay hung around the station for three days until the beggar reappeared. It turned out he *was* the lost son. He's back home with his family now.' Taos rolled up his cigarette in one deft movement.

'Why didn't he contact them for ten whole years?' asked Alida, more struck by this than by the miracle of the young man being found.

'I guess he lost his marbles.'

'Are you trying to tell me that's what's happened to Mia? That she's gone mad?'

'I'm not trying to tell you anything about your daughter. It's just a story, that's all.'

'You mean it isn't true?' Alida pressed a hand briefly to her forehead. She was starting to get too tired to think.

33

His lips tightened. 'Of course it's true. Just because someone goes missing, it doesn't mean they're dead.'

'I know she's not dead.'

'That's fine then.' He tapped his cigarette on the table.

'But I'm not waiting ten years to find her.' Alida looked up at the sky and noticed that the rain clouds had shifted away to the sides and that the centre was a luminous blue. A plane was dragging a white line across it. The most important question she had to ask nudged into her mind and she decided that Taos was being co-operative enough now for her to ask it. 'Tell me,' she said, turning back to him, 'how was Mia when you last spoke to her?'

Taos leaned back and lit his cigarette. Smoke clouded the air between them.

'She was rosy-cheeked and sleepy. She told me about a nice dream she'd had.'

Indignation flared in Alida's chest. 'Did you sleep with her?'

'I don't think that's any of your business.' He was frowning at her again, his mouth drawn into a tight line.

Alida bit the inside of her cheek to stop herself from saying something that would alienate him even more. 'Tell me about the dream,' she managed to say.

Taos smoked steadily, tilting his head back to form smoke rings which wobbled in warped haloes above Alida's head. After a full minute, she realised he had no intention of replying. Her sense of frustration and help-lessness grew. She had known it wouldn't be easy to trace Mia, but it hadn't occurred to her that people might simply not be interested in helping her.

'Do I have to wrench every word from you?' she demanded.

A large red ant scuttled across the table on rickety legs. Its body was puffed and angry. Taos flicked it away. 'You waltz in here and interrupt my artwork,' he said, his voice low and controlled. 'You ask me who I've had sex with.

You demand information.' Seeing that Alida was about to protest, he held up a restraining hand. 'I understand your concern for her. Talk to me properly, and I'll talk back.'

Alida threw up her hands in frustration. 'What do you want me to say?'

'Tell me how you feel.'

'I've already told you. Terrified.'

'That's not enough. I need more.'

Alida bit down her fury. 'Listen. If you have nothing to tell me about Mia, just say so. But don't play with me. I haven't slept or eaten for hours, I'm out of my mind with worry and I am in no mood to play your infantile power games.'

'Power games?' He seemed genuinely surprised.

Warren arrived and set down ice-cold Cokes and a steaming plateful of *aloo gobi*. 'On the house,' he said with a smile, and sloped off across the roof again.

Alida's fingers shook when she picked up her spoon. She swallowed a mouthful of cauliflower and her stomach somersaulted in rapture. She knew the food would restore her and stave off the overwhelming need for sleep.

'The main thing she was excited about was that even while the dream was happening, she knew that she was dreaming,' said Taos.

Alida watched him but kept eating, unable to stop now that she had started.

'In the dream, she was watching some sort of bridal ceremony take place in the Meenakshi Temple in front of a fertility shrine. She said that even though the colours and scents and movement all seemed so real, she was strongly aware that she was dreaming the whole scene.'

Alida learned each word by heart as he spoke. She imagined Mia waking up next to this man with her face flushed from sleep, telling him about her dream while he watched her from his invisible eyes. The image repelled her.

'Was that the last time you spoke to her before she disappeared?' she asked.

'It was.'

'Did she give you any clue, no matter how small, about where she might have been headed that day?'

Taos stubbed out his cigarette in a star-shaped glass ashtray. He seemed to be deliberating whether or not to tell her something. Tension whined inside Alida but she continued to eat as if the answer were of no importance.

'She said she wanted to see whether the fertility figure she saw in her dream really existed in the Meenakshi Temple, or if she'd just made it up.'

Alida put down her spoon. 'So you think she might have gone back to this temple on the day she disappeared?'

'I'm not saying that's the day she went missing. It was just the last time our paths crossed, that's all.'

'Where is this temple?' asked Alida urgently.

To her surprise, Taos laughed, making the goddess on his T-shirt undulate. His teeth were white and strong, and a silver piercing glinted in the centre of his tongue.

'What's so funny?'

'Stand up,' he said. He had lost his bored narrator tone and sounded almost friendly.

'I'm eating.'

'Go on. See for yourself where it is,' he said.

Alida pushed back her chair and stood. Dominating the skyline to her left were a group of wedge-shaped towers that looked orange at first glance. Then she saw that each tower was thick with statues, some blue-skinned, others ochre. They were stacked in rows, forming a wall of figures trampling on each other's heads. Each tower was topped by beasts with fangs and spherical eyes.

'Those towers?' she asked, looking back at Taos.

He nodded briefly, his flash of humour gone. His laughter had transformed his face; for an instant he had been liberated. Now his face was shuttered again. Alida's gaze rested on him for a moment as she wondered if he regretted his laughter. Why was he so reluctant to open up to her?

36

She turned back to the temple and stared at it until her eyes watered and the colours ran together. She imagined incense spiralling around a pot-bellied statue, and a bride bending forwards to make a ritual offering. She imagined Mia standing alone in a corner, her eyes opaque in the gloom as she watched from her dream.

Chapter Six

Washed and dressed in a knee-length navy silk nightie which she'd packed because it was the lightest sleep garment she possessed, Alida slid underneath the eiderdown, her breathing already as slow and deep as a sleepwalker's.

Taos had replied to her questions about the Meenakshi Temple in monosyllables. She couldn't understand his apparent unwillingness to help her: surely anyone, however disinterested, would do their utmost to help a mother searching for her lost child? And Taos *knew* Mia. As Alida rolled exhaustedly onto her side, it occurred to her that it was dreadful enough to know that Mia had disappeared, but almost worse was the fact that she had no way of knowing how all this was going to end. She couldn't know whether she would find Mia alive and well, or else hurt – possibly molested – or even dead. Or would she simply never find her, never see or touch her again, never know what had happened to her? Perhaps she would go through the rest of her life involuntarily scanning crowds at tube stations or on busy streets, wishing for Mia's face to materialise and never seeing her, not once. Despite her dizzying fatigue, Alida was suddenly angry with Taos. How could he block her out – and why? If he was hiding something, she would find out what it was. She determined to return to Hotel Guru to see Mia's room and to wrestle more information from him. Then she gave in to the heaviness of her body and drifted down into blackness.

After many hours of sleep, she dreamed she was running barefoot through deep green woods, looking for Mia. Blocking her path was a shining puddle. In it floated a flower with black petals, and when Alida scooped it up in her cupped hands she saw that in the very centre of the flower was a baby-blue eye. As she looked at the eye and it looked at her, she understood that she was dreaming. Her heart leaped at the strangeness of the discovery and she became intensely aware of moss tickling the soles of her feet, the air bright in her lungs, the gaze of this little blue eye pulling her into itself. She looked up and saw the disc-headed man sitting on a tree branch, shiny and muscular, his long legs dangling casually. He was vibrant, kind. He was waiting for her.

Alida's eyelids fluttered, then opened. The room was dark, and her mouth and throat were sour with dehydration. Her gaze fell upon the translucent shape of her water bottle on the floor, and she rolled out of bed and drained it thirstily. There was a roaring noise all around her that she couldn't identify. It made her think of the time she and Ian had climbed up a waterfall in the Black Forest with two-year-old Mia riding on Ian's shoulders.

A cord operated the long slatted blinds at the window. Alida pulled on it and discovered that the window was in fact a door and that she had a balcony. She stepped out onto it and the wind whipped the door from her grasp so that it cracked back against the wall. Her upper body was soaked within seconds. A monsoon storm, she thought with a sense of wonder. The giant lumps of Meenakshi loomed tall in the night. She slit her eyes against the wind. She wanted to throw herself into the storm like a raindrop. The sky flared and bounced and the rain came down in streams. Everywhere was noise and action: gutters singing, empty streets hammering. Street lamps turned the raindrops yellow as

39

they flashed to the ground. Alida's hair morphed into thick rat's tails which curled under her chin and filled the hollows of her clavicle with warm drips. The storm was a fat, emotional display of fury and her bones resonated with the thunder. Somewhere under this same wild sky was Mia. Alida knew for certain that she would find her. She tipped her head as far back as she could and drank the rain.

Back inside the room, the air conditioning purred coolly and she shivered in her wet nightie. It was a pleasure to feel chilly in this country of steamrolling heat and hairdryer breezes. She squeezed excess water from her hair with both hands and shook the drips onto the floor with such violent flicks of her wrists that the blood zinged in her fingertips. Mia's bag squatted on the floorboards, drawing her attention with its broad stripes of colour and its bulging middle. Invigorated by the sheer energy of the storm, Alida strode to the bag, unzipped it and started to pull the contents out onto the polished surface of the floor.

A pink sarong embroidered in silver, a hairbrush. A few paperbacks whose titles meant nothing to Alida: *The Inner Courtyard*, *Diamond Dust*, *Karma Cola*. More sarongs and T-shirts which had a musty, unused smell. A large plastic bag crammed with toiletries accounted for the bulge. She opened it and the smell of tuberose drifted out. Somewhere under the perfume, as fine as a smudge of powder, was Mia's own scent. Alida closed her eyes at once and let her lungs fill up with memories. There she was: Mia, who as a little girl would roll herself up in the sun rug so that her mother could lift the end and tug to make her roll back out again like a runaway sausage. Laughing and sneezing all over the floor. Mia, who when she was fourteen stood red-eyed in Alida's bedroom, her hair wrapped in a beige towel while she screamed her distress across the room. 'How could you keep something like that in your wardrobe?' Her towel bobbing like an ice-cream cone. 'You're deranged. Dee-ranged, Alida.'

As she opened her eyes, Alida realised with a dull shock that apart from the scent, this could be anyone's bag. She recognised nothing in it. Nothing that Mia had taken with her from home. Nothing which spoke to her as a mother. Most painfully of all, no reference to her, Alida. But what had she been expecting? A laminated heart sticker with I LOVE MY MUM printed across it? A framed picture of the two of them laughing in each other's arms? That wasn't the way it was when Mia left, so why would she have brought any reminder of her mother across the world with her?

Alida tipped the rest of the bag's contents onto the floor and her fingers searched through the scattered items. Trinkets bought on market stalls: metal bracelets, glass beads, Hindu gods painted on rectangles of frayed silk. A worn pair of blue and white flip-flops. Elastic bands, safety pins, hairbands. Unwritten postcards of places with strange names: Bangalore, Mamallapuram, Varkala, Hampi. An elephant, four inches long and carved from soapstone, its trunk sweeping low. A diamond-shaped turquoise bindi had been glued over each of the etched eyes so that the elephant appeared to have large, glittering blue eyes. Alida picked it up and touched a finger to the eyes. Why had Mia gone to the effort of gluing these bindis on? She didn't want to leave the elephant in the mess on the floor, so she set it down on the bedside table and sifted through the rest of the pile with both hands.

There was a cotton shoulder bag with a red velvet strap and nothing inside it but a rub of fine-grained sand, and strewn around and between everything else was medical paraphernalia such as rehydration salts, aspirins and plasters. As she pushed one of the paperbacks aside, Alida saw writing inside the dust jacket and read it, frowning. It was in Mia's handwriting.

I can stare at the sun without going blind, stride through the universe with planets for eyes.

The sentence made no sense. It gave Alida no clues. She

nibbled her lower lip while she studied the words again. Had Mia come up with this herself, or copied it from somewhere? She checked the other books for handwriting and between the pages of the most tattered of the three, she found a slip of paper. It read: 'The Blue Sunrise Guest House, Varkala, Kerala'. Under the address, Mia had drawn a smiley face. Alida's heart bucked. This was something real to follow up. People in the guest house might know Mia. Mia might be there now. Blue Sunrise... It sounded like Mia's kind of place. She smoothed the paper out, located the money belt that she'd bought at Heathrow while she waited for her flight to be called, and stashed it in one of the small front pockets. She would have a look around the temple the following day, and if she had no luck there, then she would go and find this guest house.

With renewed hope, she emptied out the bag of toiletries and categorised the items rapidly. Snaking between shampoo and moisturising cream was a thread of silver. Alida snatched it up. It was Mia's necklace. Ian had given it to her on her fifteenth birthday and she had never taken it off. Why had she now? Alida let it slide through her fingers, considering its weight and coolness. Impulsively, she hooked it around her neck. Then she remembered the picture, which was leaning against the wall. She pulled the string knots apart and unwrapped the linen covering as carefully as she could, wondering whether the police had wrapped it like this to prevent it from being damaged, or whether the person who had sold it to Mia had done it. An image came to her of Taos blowing smoke rings insolently over her head.

When the linen slipped to the floor, she saw that it was a crude painting of an orange bear looming over a small replica of itself. The background was in dark blues and blacks, and in the top left-hand corner someone had glued a postcard of an elephant statue and then had lightly painted over it. There was no name on the canvas. Peering

42

more closely at the painting, Alida saw that the bears had fur made of dried orange petals. She sat back on her heels, not sure what to make of the picture. It must have spoken to Mia in some way, otherwise why would she have bought it? She thought of Taos again, unwillingly. How well did he really know Mia? In any case, she would keep the picture safe for her.

Looking at the splatter of possessions at her feet, she realised how cold she was in her rain-soaked nightie. Every inch of skin seemed to have shrivelled into goose-bumps. She struggled out of it too hastily and the straining material at the armpit ripped. Exasperated, she threw it down on the floor. The floor was getting to be her favourite part of this room, she noticed, the part where all the action happened. Something about hotel rooms always gave rise to this kind of behaviour in her. And why not? She was alone; she could do what she liked. She towelled herself dry and put on fresh cotton underwear from her suitcase.

One of Mia's sarongs caught her eye, a green one with fish skeletons printed all over it in blue. Alida remembered the wary faces of the young travellers in Hotel Guru and wondered if it really made a blind bit of difference what she wore. She was separated from them by her age and her obvious ignorance of India as much as anything else. Winding fish-bone-print fabric around her hips would hardly make her more approachable. Why had Mia chosen such a strange design? She scooped up the wide rectangle of material and wound it experimentally around her waist, securing it with a knot at the hip. She pulled one of the musty T-shirts over her head. Mia was bigger than her; she had breasts that preceded her into rooms. This T-shirt must have been tight on her. On Alida it was a pleasantly loose fit. Already she felt warmer. She slid her feet into the flip-flops and her toes tried to wriggle into the hollows left by Mia's toes and found they didn't quite fit.

Alida stood some distance from the wardrobe mirror and

squinted hard. Her daughter's skin was lush and young, velvet soft. Mia's lips were slim, unlike her own, and she carried herself well, standing tall. Mia liked wearing dangly earrings with semi-precious gemstones such as amethyst, malachite, and garnet. She would fiddle with the earrings, or pull one of her dark curls around her finger, her hands constantly in motion.

The chin a little lower. One hand up beside her ear, twiddling a strand of hair. A foot splayed sideways. A wide, air-catcher of a smile.

Alida could almost see her.

Chapter Seven

September 1998
Dad comes home from work every evening wearing a clattering smile. He lifts me up and swoops me through the air until I shriek, but Mum sits very still and watches him from eyes which shrink into points. He has a new scent that even she can smell. It tastes of a jelly bean that has just been thoroughly chewed. It clings to his chin and the palms of his hands. I can see that it makes my mother nauseous. She watches him as if she has just realised that he isn't himself at all, but one of Poppy's trolls. The look in my father's blue eyes is a terrible sight. He looks scared and giddy, like someone about to jump from a plane. And the smell is all over him, turning him into a walking jelly bean, a sugar man melting in the heat.

Every night, as soon as I am tucked up in bed, they sharpen their store of words and hack at each other. Every night I press my hands over my ears so tightly that every swallow is magnified and fills my head like the gurgles of an underwater cave. But the ashy texture of the air doesn't change. I am nearly nine years old, too old to need soft toys, but every morning I wake up to find my black and white panda crushed beneath my chest.

This time their voices go right through my hands.

I slither head first from my bed and press my ear into

the hairy darkness of my carpet. My hearing fans out over the surface of my bedroom floor.

I close my eyes and picture them in the kitchen. I work with the information I have: the way they looked before I went up to bed this evening, and the texture, weight and shape of their voices. Dad is leaning up against the fridge in the suit that makes his eyes shine from his face. His arms are folded across his chest and, when he shouts, his anger hits the air in concrete blocks and turns everything blotchy lobster red. Mum stalks around the kitchen table in a long cream cardigan which trails wisps of wool. Her hair is wild, and barbed wire snaps from her eyes. Her voice spatters the air with black ink. Are they arguing about the way Dad smells? Sticky pink sugar all over his bone-deep baked-potato scent.

'Don't imagine I can't see right through you,' she is shouting. 'Don't think I don't know what's going on.'

His voice is harsh. 'I don't care any more what you do or don't know. This is where it all stops.'

When he says that, everything does stop. Mum's shoes stop their angry clacking on the kitchen floor. The hum of the house stops. My breath stops in my chest.

'You're leaving me, aren't you?'

There's a rumble, a half-groan from him. Even from here, I can tell he's agreeing with her.

My palms are oily with sudden sweat. My mother says something low and vicious. Then her voice explodes up to ceiling height again.

'And what about Mia? She wasn't even six when the first *bloody awful* thing happened in this family.' When she says that, I taste blood between my teeth. I see blood trickling from my parents' eyeballs, oozing from their noses in dangling red clots. They are making each other die.

'I can't live my life for someone else.'

'Not even for your eight-year-old daughter? She needs

you, Ian. She needs *us*. We agreed to see this through.'

'I can't,' he shouts. 'It's too hard, and you know it.'

A silence grows around us, pressing ashes into my throat. Under my ear and cheek, the carpet prickles like tears in the back of the eye. This is the bit I dread, the gaps between the words. This is the part where, every time, I fail to understand what passes between them. My parents become invisible, silent, untouchable.

I wait, and ashes drift across the bedroom floor.

Then there's a flurry of movement: a chair is pushed aside, boots cross the floor.

'Where do you think you're going? Don't you walk away from me, Ian. Get back here!'

I snatch my head from the floor and clamp both hands over my ears. That high shriek hurts me in my kidneys. The front door slams shut, sending a dull vibration through the house. I jump up and hurry to my window. Pushing the curtains aside with both hands, I see Dad striding down the garden path, struggling into his coat as he goes. There are glowing pinpoints in the air around him, like sparks from a fallen firework, white hot.

The front door is torn open and light spills onto the lawn. My mother's voice crackles through the air. 'Coward.'

Dad bangs through the gate without looking back, and the pinpoints of fire surrounding him turn to ash on the wind.

October 1998

I can stay alive without breathing.

My breath waits inside me in a fine pink mist. It holds me so still that for a moment I become just a pair of eyes. It's a slimy autumn leaf day and the van, packed tight and high with Dad's things, has rolled out of earshot. Through the kitchen hatch I can see my mother's face reflected in the silent splash of the hall mirror. She has pushed herself up close to the glass and for the first time in my life she looks ugly to me. Her eyes are knotted tighter than wet string and something struggles under the surface of her skin. The primroses which Grandma pressed and glued into the frame of the mirror before I was born circle her face warily.

'Selfish man,' she hisses, and the air caught tightly in my lungs turns smoky purple.

I'm starting to breathe in colour. The world begins to look magical, doubly alive. It gathers itself into cubes of brightness, and there's a feeling pouring through me, as if anything could happen. I can beat death.

Then Mum balls her right fist and swings it savagely. With the raw carrot snap of the glass, her features shift. She is a car crash victim, face slashed open, eyes howling off on separate tangents.

The air around me jumps with boiling triangles which burn me all down my arms. The breath in my lungs is darkening in flakes. I can't take my eyes off the nightmare face in the mirror.

She steps back fearfully, as if she has done something she never wanted to do, or seen something she never wanted to see.

'Mia!' she shouts, staring wildly up the stairs, where I am not. 'Mia!' She takes the stairs two at a time.

But I cannot answer her. The air inside me is black and rotten. Pieces of it flutter at the edges of my vision. The mirror still seems to hold her broken face. As slow and steady as velvet, the room tips over and the floor pounds once, urgently, on the side of my head. I lie for a moment, my gaze too far away to call back.

Then I remember to breathe in again, and it's like biting into a lemon.

Somewhere above me, my mother runs across the humming carpets, calling my name.

Chapter Eight

Music jangled from loudspeakers positioned on stone columns, and the temple thronged with pilgrims and devotees. Alida was a barefoot guest among thousands of barefoot guests, and the party looked set to continue all day and all night. Colourful assemblies of sari-clad women sat cross-legged eating rice off wide green leaves while small children scampered around them. Dressed in Mia's green and blue fish-bone sarong and a stone-coloured T-shirt, Alida felt far less conspicuous than she had the previous day. People stood before shrines with flowers dangling from their fingers, rubbing ghee into fertility statues so that they glistened. The air reeled with frangipani and gardenia as incense smoke poured and turned from every corner. The walls sprouted many-limbed gods who twisted and danced in supernatural ecstasy. Alida looked up and saw circular mandalas painted on the ceilings. She looked down and saw her pale feet peeling off the flagstones. This was the beginning of her first full day in India and she wanted to get as close to Mia's experience of Madurai as she could. She walked without knowing where, trying to feel what Mia had felt.

In one large hall, an excited crowd of women were bunched tightly together, arms straining towards something that Alida couldn't see. She stood on tiptoe and peered over their heads but found herself none the wiser.

'Holy water,' explained a cultured male voice beside her. She looked around into a sharp-featured face with a trim moustache.

'Really?'

'Yes. Fetched from the temple tank and blessed by temple priests. They wish to touch the holy droplets. This brings good fortune and happiness.'

A great shriek went up from the women as the holy water was distributed. Alida swayed on her toes. The scene reminded her of teenage fans at a pop concert. The women were elbowing each other in their scramble for benediction. Then, just as suddenly as it had crunched together, the crowd quietened down and dispersed.

'Is it your first time in the Meenakshi Temple, madam?' enquired the man politely. Alida sized him up. He was dressed neatly in a shirt and trousers. She noticed streaks of grey in his thick black hair.

'First time,' she said. 'Are you from Madurai?'

'Bangalore is my city,' he said, looking pleased. 'May I be of service?'

Alida hesitated. 'Well, I'm looking for a fertility shrine.'

'There are many, many fertility shrines here. You are in the right place. Meenakshi is generous to those who sing her praises. Babies will come to you, of that I am certain. The only important thing is asking with the heart open.'

'Oh, I'm not here because I want a baby. I'm nearly thirty-eight and I already ...'

The man waved a hand, smiling broadly. 'It is never too late. Meenakshi is bounteous.'

'No, no, I'm here looking for my daughter,' said Alida, tucking a loose curl behind her ear and meeting his gaze squarely. 'She's gone missing. Someone I met yesterday said he thinks she may have come to this temple to find a fertility shrine she saw in a dream. It was a shrine new brides went to for blessings.'

'Ah.' He dropped his eyes from her face momentarily, and when he looked up again he spoke with grave calm. 'Meenakshi the merciful will surely find your child.' He bowed slightly. 'I am Mr Bhawan. I know of such a shrine. Please follow me.'

Alida allowed herself to be led through halls and down corridors. Scenes caught her eye as she walked: a woman in a green and gold sari smearing vermilion over the breasts and navel of a statue; a blind man holding a rope of flowers above his head and muttering as tears slid from his egg-white eyes; a toddler jiving to the temple music while his parents laughed and clapped encouragingly. The temple somehow contained the whole of life, cathartic activities blending easily with the mundane.

Mr Bhawan led her into a hall with high windows through which sunbeams touched the ground. People were seated on the floor watching a ceremony take place around a central shrine propitiously lit by a sunbeam. A queue had formed, and one by one devotees stepped before the voluptuous statue to place their offerings. Once they had bent to touch the statue with powder or adorn it with hibiscus blooms, they straightened and walked through the shaft of light, dust motes glittering around their frames. Alida realised that many people in this temple had come seeking a balm or even a miracle. Some might have come to thank the goddess for her generosity or to ask for a happy marriage, she thought, while others might be making offerings on behalf of a dying child. Their prayers whispered up to the ceiling mandalas and floated off the long strings of incense smoke.

'Is this the shrine you meant?' she asked Mr Bhawan. 'Even if it isn't, I think I'd like to sit here for a while.'

His moustache stretched the length of his smile. 'This is the self-same shrine. Please, sit down. One moment and I will return.'

Alida sunk to the ground at the base of a column and

leaned back into its ridged surface with a sigh. She sat cross-legged and cupped her hands around her toes, which were dry and dusty. Mr Bhawan came back shortly with a jasmine garland which he handed to her respectfully.

'I myself come for my daughter,' he said. 'I pray that it goes well for her when her child comes into this world. And you pray for your daughter's safe return to her mother. We have one and the same wish: the well-being of our beloved one. May good fortune go with you.' He bowed again. 'Might I know your good name, madam, before we part?'

'Oh, how rude of me. I'm sorry. It's Alida Salter.' She smiled at him. 'Thank you so much for bringing me here.'

She watched him disappear into the crowd. The jasmine garland was fat with clean, starlike white petals. Alida hung it around her neck as she had seen others in the temple do. Its scent enveloped her at once. She took out the framed photograph of Mia and propped it on her lap. The idea of tapping random people on the shoulder and showing them the picture seemed ridiculous, and suddenly she was at a loss. There was an impossible number of people in this country. Driving across Madurai in an autorickshaw was like plunging through an unending bazaar, and people were streaming from every orifice of this vast temple. Who would remember a young English girl threading her way through this relentless crowd? She gazed over at the praying devotees and considered the way the sunbeam swallowed them whole as they departed.

The sun was burning away the clouds with increasing ferocity. Alida had found her way to the temple tank, which resembled a large, bottle-green swimming pool. There were many backpacker types perched on the steps, smoking or writing in their diaries. The diary-writing reminded Alida of the spiral-bound notebook she had in her bag. She had been a diary writer as a girl, recording

52

anything from dreams to spats with her best friends at school, and she had written short stories while Mia was small, for the pure creative buzz of building pictures with her imagination. Since she had started spending hours proof-reading other people's writing – anything from gardening articles to doctoral theses – she had entirely lost the habit of writing for herself. Now, looking at the scribbling pens around her, she decided to jot down that morning's dream.

The air was warm and dense and perspiration prickled the backs of her knees as she wrote. The lucid moments of her dream returned to her as a mounting sense of space and concentration, and before long the words flowing from her Biro were virtually creating themselves. When she had finished describing the dream, the blue-eyed flower kept staring at her, only now the eyes belonged to a human face and the blue was seeping everywhere in wet splashes and Alida's pen kept moving. It drew together threads from memories and old dreams as she watched the images unfold in her mind's eye. It rushed across the page the way it hadn't in years, and Alida had trouble keeping up with it.

From eyes to water, the blue is seeping everywhere. It's that exact shade of luminous blue that makes me sad, the colour – so beautiful – of a mosaic-tiled swimming pool laid out in the sunshine. That blue can still make me rage (shamefully, secretly) at my daughter. I remember running, no breath left in my lungs, and arriving too late. Mia has been dreaming of fertility figures, of the archetypal Mother. I have been dreaming over and over of losing a baby through carelessness. I sprint my way back to the baby but it's always just too late; the cliff edge she's playing on collapses into the sea, or the café I left her in explodes in a bomb blast. I am left staring at a floating nappy or the starfish form of a tiny severed hand.

Once, when Mia was five, a film clip from the Vietnam

53

War came on the television. A boy was held up by a US soldier and a gun was put to his head. I jumped to my feet, but before I could turn off the television, the boy's brains blew out of the other side of his head and turned to confetti in the air. 'Try to forget you saw that,' I told Mia, knowing that images are the hardest thing for the brain to forget, harder than words, harder than a memory of physical pain. When I think of what both of us saw less than a year later, I want to rip the sky in two, alter the fabric of time so that it didn't happen. If I had got there just one minute sooner, it could never have happened.

The feeling which stretched out that split second when I leaped to turn off the television is the same as the feeling in my dead baby dreams. It's the feeling you get when you know that no matter how fast you move, you won't quite make it in time. That's how I feel every minute now. I am sprinting again, running with outstretched arms through a whirl of possibilities, hoping that this time I won't be too late.

Alida snapped the notebook shut without reading what she had written. She looked across the tank to where a drooping old woman was peeling a mango, but she didn't see her. Instead she remembered a pair of bright blue eyes watching her unblinkingly. She had to call Ian.

All over Madurai town centre were red and white signs on random shops declaring STD services. That morning, splashing to the temple in a rickshaw, Alida had reached the uneasy conclusion that these were places where doctors were available to diagnose and treat sexually transmitted diseases. Now the rickshaw she had taken from the temple pulled up in a busy side street outside one of these signs and the plump driver was motioning her to go inside.

'Wait, wait,' he added confusingly. Alida hesitated in

the hot street, looking askance at him. 'Going, going, I waiting!' He waved her away with both arms, laughing richly.

Standing against the blackened boards of the building, just by the entrance, was an Indian woman, begging with her little daughter. The daughter, in a frayed and sun-bleached dress, was very pretty, with enormous black eyes and rosy lips. The mother's face was featureless, inhuman. On first glance, this face, ruined by fire, made Alida think of a frozen waterfall, or a face seen through water, the lines blurred, slurred, unreachable. Distressed, she took out some rupees and handed them to the little girl. The child favoured her with a smile of such joyous proportions, astonishing in its beauty, that Alida faltered, not because of the contrast with the mother's burned and immobile face, but because this child, who must have a terribly hard existence, could still smile in that life-affirming way. There was beauty everywhere, she thought, if only you looked for it amongst all the rest. Glancing around her now, she could see the rain-bloated body of a dead rat in the gutter, but here, too, was the incongruent beauty of a pale, hump-backed cow standing sideways on in the narrow street, chewing the cud and eyeing the sweltering traffic jam it had caused.

Inside, cool air hit her face and arms and the band of sweat on her forehead seemed to freeze instantly. Alida sighed in relief.

'Can I make an international call from here?' she asked the girl at the desk.

The girl waved a slender arm. 'STD, ISD, come behind, please.'

Behind were rows of telephone booths. The girl joined her with a bulky black stopwatch and dialled the number for her. Alida calculated that it would be 7.25 a.m. in London. She hoped he'd be up.

Ian picked up on the second ring, sounding tense.

'Yes?'

'Ian. It's me.'

'Oh, you've finally decided to get in touch, have you?' he asked bitterly. 'I called you all day yesterday. I got no answer in the flat, and you'd considerately turned off your mobile. I'd be interested in knowing why you make sure you're impossible to contact when your daughter vanishes off the face of the planet.'

'I know, I'm sorry. I should have called sooner, but I got on a flight to India.' She waited for a reaction, but none came. 'I'm in Madurai. I went to the police station yesterday afternoon and got Mia's bag. There aren't really many clues in it, apart from one address which I'll follow up.' She heard him releasing a whoosh of disbelieving air down the line.

'You're really in India?'

'Yes.'

'That's why we've got this time lag, then. I thought it was your mobile playing up.'

Another long pause. She had taken the wind out of his sails, and felt strangely guilty for it.

'What did the Embassy say?' she asked.

'Well, they won't look for her. That's the job of the Indian police, they say. They did mention that a suspicious amount of backpackers have gone missing in the area of the Kullu Valley, but that's right up north in the Himalaya somewhere, at the opposite end of the country. It's a bloody big place.' He sighed. 'I'm going to buy a detailed map of India this afternoon. You should do the same. Now, tell me exactly what you've found out since you arrived.'

Alida twisted the telephone cord around her left index finger while she told him about Hotel Guru, Mia's dream, the carved blue-eyed elephant and the Meenakshi Temple. She didn't tell him about the discarded necklace. She didn't mention the dizzying number of people swarming everywhere, turning Mia into one lost among millions, reducing the search to pure luck.

'What's it like out there?' asked Ian when she'd finished.

'I don't know. Hot.' There was no way of summing up what she had seen of India in a few words, and Alida was in no mood to try to describe it as though she were on holiday there.

'It must be more than just hot.'

'Well, it's chaotic.' She hesitated, thinking of the blur of saris on the streets, the painted mandalas on the temple ceilings. 'Colourful,' was all she could think of to add, aware of the paucity of the description. But Ian seemed satisfied.

'I want you to email or telephone me every day,' he said.

'I'll try, but don't panic if I don't. There might not be facilities everywhere I go.'

'Just make sure you stay in touch,' he warned. 'I never insisted that Mia did.'

Alida closed her eyes. 'Neither did I.'

Alida returned to her hotel damp with sweat and laden with bottled drinking water, intending to have a bite to eat in the restaurant before heading to Hotel Guru to talk to Taos. As soon as she walked into the foyer, the receptionist at Hotel Raj handed her a telephone message which stopped her in her tracks.

'From police station,' he told her. He looked frightened.

The message had been written in block capitals with a failing red Biro: 'BODY FOUND. VISIT MADURAI CITY HOSPITAL MORGUE, SIVAGANGAI ROAD, AT EARLIEST CONVENIENCE.'

Chapter Nine

The rickshaw was bumping through a mist of colour and sound to the city morgue. When your child dies, thought Alida, you don't recover. You walk on with your memories. You try not to shatter. You long for her in your stomach, your lungs, your bones. The body weeps but the heart beats on.

She remembered how insubstantial she had felt the last time she had stood next to her strong, full-figured daughter. Alida wondered now whether in that same moment Mia might have felt superfluous standing next to her. Normally Mia's golden-brown eyes were gentle, but that day they had an impatient edge, and her expressive dark eyebrows were knotted into a frown. An argument had erupted between them yet again about Mia's insistence on travelling alone and unprotected in India, but both of them knew that it was a pointless argument: Mia's flight was leaving in four hours' time. Their anger had subsided and remained only in the flush of their cheeks. They stood side by side in grim silence in front of Alida's flat and watched Ian's blue Peugeot rattle up to take Mia to Heathrow. Mia's keenness to get away from Alida was palpable, rising off her in waves and visible to Ian even from a distance. The front tyre squeaked against the pavement as he stopped and Alida wanted to take Mia's hand and make a bridge with their arms but she didn't. There was just a brief, awkward hug and the scent of tuberose. Then Mia was gone.

The rickshaw stopped at a traffic light and an old man shuffled up. One leg finished in a dirty rag at the knee and he was using a splintered stub of wood as a crutch. He pushed his free hand out to Alida and mumbled through broken teeth. One of his eyes was bright red, drowning in blood. Alida fumbled in her bag for a coin and passed it to him. She didn't smile and neither did he. She turned away and the lights changed to green. If the girl in the morgue was indeed Mia, how would she survive it? Could she drag herself through life as that contradiction, a childless mother?

Women in rainbow saris formed clusters of colour which bobbed along the pavements or wove between the lanes of traffic. The air was rough with fumes. Alida leaned her head on the metal sidebar and allowed it to be jogged by the motion of the rickshaw. She wondered what happens after suicide. It was a question that had tormented her in the past. *Is suicide really an escape to something better? Isn't the risk great that some wandering part of the soul will still feel the same leaden hopelessness?* Alida looked up at the sky, where one soft-bellied cloud hung. Its underside was opaque but its edges were unravelling quickly in the hot sunshine.

It can't be that easy to throw off despair.

The rickshaw pulled up in front of the main hospital entrance and she jolted upright in shock. Her palms were sweating so she wiped them on her sarong and was comforted by the feel of her thighs under her palms. Living flesh on living flesh. It might not even be Mia, she reminded herself. The driver's English was very limited, but he appeared to agree to wait for her.

Inside, Alida found herself wading through a river of people whose voices flowed over her while they themselves flowed around her. The walls were yellowing and cracked. The smell of disinfectant and stale coffee hung in the air and several people seemed to be arguing about something. A woman with a puffed face was crying into a corner of her sari. Alida let herself be found by a man in a jade-green tunic who read the telephone message the hotel had given her and asked her to follow him down to the morgue. There was a corridor that took them away from the crowd, and Alida's feet, in Mia's large flip-flops, clacked insolently against the sudden silence. She curled her toes to try to reduce the noise, but without success. A lift took them down into the bowels of the building. The man led her along another passageway, then unlocked a white door and entered the room beyond it.

Inside it was very cold and very still. Alida got a confused impression of rows of tables. Upon some of them were white shapes draped in hospital sheets. Feet protruded from the ends of the sheets. It resembled a youth hostel dormitory full of motionless sleepers. Alida looked to her right and saw a young-looking pair of female feet with red nail polish on the toenails. She imagined the young woman hunched over her feet, stroking the nails to crimson beauty and blowing at them through soft lips to dry them. The floor tipped slowly to one side. She bit the insides of her cheeks hard and her balance flipped back as if it had never gone. The man was walking further into the room, glancing around. He's looking for a pair of white feet, thought Alida, and felt she might turn and run.

'Here,' said the man simply. Alida pushed herself forwards. There were black spots dancing in her vision. She looked at the slim, pale feet and didn't know if they were Mia's or not. The nails were bare of polish and there was a thin silver toe-ring on the second toe of the left foot. She tore her gaze away. The man was easing back the sheet to expose the head. In the beat of time before she looked, Alida felt weightless. Then she looked and saw the spiralling curls, the pallid skin and bloodless lips. To her horror, the whole face was blotted with black spots which flashed and bled as the room folded in on itself.

Chapter Ten

November 1998

My mother sees the calendar year as a wiggly ribbon in the shape of a horseshoe, divided into twelve sections. Grandma, who smells of honey porridge and wears a ring on every finger, said time shaping can also be a sign of synaesthesia. She has been reading about it more than ever since she moved in with us, but when she said that Mum just laughed and said she was sure that most people imagined time into a shape they could easily understand. Grandma is going to stay with us until we move into a smaller house. She has her own coloured alphabet, different from mine, and she thinks Middle C on the piano is butterscotch brown, when it is clearly aubergine.

Grandma didn't know she had synaesthesia until we found out that I have it. She thought everyone saw the colours of letters and musical notes, and never bothered to ask anyone about it. She says that my synaesthesia is much, much stronger than hers.

Sometimes I try to shut down my senses, to see what it must be like to be Dad or other people. It must iron the bumps and colours out of the world and turn it into a smooth, bleached sheet, and mostly I think this must be quite boring. But then sometimes I think it might make life clearer, less cluttered.

Twice, I've lost myself in feelings so wide that I

couldn't see past them. Both times it happened when a winged insect attacked me.

The most recent time was about six months ago, when I was eight and a half. I was doing cartwheels in the garden and a wasp panicked me by flying straight into my face. I fell to the ground and squeezed my eyes shut and clamped my mouth into a silent line and blocked my ears because the panic hit the back of my throat like lumps of black sewage and the buzzing turned the air into charred ping-pong balls which rubbed and bumped against my skin and everything smelled of wet dog.

Dad says it's called 'sensory overload'. It feels as if *everything is happening now*, and as if I am everything and everything is me. It feels as if it'll never stop. When it happens, I can't think any more. There is only the distortion and the colours and the sounds which prick me with their javelin spikes.

I'm very careful, now, with things that fly. They're very pretty to watch from a distance, but you can never tell what they're going to do next.

January 1999

When my grandpa heard that I was growing inside Mum, who was an unmarried teenager at the time, he had a series of heart attacks and died. He was forty-seven. Grandma always shakes her head when she thinks of this. The other day she said to me, 'The irony is that he would have loved you so, Mia. You're just like him, the way you size people up and work out the world.' But whenever I think about Grandpa, I get dirty green spots in front of my eyes, because it was me who killed him.

Dying is when you stop breathing, and I want to beat death.

Since that first time, the day Dad left, I've tried lots of times to hold my breath for ever without dying. Every time I start, I think I can do it easily. I start to breathe in colour and there comes that moment when the world goes all bright and alive, and anything and everything seems possible. But then I end up dizzy and black, or on the floor again, like now. I am just finding my eyes when Mum's face bends over me, red with worry.

'Mia. What's wrong?'

The black dots flutter out of sight as I blink, and her face comes into full focus.

'Nothing. Just an experiment,' I say.

'What sort of experiment?' Popping brown spheres very close to my face.

'I'm learning how to stay alive without breathing.'

She pulls me roughly upright by my shoulders and fixes me with dragon eyes. 'You should know damn well that no one can live without air to breathe.'

'I'm trying to beat death.'

'You can't beat death,' she cries. 'It swoops in when you least expect it and it's stronger than the will of anyone in the world.'

'But if I—'

'Death, Mia, is impossibly merciless and impossibly random. Some people actually want to die but death won't come for them, and others have every reason in the world to live but they are snatched away.'

She releases my shoulders and sits back on her heels. There's something wild in her face that makes me remember another time I saw her like this. 'Promise me you'll never pull a stunt like that again.'

'I promise.'

For a long time, neither of us says anything. Her breathing runs through her whole body in waves. I sit and watch the dark flash of her eyes as she thinks things through.

Eventually she breaks the silence. 'Do you miss your dad?'

First time she's asked me that. 'Yes.'

She is calm. Her curls bob as she leans forwards and draws me into a deep vanilla hug. 'Well, my sweet,' she murmurs into my hair, 'you'll see him again on Saturday, and he still loves you just as much, but as for him coming back to live with us, there's no point in either of us holding our breath for that day.' She lets go of me abruptly and starts to laugh and laugh. I join in even though it's not really funny, because Mum's laugh is so beautiful that it makes the space between us come alive with soaring buttercup-yellow lines. When we're finally quiet, we sit grinning at each other and Mum tickles my toes through my socks to start me off again.

Mum shows every feeling she feels, and her feelings change all the time. She goes from Jack-in-the-box anger to pools of giggles and she never lies about anything. There's only one thing she never lets me talk about, and that's the thing that happened before I turned six. Sometimes I still find her crying about it with rolling marble tears. Once, she was up a ladder, fitting a hook so that we could hang up a wooden moon in my bedroom. When she had drilled a thin floury hole in the ceiling she caught me looking at the tears tracking down her cheeks. That was the only time she said anything about it. She wiped her face on the sleeve of her shirt and said, 'It never goes away.'

I darted forwards to hug her legs but she nearly fell off the ladder and she told me to leave her in peace.

February 1999

It turns out that Dad's jelly-bean flavour comes from a woman called Maggie. Dad wants me to meet her but Mum doesn't. Mum works endless, vertical days, because Dad's money walked out of the door when he did. Every corner of the house smells of honey porridge and the voices that float up to me at night are as round and soft as silken juggling balls.

But I only see my dad on Saturdays, and I miss him the whole week long.

No one alive has eyes that blue.
I need him to look at me.

Easter 1999

I am breathing underwater, and I'm not drowning. This is another world, one where prehistoric fish swim through aquamarine light and starfish rest like sunbathers on the rocks. I push off from the sandy ocean floor and drift upwards past octopuses and fragile seahorses. I am looking for a long-lost treasure, but I don't know what it looks like. All I know is that I haven't seen it yet. It might be a mermaid, or even a water baby.

Something draws level with my face. I turn to see a miniature elephant swimming beside me with galloping kicks of its legs. Its trunk is curled into a wormlike spiral and it has blue eyes.

As soon as our eyes meet, I know this is a dream. I don't want to wake up.

'I've found you at last,' I say to the elephant. 'Come and swim with me.'

It hesitates, treading water and watching me shyly.

'No one alive has eyes as blue as yours,' I say. This is a password, and the elephant somersaults for joy. Together we dive past sea anemones with whispering tentacles. The water clings in glass bubbles to our skin.

Chapter Eleven

It was the day after the morgue visit, and Alida walked right up to Taos before he noticed her, as he was at the far end of the roof, painting in the weak morning sunshine. He had set up a battered wooden easel and was deep into the work. Alida saw that he was at least six feet tall, and the curve of his neck as he leaned towards his canvas carried the same hard-lined tension she had noted when she first met him. He had golden hairs on his forearms and large, sun-browned hands, and he was painting the falling tiger she had seen in sketch form two days before. The tiger's eyes were concentric rings of yellow and its expression was somewhere between savagery and shock as the sea approached. Suddenly becoming aware of her presence, Taos turned and did a double take when he saw her.

'You look different,' he observed.

'You look the same.' She nodded at his sunglasses and the goddess T-shirt.

'I didn't just mean your clothes. Your eyes have come to life. Have you found her?'

'No, thank Christ.' She told him about fainting in the morgue, how the dead girl's face had looked so unlike Mia's that she had returned to consciousness with shouts of relief echoing through her mind. How she'd stepped away from the rows of corpses with carelessly loud flip-flop steps and a bruise on the back of her head. She described the feeling of bursting out into the sunlight where the rickshaw was waiting for her.

'All those colours everywhere, the flower-sellers, the roar of the traffic. Everything was astonishingly alive, more alive than I've ever seen it. Do you think maybe I was concussed? I went back to my hotel and slept for fourteen straight hours. That poor girl's parents ... But you know, I'm just so incredibly relieved that it wasn't Mia asleep in that place.'

Taos nodded. She could feel his gaze lingering on her face and suddenly felt she had revealed too much. 'I was looking for Warren, but he's not around,' she said quickly. 'But I'm glad I've found you.' She hesitated. 'I was wondering if I could ask you something, actually.'

'Go ahead,' said Taos, folding his arms and leaning back against the wall. He was still holding his paintbrush, which was slick with white paint. He seemed more open towards her today, and Alida felt encouraged.

'I've lost my daughter,' she said, twisting the topaz ring on her middle finger in slow circles. 'Anything could have happened to her, and you've met her, yet you don't seem to care whether I find her or not. I've been thinking about it, and I can't understand why you were so reluctant to talk to me the other day.'

Taos studied her unsmilingly for a moment. 'If you want the truth, I didn't much appreciate your bossiness.' Ignoring Alida's frown, he continued quickly, 'And I did spend a little time with Mia. She didn't say much, but I got the definite impression that she'd had a tough home life; that there had been unpleasant events in the past.'

'Oh.' Alida's face creased with pain and she looked away, her gaze travelling back through time to a memory of her daughter's gold-flecked, tearful eyes; Mia's small face mute with the horror of what the two of them had seen.

Taos shifted his bare feet. 'I'm not suggesting it was all

67

your fault,' he said. 'But some travellers come to India to escape their families, and I have respect for that.'

Alida looked at him uncomprehendingly. 'But others get abducted or murdered or lost, and they need to be found,' she protested. 'And so far, I'm the only person looking for her. It would be good to have some help, you know?' She was close to tears.

He chewed on his lower lip, his eyes obscured by his sunglasses. Then he nodded. 'Fine.'

'I'm leaving Madurai this afternoon,' Alida said, swallowing to ease the lump in her throat. 'Before I go, perhaps you could tell me the best spots in town to pin up "missing" posters for Mia? Backpacker cafés, that sort of thing.' She reached into her bag and extracted her notepad. 'Look,' she said. The pad was folded open to a page with words written in a firm, rounded hand:

Have you seen my daughter?
Mia Salter, eighteen years old. Last seen in Madurai.
Any information, please contact Hotel Guru or Madurai
police station.

'Do you have a picture to go with it?' asked Taos.

'Yes, I'll photocopy one of the photos I brought with me.' She fished out the silver-framed photograph and showed it to him. He leaned forwards to examine it and she caught a whiff of tobacco and paint and something else: a freshness. Lemon grass?

'Photographs don't copy well. It'll be indistinct and full of shadows.' He put down his paintbrush, took the pad from her hands and sat at a table where he started to scribble and shade with a soft pencil. When he held up the pad a few minutes later, there was a grey and white portrait of Mia laughing off the page. Alida found herself smiling her first real smile in days. This was more than just an image. The pencilled lines had captured something essentially

Mia. The curve of her eyebrows, the cheekiness of her wide smile. It was wonderful to know someone in India who knew her daughter.

'That's quite a gift you have,' she told Taos. He said nothing, but gathered up his paint pots and started clearing his rags and water jars away. 'Did you, um ... Did you ever give or sell any of your artwork to Mia?' she asked.

Taos swung his head around sharply. 'No. Why?'

'There was a painting in her room, along with the rest of her stuff. I just wondered where it came from, that's all.'

He frowned, seeming to deliberate for a moment. Then he shrugged. 'I'll take you to the traveller haunts myself, if you like,' he said.

Alida looked at him in surprise. 'I don't want to interrupt your painting,' she said.

Taos paused, his hands curled around a thick stack of paintbrushes which he was in the process of transferring to a plastic bag. 'You know, it's really fine, Alida,' he said, and she was gratified to see that he had remembered her name. 'I can come back to it later. I already have the sketches, so the rest is easy. Finding inspiration for the sketches is the creative part.' He pushed the brushes into the bag and wiped his hands on a rag.

'How did you think up the falling tiger?'

He tensed. 'I remembered how I felt after something very bad happened to me.' He tossed the rag aside and moved past her before she could question him further. 'Shall we go?'

They were sitting in a tiny café whose walls were plastered with Technicolor pictures of Hindu deities, framed in fairy lights. Two adolescent boys were serving fresh *masala dosas*. The 'missing' posters had been perfected, with Taos's drawing and a copy of Alida's photograph both incorporated into the design. The relevant phone numbers had been added, and they had made a hundred copies. For the last hour, Taos had been introducing Alida to café proprietors, coconut-sellers and second-hand bookshop owners. They had already stuck up more than fifty posters in strategic traveller haunts and guest-house foyers. Despite the sombre nature of the task, since visiting the morgue Alida felt that Mia's death was not only unthinkable, it was an impossibility. She was convinced she was on the verge of finding her.

In her mind's eye, Alida rounded a corner and bumped so solidly into Mia that the stack of posters flew from her arms. She envisaged the wonder in Mia's dark-gold eyes. She pictured the two of them hugging tightly. A gust of wind would send the redundant posters cartwheeling down the street, flattening them against the flanks of wandering cows and whipping them under bus chassis. Mia would stretch out a ringed hand and touch Alida's hair, which was stiff with the glue of dust and humidity. She would laugh at the sight of her mother in one of her sarongs, and at the withered jasmine garland hanging around Alida's neck. Her disappearance would be a simple misunderstanding – she had been away on a sightseeing trip and had simply forgotten to take her passport with her. None of it would matter, and Mia would insist that the two of them go to the beach together for a week before returning to England. They would swing in hammocks or sit barefoot on the sand together while the sea lapped at their feet.

'What went through your mind while you were being driven to the morgue yesterday?' asked Taos abruptly. His fingers were engaged in the final stages of rolling a cigarette.

Alida tore herself away from the feeling of her toes wriggling in wet sand. 'I thought about the last time I saw Mia,' she remembered. 'And I found myself thinking about suicide.'

His head jerked back and she realised how that must have sounded. 'I don't mean I was suicidal,' she said hastily. 'I was just turning the idea around in my mind.'

Taos had frozen with his unlit cigarette in mid-air. 'And why would you do that?'

'I was just considering it as a concept.'

'Suicide isn't a concept. It's an irrevocable act.'

'Whatever.'

His melodramatic immobility annoyed her. To compensate for it, she shifted in her seat. He looked like a DVD on pause. She waved an arm at him. 'Don't you ever take those things off?' she asked irritably.

'These things?' Taos removed his sunglasses slowly and laid them on the table. His eyes were deep set and hazel and starred with thick lashes. There were lines scored around them, fanning out from the corners. Without the barrier of his sunglasses, there was a vulnerability about his face; his eyes shone with something like sadness, or perhaps compassion. He was good-looking, Alida realised, his eyes compelling under dark-blond eyebrows, and he was older than she had first judged him to be. He could be thirty-five or thirty-six, a year or two younger than her. He was looking at her very seriously.

'So you do have eyes under there somewhere,' she said, and forced her own eyes to turn away. After spending the morning talking to twin orange ovals, being faced with his bare gaze was unsettling. She looked instead at the table-top, which was an ugly rust colour. Ants scrambled along its edges.

'I've got something—' he began, but Alida, frowning at the ants, interrupted him.

'Listen, I have no intention of killing myself. It's something I would never do.'

'How do you know that?' He lit his cigarette and the stray strands of tobacco drifting from the end crackled and sparked as he inhaled.

'It's just something I would never do,' she repeated.

'How do *I* know that?' He leaned back in his chair and watched her.

'You don't have to know anything.' She met his gaze in exasperation. 'I know it, and that's good enough.' If I were the type of woman who slits her wrists when life becomes unendurable, she thought, I would have done it thirteen years ago.

Both of the waiters bore down on their table and set down banana *lassis*, bottled water, and two triangular *masala dosas* which flopped over the edges of the tin plates. Alida looked hungrily at her food, which was crisp and hot and smelled of curried potatoes. There was no cutlery, and she was wondering whether she was supposed to eat it with her fingers when a waiter returned with two forks for them.

They started to eat, and Alida's mind looped back over their conversation. 'What were you about to say just now?' she asked Taos suddenly. 'You've got what?'

He looked up. 'I've got something of Mia's that you should probably see.'

Involuntarily, Alida's hand tightened around her fork. The quickening of her heart told her that this was something important, something that Taos had been keeping back from her for whatever reason. She forced herself to appear casual; she didn't want to frighten him off.

'Oh really, what's that?' she asked, keeping her tone light.

He shook his head. 'You'll see when we get back to the hotel.'

Chapter Twelve

Taos stopped outside a padlocked door in Hotel Guru and took out his keys. Alida noticed that his T-shirt was ragged at the hem and flecked with paint the colour of dried blood. She suppressed an image of Mia, gagged and with screaming eyes, tied to his bed. Taos unlocked the door and stepped into the gloom. Peering after him, Alida made out right-angled shapes and a stiff, sharp smell.

'Welcome to Hotel Guru's broom-cupboard-come-art-studio,' said Taos over his shoulder. 'Look to your left.' He pushed open the shuttered windows and sunlight crashed in.

Through spiralling dust motes, Alida looked left and saw a semicircle of canvasses, each about eighty centimetres tall, propped against what looked like a rusting air condi-tioner and pieces of discarded furniture. The colours in the pictures – raspberry, lime, chestnut, apricot – dazzled her momentarily before settling into definite lines so that images sprung up around her. The first thing that struck her was that these were by the same artist who had painted the one now owned by Mia. She swivelled her head from far left to far right, pausing on each of the four images.

A frail figure cringing from a large, diving insect.

A pregnant woman in a bubble, something clumped white and still inside her belly.

An elephant carrying something ungainly on its back.

A child standing on a beach as the waves powered in.

'Are these yours?' she started to ask Taos, but she noticed something and immediately her lips clamped down over the words.

The child on the beach had no arms.

She sunk down into a crouch. 'Oh my God, I remember those nightmares. These are Mia's, aren't they?' She didn't need to see Taos's nod to confirm her thoughts. With her fingertips she traced the frowning ridges of paint that formed the child. 'Ian and I would be downstairs in the evenings, sipping wine and trying to avoid ... a certain subject. Sometimes, though, a half-spoken sentence or an unguarded look would wrench it all up again. We would argue, and worse.' She glanced quickly up at Taos, but he was watching the tentative movement of her fingers on the canvas and didn't speak. 'Then all hell would break loose from Mia's bedroom. Screaming, incoherent yells. One of us would rush upstairs and she would be fast asleep, kicking her legs – really drumming them against the mattress – but with her arms immobile at her sides. She told us that in these dreams she was a girl with no arms, but we never managed to persuade her to tell us what else happened in them.'

Alida's hand retreated from the painting. She sat back on her haunches and hugged her knees. Mia had painted a struggling sea, one which chewed at the shore. It would carry the roar of a landslide and the surf would swallow up the sand with the hiss of tyres on a wet road.

Taos came to her side and leaned down. Alida looked up at him, but again he was staring at the picture. She followed the line of his gaze. 'Is that an arm?' he asked abruptly.

Alida saw it as soon as he said it: a thin, sorry brush-stroke with five splayed digits, disappearing beneath a wave.

'Why didn't you show me these the first day I came

here?' she asked him with sudden bitterness.

'I didn't know you.'

She stared at him. 'Taos, I'm her mother.'

'I know that.' Clearly agitated, he moved away from her as he spoke. 'But art is very personal. At first the artist is outside, but as the work develops, he wades in, deeper and deeper, until at the end he's wholly inside the image. It's as if—'

'All the more reason to show me these at the first opportunity,' snapped Alida. She stood up, her knees cracking uncomfortably, and faced him. 'These paintings will tell me what was on Mia's mind before she vanished like that. Seeing these is far more important than putting up posters or visiting bloody useless morgues.'

Silhouetted against the brightness of the window, Taos raised both hands in a calming gesture. 'We'll photograph them,' he said. 'That way you'll have them with you as you travel around searching.'

'I'm not on holiday. I didn't bring a camera with me to India.'

'I'll get mine.' He made to step past her, but Alida moved her arm to stop him.

'One second. How did you know these pictures were here?'

Taos frowned. 'Mia was interested in the idea of painting dreams and memories, and she asked my advice.'

Alida stared at him. 'Did you spend a lot of time with her, then?'

He shrugged. 'I encouraged her to find her own way of speaking in images.'

'But if you spent time with her, then why the hell didn't you report her missing when you didn't see her for a week?'

Taos shifted uncomfortably. 'I didn't feel the need to report anything. She's a free agent.'

'A free agent? She's a young girl alone in a foreign

country, Taos. If people who see her on a daily basis don't report her disappearance, then who will?'

'I didn't know she wasn't going to come back.' He turned his palms upwards in a quick, helpless gesture.

Alida stepped away from him, her gaze swinging back to the pictures. She shook her head. 'That's no reason,' she mumbled.

'I'll get the camera.' He stepped past her and was gone, slipping through the door in guilty haste.

Left alone with fragments of Mia, Alida looked into each one. They weren't paintings, she saw that now. Or not entirely paintings. Like the one she had in her hotel room, among the thick crusts of paint there were other materials: strips of silk, raised oblongs of paper, the sparkling plastic bindis Indian women sometimes wore in the centre of their foreheads. These were collages.

The elephant wore crow feathers, stiff with white paint, which rose off its back in two outstretched wings. Its eye was composed of turquoise bindis arranged into a tilted square, so that Alida was instantly reminded of the carved, blue-eyed stone elephant she had found in Mia's luggage. The white clump in the woman's belly was a skeleton made of pipe cleaners, its ribs black stripes on paper, its eye sockets sooty jabs of paint. In the top left-hand corner of each collage there were images of places in India, apparently snipped out from postcards, each veiled by a dry saffron brushstroke so that it was like looking at them through a sandstorm.

Alida saw that the small figure under attack from the insect was being bombarded with word-bricks fashioned from curls of paper. 'Popping chartreuse', she read, bemused. 'Bells'. 'Silver hammers'. Worm-words were squirming their way into the figure's ears. Grains of coloured sand stained the air above. This, she realised, was Mia's auditory, textured vision. Only the beach painting had no synaesthetic embellishments, and yet it was the one

76

that Alida's eyes kept jumping back to. She wanted to pluck the silent figure from the beach, retrieve her arms from the waves and make her whole again. It was something she should have done years ago. How could she have thought that ignoring Mia's suffering would make it go away?

Digital camera in hand, Taos crouched to photograph each picture whole, and then he broke them down into details. Here, the elephant's diamond eye. There, the macabre contents of the pregnant woman's belly.

Alida waited in a trance, Mia's images and her own adjoining memories taking up all the space in her mind. She could feel Mia's presence as acutely as if she were standing beside her. She was flooded with the colour and perfume of paint. When Taos straightened up and favoured her with a rare smile, Alida stirred herself.

'I'm leaving for Kerala in a few hours,' she said.

There was a pause then, the smile on his face softening to something that made her heart jump in recognition. He had sunk his gaze into her own – or perhaps she had initiated it with her own far-off stare – and now they were looking right into each other. Ian used to do that all the time, in the early days. Sink his gaze through the refractive liquid of her irises and look deep, until he found her. For the briefest moment, Alida looked far into the steady darkness of Taos's eyes.

'Would you... Will you come with me?' she heard herself asking him then.

Chapter Thirteen

March 2000

I'm practising being an iguana in the cherry tree at the side of the new house where I live with just Mum. In the new house I have a yellow bedroom with a window seat where I can sit and see what's happening in the neighbour's garden. Nothing much does happen – grey and white washing turns on the line and sometimes an old woman comes out and bends over the flowerbeds. When we moved here, Grandma moved back to her own flat to give us our space, but I wanted her to stay. Mum is full of scarlet and black steam; I watch it build in her and it all comes shooting out every time something reminds her of Dad.

'He's a bad luck man,' she says as she hammers nails into walls while I wait to pass her the picture she wants to hang. 'He's brought me nothing but trouble.'

But it's not Dad who's a bad luck man; it's me who's a bad luck girl. If the thing that happened when I was nearly six had never happened, we would be a happy family.

I can feel the branch of the cherry tree pressing like walnut shells along my chest, stomach and legs. My arms are locked around it in a steadying hug and just where the branch forks, my face hovers with a view across to the gravel rectangle where Dad will park his car. I am very still, a ten-year-old iguana girl invisible to the untrained eye.

The gravel crunches, rich as toffee, as he rolls in and stops, the sun slapping his car roof a silvery blue. He sits a while before he gets out, and past the glare on the windscreen I can see him frowning in the direction of the front door. I'm an iguana girl, I remind myself quickly. I'm a magic maker, and this is where the magic must start. I imagine the magic covering Dad as he trudges to the door of my mother's house, his shirt as blue as his eyes, his hair dark gold and wavy. The magic gives him a lemon sherbet-tasting sheen. It's all slow motion now, the press of the doorbell, the door swinging open, my mother movie-star beautiful in the red dress I persuaded her to wear today. I try to imagine the magic swarming from Dad to her, but just seeing them standing on one spot together is distracting me. They exchange a few words and I catch the sound of that special double tone their voices make, song on song. Baked potato plus vanilla equals something that makes my veins go limp with love. I am melting into the tree branch.

'Mia!'

My body stiffens again. My mother has turned back into the house and is calling me sharply. Dad looks irritated and I can't taste the lemon sherbet any more. It's hard for iguanas to move once they've taken up position, and they don't like to move backwards. I struggle down the branch and end up slithering pretty fast down the trunk. I think some of the sequins on my green top have probably torn away. As I land on the ground, Dad sees me.

'There you are, rascal,' he says impatiently. 'Been spying on us while we try to find you, have you?'

'No,' I protest, smoothing my clothes down as I walk towards him.

'Oh, Mia, there you are,' says Mum. She has my overnight bag with her. We meet in front of the car in an uneasy three-some. The magic has almost all gone; only a shimmer remains behind Dad's ear. He draws me to him and kisses me on the cheek. I haven't seen him for two weeks because he was too busy to see me last weekend. He smells of himself and of Maggie. I think Mum can smell it too. Her lips are pale as she passes me my bag. 'Have a lovely time,' she says, sugary bright. I think of the way she called Maggie 'The Maggot' last week, and the thought helps me to smile at her when she kisses me on the forehead.

Then I'm in the car which reeks of Maggie and the magic still hasn't worked and Mum's waving all lonely in her pretty dress and it's that weekend feeling again and I only just manage to stop myself from turning to Dad and shouting, 'When are you coming back to live with us? When?'

Summer 2000

Maggie's OK. All of her limbs are round, nothing like Mum's hard beauty, and she has robin-dark eyes and a hurtling laugh that makes me smile even when I don't want to. Dad never wants to see me on my own, without Maggie. While I'm showing him the weather project I did for geography with Poppy, where we kept temperature charts in our gardens for a month and Poppy faked her results all through the last week because she was too ill with a chest infection to go out every morning and measure dewfall levels, Dad's gaze keeps skittering off my graphs and charts so that he can touch Maggie's face with his eyes. When I ask him if he'll take me to the zoo, he asks Maggie if *she* wants to go to the zoo, and she doesn't, so we don't go.

He still looks and sounds like Dad, but he's different now. I don't think he loves me as much any more.

Chapter Fourteen

The driver revved the engine until the bus shook and, as he began to edge it forwards out of the bus station, all the peanut-sellers scrambled off, while last-minute passengers forced their way on, clambering over all the luggage stacked in the aisles. Alida looked at the dusty, flip-flop clad feet, the flapping silk of saris, the women's hair greased with coconut oil and pulled into such tight buns that the comb marks were clearly visible, scoring the hair in deep lines.

Some of the women stared at Alida with frank dark eyes. Others smiled at her, so she smiled politely back. This was her third day in India, and she had known about Mia's disappearance for four days now. It occurred to Alida that it was, as always, both astounding and banal to see how life continues despite the cruellest circumstances. It was impossible to live at an emotional peak day after day. A semblance of normality creeps first into the stomach, which gets hungry, then into the voice, which relaxes its constricting grip on all those tears stored up in the throat, and finally normality reaches the facial muscles, so that automatic smiles appear in response to the smiles of others. Still, there was a weight in her chest, as if a flat river stone were wedged up under her ribcage. Alida knew this weight, the uncompromising lines of it. This weight, she knew, would stay with her. A few seats ahead, a toddler with a shaved head was screaming, dropping his head back so that his mouth was parallel to the roof of the bus. Alida rested her cheek against the grimy window and watched Madurai swarm around them as they pushed their way out of town. There was an overpowering smell of sweat and engine oil, but she was following her first proper clue and her feeling of hope was strong.

Her stiff old suitcase would have been impractical on this trip, so she had left it locked up with the rest of her belongings in the luggage storage room at Hotel Raj, and brought Mia's bag instead. She had packed some of Mia's sarongs and T-shirts to wear, as well as the fan of blank postcards that Mia might have been planning to write to her or Ian, the silver necklace, which was still fastened around her own neck, and the carved elephant because there was something very Mia-like about Supergluing sparkling blue eyes onto soapstone. None of the rest of Mia's possessions seemed worth bringing along, so they were also in storage at Hotel Raj along with the collage of the two bears. The wide blue strap of Mia's bag dangled from the luggage rack and rocked with the motion of the bus.

The driver put on an Indian pop music video and turned the volume up to distortion level. Alida read the English subtitles.

Oh slim girl! Why do you need a girdle? A tiny ring will do!
Oh fire boy! You are a rabbit that just wants a love rush!

Alida found herself humming under cover of the tractor-like grind of the engine and the wail of the music video, partly to alleviate the weight in her chest and partly because she could do so unobserved. She couldn't hear the sound that she was making, but she felt it in the vibration of her chest and vocal cords. She remembered doing the same thing as a child on windy car journeys with her parents, making a noise which nobody could hear, not even herself, but which she could clearly feel. There was a certain satisfaction to performing an external action that was imperceptible even to people close by, a bit like pulling ugly faces in the dark. And then there was the freedom of burying her noise in the greater noise of the bus. She hummed in broad swathes of sound, disturbing no one, and let India fill her eyes as the bus rolled onto the highway in a cloud of mustard-coloured dust.

Taos was frowning into his book, his long legs sprawled out by necessity into the aisle. Alida stole a glance at him. She had offered to pay for his bus fare and accommodation, but he had waved her aside with a look of such irritation that she hadn't insisted. It worried her slightly, though. What was in it for him, after all? She didn't see why a virtual stranger would subject himself to a seven-hour bus ride across India with an anxious mother. She knew nothing about him or his past. Although he seemed comfortable directing personal questions at her, Taos was non-committal to the point of rudeness when it came to talking about himself. Most people emerge mushroom-like from their past and carry the scent of it in their shape and bearing. Taos had an anonymity about him, a separateness, which made Alida uneasy. Here was someone who for the past few months had chosen to live in a backpackers' crash pad in India and who devoted his time to filling a broom cupboard with paintings. In addition to teaching her daughter the art of art, of course. Hadn't she read somewhere that most murder victims know their attackers – or was that rape victims?

Alida closed her eyes briefly to halt this unsavoury unspooling of her thoughts. Taos was all right. A bit private, a little moody at times, but he was a solid, breathing person beside her. Whatever his reasons, he cared enough to accompany her, and that was good enough for now.

After three hours of sucking up India with her eyes, the stream of images could hold Alida's attention no longer. Rice fields, cyclists and waving children ran together like raindrops on a windshield. The bus roared and blared around her. Her head lolled against the window pane and she fell away from the noise and movement. She dreamed she was in a muddy field, lecturing teenaged girls about how to avoid pregnancy. As she spoke, some of the girls climbed onto the edge of a well with thick stone walls. Their erect, immobile posture made her think of marmots sniffing the air. One after the other, the girls sprang into the centre of the well and were lost from sight. Beyond them, sitting cross-legged on a post, was the disc-headed man. As soon as she saw him, she knew this was a dream, and she flew to him with the wind on her skin. His body was bronzed and wiry.

'I'm dreaming again,' she announced, her smile glistening on her face.

He extended his hands to her and she gripped them impulsively. They were warm and strong and very real. She saw that four etched words were continually rising and fading across the silver disc of his face. Leaning closer, she tried to memorise them for when she woke up. Blood. Belly. Baby. Blue. As she watched the words she could feel the tidal rhythm of his breathing.

'Will I find Mia?' she asked him.

There was a moment of silence, like watching ripples spread across a lake. Then he released her hands and everything disappeared.

Alida opened her eyes a crack to see Taos reading his book, sunlight glinting off the golden stubble on his scalp. She was perspiring and the combined noise from the bus engine and the music video was overwhelming, but her dream images hung clearly in her mind and she didn't want to let go of that feeling of absolute awareness. She reached for her notebook and a pen. Eyes still only half open, she recorded her dream in a script which mirrored the jolting of the bus. As she wrote, she dropped into herself, moving again towards the feeling of her dream, and her dream images began to change before her eyes; the girls jumping into the well morphed into an image of herself as a pregnant teenager, her eyes ringed with black eyeliner, foundation caked in small lumps over the persistent spots on her chin. Was her own early pregnancy really the reason she had begun lecturing adolescents about contraception? She supposed it was; yet you could never get through to the ones who didn't want to listen. Raw experience was the only way they learned. As she wrote to the end of her dream, the words the disc-headed man had shown her stood out in glowing silver in her mind; lexical breadcrumbs laying a trail. The words and her pregnant self were producing new images between them, and Alida bent her head closer to the page. Too rapidly to think about what she was writing, she described the story that the images told.

Once there was a girl who fell in love like a marmot jumping down a well. She gave herself to a boy with a motorbike the colour of blood. He loved to curl his fingers into the cleft of her buttocks, taste her breasts with his tobacco tongue. The two of them were the first lovers on Earth, living with an intensity that shot all reason from their heads.

Soon, the girl's belly hardened and stretched with balled-up life. It swelled into a sphere which protruded incongruously from her narrow hips. She was doubly alive, a quadruple X chromosome, woman harbouring woman.

They sat by the river one evening watching the silent flash of a kingfisher. The boy's hands moved over her belly, reading it like Braille. She had never felt so full. Then her body rippled and fire ringed her midriff. By morning, her muscles were jelly, her thighs sticky with blood, but she held her daughter in her arms. 'Mine, you are all mine, my treasure, my baby,' she whispered. Through the fog of birth the baby looked back at her, and both experienced the lock-on jolt of recognition. For a time the girl, the boy, and the baby lived in a taut circle of love.

Gradually, the circle slackened. The girl turned the full blast of her love to her child, who cried and laughed and grew strong. The boy found himself watching the insouciant, long-legged strides of childless women as they passed by. He climbed a ladder of thoughts until he was half inside, half outside the circle. The girl sensed this and tried to tug him back but his eyes were wide and shining, reflecting the freedom he saw. She found herself wishing for a new child to tempt the boy back into the circle. Her wishes turned to prayers, but no baby came.

Dissatisfaction turned the circle into a prison. The boy escaped once or twice and returned smelling of the childless women he admired. At times like these, violence smeared the air. It vibrated in their angry voices. It echoed like trapped screams. The two of them said and did things that they should not have said and done. The girl slammed a fist into the boy's blue left eye. He pinned her to the floor and bellowed into her face until she was giddy and deaf.

Now that these first steps had been taken, it was easy enough to repeat them. They explored different ways of hurting each other. They selected weapons which would slough off the skin and expose the flesh. They scratched and dug for blood. Their battles seeped into their child's dreams and it became hard to pretend that the circle had not suffered irreparable damage. For her sake, they tried.

But the circle looked different now. Punctured with holes where the boy had escaped, yet choked with the sour air of disintegrating love, it stopped the child's laugh. They were waiting, all of them, for the denouement, the final high or low that would decide the family's future. When it came, it was at first so sweet and finally so cruel that the memory of it would never leave them.

*

86

'What were you writing about?' asked Taos as soon as she had slipped her notebook back into her shoulder bag.

Alida hesitated. 'Oh, nothing. Just a sort of mini-story. Writing stories was a hobby of mine in my early twenties, but the habit died.'

'What's your story about?'

Feeling faintly awkward, she glanced out of the window. They were overtaking a bullock cart driven by a skin-and-bone man whose face was screwed up against the dust. 'Marmots,' she said evasively.

Taos raised an eyebrow. 'You wrote a story about whistling rodents?'

'Mmm.' Alida fiddled with the metal spiral binding of her notebook, hoping for a change of subject.

'Well, I'd like to read it, if you wouldn't mind,' he said doubtfully. 'My book's going nowhere.'

'Actually, it's quite personal. I had one of those aware dreams, you know . . .'

'A lucid dream?' He twisted his head further around so that he could see her better.

'Yes. It's the second time it's happened. I first realised I was dreaming the night you told me about Mia's dream.'

Taos shrugged. 'It's often the way. You hear that something is possible, and you do it.'

'I suppose so.' She glanced rapidly out of the window, wondering whether to tell him more, and then decided to. 'I keep dreaming of this disc-headed man.'

'Disc-headed?'

'Yes. A big round, silver disc.' She sketched the size of it with her two hands. 'He's magical, and I've never had a figure like him in my dreams before.'

Taos seemed interested. He closed his book, keeping his page with his thumb. 'How does he make you feel?'

'As if I have a friend,' said Alida simply. 'He's showing me he understands.'

'I'm no dream theorist,' said Taos with a quick smile,

'but I'd guess Freud would call it a classic case of wish fulfilment – you've created a dream friend so you aren't alone during this ordeal. And Jung might say this is an archetypal figure that represents the integration of some aspect of the psyche.'

Alida took a moment to absorb this. 'Whatever he does or doesn't represent,' she mused, 'he's very real, in his own unreal way. When I look at him, knowing that I'm dreaming, his realness only seems to increase. And there's a great deal of humanity in him. I feel he knows me, and he's full of compassion. When I dream of him, I find myself feeling brave enough to write about things that I've been trying to forget for years.'

'It's funny how both you and Mia started having lucid dreams in India, and that she collaged hers, while you write about yours,' he remarked.

Interested by this connection, Alida sat up straighter in her seat. 'That's true.'

'And another funny thing,' said Taos, looking closely at her face, his eyes resting briefly on her lips before he moved them away, 'is how young you look for the mother of an eighteen-year-old. Mia never mentioned you being so young.'

'Oh, even though I had her when I was very young, to Mia I'm an old fogey, just as all parents are to their kids,' Alida said with a grimace. Her eyes skittered to the window. 'I do wonder sometimes how I come across to her – I've always been the authority figure in her life, same as Ian, and that must give her quite a different perspective of what goes on in my head.'

'Which reminds me,' said Taos, closing his novel completely and wedging it under his leg, 'I'm curious to read this story of yours.'

Alida felt absurdly panicked. 'Why should you read it? Writing is private.'

'No more so than painting is,' argued Taos. 'I communicate

in images, and I exhibit my work in galleries.'

'Hold on there – you didn't even want to show me my own daughter's artwork.'

'It wasn't mine to show.' Taos looked at her steadily.

'Well, all right, but I still say that writing's a particularly private activity.'

'How's that?'

'Writing exposes you,' she said nervously. 'If you write so fast that you barely have time to think, your unconscious slips onto the page without you even realising. Once it's there, there's no disguising it. You become transparent.'

'Same as art, then.'

Alida shrugged, unwilling to continue the discussion.

'Anyway, why wouldn't you want to expose yourself in your writing?' asked Taos. 'I would say that's the whole point. To cultivate the kind of honesty which allows your mind to travel wherever it needs to go.'

'Fine,' said Alida, piqued into a response in spite of herself. 'But it's one thing to expose yourself to yourself, and quite another to expose yourself to others.' She twisted a ringlet of hair around her forefinger and pulled at it gently, as if testing its strength. 'It's the same with any form of exposure. I mean, some people like to sit around naked on beaches, while other people prefer to keep their swimming costumes on.'

'That's just prudishness.'

'Not necessarily. Maybe they've suffered some damage. Maybe they lost a breast or a testicle through cancer and don't want other people to see their scars.'

'They have something to hide, you mean.'

'Something to hide, or just something they don't want to expose to prying eyes.'

'Not all eyes want to pry.' Taos looked at her for a moment. 'Why don't we do an exchange? You let me read your story, and I'll show you a few of my paintings. Go on.' He nudged her very slightly with his shoulder in a gesture which she found disarmingly personal. 'I'm dying of boredom in this lumbering tin can.'

'How can you possibly show me your paintings? We're on a bus.'

'They're on the digital camera, same as Mia's stuff. It's a bit small to look at but you'll get the idea.' He struggled to his feet and started rooting around in his rucksack.

Alida watched him. Hearing him say Mia's name so casually made it sound as if Mia was right beside them. She liked that, liked it very much. She imagined Mia's tousled head appearing around the seat, her eyes gleaming in the sunlight which swung across the upholstery. It was this feeling of intimacy more than any argument that Taos could muster that made her hand over her notebook.

While he read, she beeped through the photographs of his artwork. While Mia's collages were powerful, they had an amateur crudeness about them. Taos's paintings were subtle, training the eye on details without forcing the issue. Alida held the camera close to her face and shielded the tiny screen with her cupped hands to deepen the contrast. She wished she could stand before the canvasses themselves and feel the full thrust of the images. There was sensuousness here, but something more besides. She beeped onto a portrait of an Indian flower-seller whose melancholic eyes were ringed with dark circles. The sumptuousness of her wares seemed to efface the woman. Her shoulders were slumped, her eyes unseeing of the bright heaps of jasmine and marigold. She doesn't enjoy the colours and perfume of her flowers any more, Alida realised. Taos went inside her mind. He walked through it until he understood. Then he painted what he knew. She found herself remembering the depth of the look they had shared at Hotel Guru. When he looked inside her with his painter's eyes, what did he see?

Taos had finished her story, but he didn't speak. Alida lowered the camera for a moment, aware of his stillness. To her indignation, he started flipping casually through her

90

notebook. Before she had time to think about it, her arm had whipped up and grabbed it off him in a flap of pages. 'That's private.'

Taos looked amused. 'Your story wasn't about marmots at all.'

'It started with a marmot simile,' she countered, squeezing the notebook back into her bag and wishing she hadn't let him read it.

'And where did it finish? Where's this denouement thing?'

She threw him a wary look. 'I'm not going to write about that.' Their conversation was edging uncomfortably close to danger. To shift the attention elsewhere, Alida frowned down at the camera display and beeped it on to the next image. An armless child on a beach. She had reached Mia's collages. Taos had stopped by Hotel Raj to photograph the collage of the two bears as well before they left town, so they had the full set with them.

'Did your ex-husband hit you?' he asked suddenly.

She gaped at him. 'I'll pretend I didn't hear that.'

'Sorry. Your life seems interesting, that's all. I'd like to know more.'

'Violence is not interesting, Taos, it's just nasty.' She paused. 'I know virtually nothing about you, do you realise that?' It seemed unfair to her that he was gradually uncovering her ancient past, the events that had shaped her life as it was today, while he remained aloof.

'You saw my paintings.' He nodded towards the camera on her lap. 'That's me.'

'Well, you read my story, and that's me. Was me, anyway.' She looked out of the window again in annoyance. She hadn't meant to admit to anything.

She could feel Taos watching her, but she didn't turn around.

91

Chapter Fifteen

'Wake up. This is Trivandrum.' Taos was nudging her shoulder with his arm. Alida forced her eyes open and gathered her possessions together. Passengers were filing bleary-eyed down the aisle. Outside, the bus station was busy despite the late hour. Hawkers and sellers pressed around them, offering accommodation, taxis, trays of sliced coconut. Alida clung to Mia's bag and edged her way through the crowd behind Taos. She was hungry and sticky, and the night air draped itself suffocatingly around her. The humidity was so high, it barely needed to rain.

'Before we get on the train to Varkala, I want to call the guest house to see if they've got rooms free and don't mind us turning up after midnight,' said Taos over his shoulder.

'In that case, I'll phone England.'

After some confusion, they found a place that did both national and international calls, and ducked into separate booths.

'Ian, it's me. No news here. How are things there?'

'Fine, fine. Did you get my email?' His voice was rapid, but distant, as if it was being flung away from her on the wind.

Alida pressed the receiver hard against her ear. 'No. I've been on a bus most of the day. I'm on my way to that guest house address in Kerala to see if I can turn up any information. Why, what did you want to tell me?'

'Only that I've been finding out about other cases of travellers who have gone missing in India.' His voice broke through whatever interference it had been swamped in, and emerged deep and grainy in Alida's right ear. 'People have been disappearing into thin air up in the Kullu Valley, and one of the theories being thrown about is that these backpackers are just getting out, you know, of their own accord. Disappearing on purpose to live a simpler life.'

Alida pushed her hair out of her face. 'And do you think Mia would do something like that?'

'I don't know, 'Lida, but it's a more pleasant thought than the other possibilities, isn't it? She could be staying in a meditation centre, or living in a mud hut somewhere off the beaten track. There are other parents in our position, you know. They're out there like you, searching for their kids all over Asia. I've read some worrying stories. One lad disappeared for eighteen months before finally showing up in Rajastan. He says he was drugged and robbed, and this drug he was given was so mind-bending that he spent months wandering around in a trance, not knowing who he was. He reckons this has happened to more than a few travellers.'

'Oh, Christ.' Alida leaned heavily against the wall of the booth. 'But what about girls? They're so much more vulnerable than boys. Do they ever turn up? If men drug women, they usually do more to them than just rob them. What if she's drugged up in some lair—'

'It won't help to think like that, Alida. All I'm saying is that she might well be out there somewhere, not knowing exactly who she is any more. It's just another possibility to bear in mind, that's all.'

'OK.' She let air escape from her mouth in a cool tunnel.

'I don't like it that you're all alone out there. I want to come over and help you find her – I'm sick of just sitting around at home like this.'

Alida straightened her spine. She didn't want him with her. Ian would argue about strategies, undermine her decisions, drive her mad. 'No, you need to be in London, Ian, in case she gets in touch,' she said firmly. 'And I'm not alone any more. I'm travelling with an artist Mia met in Hotel Guru. He's helping me search for her.'

'An artist?' He sounded instantly suspicious. 'What is he to Mia, a boyfriend or something?'

'Not as far as I know. He's just helping me look, that's all.' Alida was aware of Taos standing in the booth next to hers. 'Believe me, it's better if you stay put so that you can be on hand if Mia needs you. If we're both gallivanting around the country, how can she possibly contact us?' With this logic, she hoped to convince him.

'I know all that, but I feel so useless,' he complained. 'It should be me out there. And it would have been, if you hadn't beaten me to it.'

Alida bristled inwardly at his assumption that it should be him leading the search, as though he were the more capable parent, but she forced herself to adopt a placatory tone. 'Look, it makes no difference which one of us is out here. Just keep doing what you're doing. Get as much information as you can, and get other people involved.'

'Oh, I am doing. I'm in touch with the Foreign Missing Persons' Bureau and I've faxed details and a photograph of Mia to every police station in the bloody country, just about. I hope to God we'll get some sort of lead soon.' He paused. ''Lida?'

'Yes, I'm here,' she said quickly.

'Do you think our girl's still alive?'

Tears stung Alida's eyes, blinding her momentarily. 'Yes. Yes, of course I do.'

'I thought we'd been through the worst.' Ian's voice had dropped and it was low and whispery. Alida's heart ran to him. She squeezed her eyes closed and cradled the phone with both hands, hoping he could feel that he wasn't alone;

she was with him and she knew exactly how it felt, life spinning out of kilter for the second time, snatching them up like a whirlwind so that they could be dropped anywhere, mangled, lost.

'So did I, so did I.'

Taos was sitting on his rucksack reading his novel when Alida finished. If he had heard her side of the conversation, he gave no sign. He had a tired face, and Alida felt a surge of warmth for him which pricked tears into her eyes all over again. Her emotions needed some outlet, she supposed. She wanted to hug him.

He looked up, and his hazel eyes shone at her briefly. 'Ready?' he asked.

Alida woke soon after dawn itching all over. She counted nine fat red mosquito bites down her legs and arms, and two on her neck. That's the last time I go to sleep in this country with no bedcovers, she thought sourly. She lay in the grey light trying not to scratch or think about malaria. Instead she focused on the sound of the ceiling fan chugging above her head. At various points in the night it had made a sound like a death rattle. The Blue Sunrise Guest House had been a disappointing end to a long day of travelling. They had arrived at around one in the morning, in a rickshaw from the train station. While they'd waited for someone to answer the back door, where they had been told to knock, Alida had noticed the bodies of half-a-dozen cockroaches littering the ground around the dustbins. They were the size and colour of split-open dates, their legs curled up in death. She had stepped quickly away; she couldn't bear to be reminded that such creatures existed. Her distaste and fear for beetles, moths and spiders was deep-seated.

Eventually, a small, sleepy boy had let them in, and then Alida had found herself alone in a boxlike room with a mattress covered by a faded floral sheet. There was no other furniture. A greasy light switch operated a single, naked bulb which dangled unattractively from a knot of coloured wires. The hotel had no hot water, not even a proper shower, it seemed. It had squat toilets and the paint was peeling off the walls. She had done her best to get clean with a bucket of cold water and no soap. Then she had lain on her mattress in a T-shirt and knickers, rolled herself into a ball and slept.

There were voices outside: loud, male, English voices. Alida got up and eased her tiny window open. She could hear the hissing mass of the sea below the cliffs. A circle of backpackers sitting cross-legged on the hard ground outside were passing around a chillum. 'Boom-shanka!' they shouted before they inhaled. Columns of smoke soared from their lips.

They were young: Mia's age.

Alida ducked back inside and got washed and dressed as quickly as she could. Then she let herself out into the cool air, scanning the grass for snakes and scorpions as she walked towards the group.

'. . . it was like vomit. This hot, lumpy liquid just spurting out of me. That's amoebic dysentery for you. Stomach-ripping agony.'

The others were recoiling in amused disgust at this description.

'Like we really wanted to know that, Nic.'

'What makes you think we're interested in your diarrhoea.'

They noticed Alida falter beside them and looked her way with friendly, red-rimmed eyes.

'Hi,' she said uncertainly. 'I'm looking for my daughter. I think she may have stayed in this guest house at some point.' She handed the photograph to the nearest boy. 'Do you recognise her?'

Mia was passed around the circle to stoned headshakes.

'Sorry, we only got here three days ago,' said a boy with an orange bandanna. 'But if she stayed at the Blue

Sunrise, the owner will remember her. She's probably just finishing her dawn yoga session along the cliff in Babu's hut. She's an Indian woman about your age.' He peered at her. 'Or maybe older, actually. Anyhow, her name's Five-toes. You can't miss her. Everyone knows her.' He returned the photograph to her.

'Fytos?'

'No. Five. Toes. Like, some of her toes have been amputated—'

The boy across from him snorted. 'Yeah, five of them to be precise. Maths was never your strong point, eh, Benny?'

Their laughter had a canned, echoing quality, and their eyes were identical reddened slits. They were all some-body's sons, fresh from A levels, enjoying their freedom. Alida thanked them and strode away. Their silliness was infectious. That and the salty breeze lifted her spirits as she walked in the direction they'd pointed in with the sea lounging huge and blue on her left. Palm trees lined up along the cliff edge leaned precariously out over the beach, their leaves rattling in the wind. It seemed a day for new beginnings; a day for finding Mia. Alida took deep, power-ful breaths and felt the sweat pores prickle across her back as she walked past closed wooden cafés and huts. A sign pointing to a French bakery made her stomach roar, but she hurried on.

A Swiss couple on their way down to the beach for an early-morning dip pointed out Babu's yoga hut, and Alida skulked near the entrance, waiting for the session to finish. The hut had no door, and she could see the teacher, presumably Babu. He was naked apart from a white cloth wrapped around his waist and passed between his legs. His hands were clasped above his head. With a look of intense concentration on his face, he contracted his stomach until it disappeared under his ribcage and seemed to stick to his spine. Then he puffed part of it out and, using only his muscles and his breath, proceeded to rotate that protruding wedge of flesh so that it looked like a guinea pig running in circles under a sheet of skin. Afterwards, he described breathing techniques to his students, urging them to 'pant like dogs' and then getting them to emit deep sounds with each breath, as though they had been winded. It was impossible for Alida not to be aware of her own breathing and she found herself performing a muted example of what the students were doing. Using her stomach muscles to force air out of her lungs made her light-headed and she leaned back against the bamboo wall.

When the class filed out, there were only two Indians among the students and only one of them was female. She wore a lavender T-shirt and a pair of black leggings. Alida's gaze dropped to the woman's feet. The right foot was exquisitely hennaed, with delicate ankle chains slipping over it, and meticulously painted toenails, each adorned with a silver toe-ring. The other foot, undecorated, ended in a dusty stump. The woman walked cautiously, but with no visible limp.

It seemed impolite, somehow, to ask her if she was Five-toes. Alida approached her. 'Are you the owner of the Blue Sunrise Guest House?'

'I am,' replied the woman. Her voice was deep and throaty, with only a slight accent. Her hair was scraped back into a bun so tight that it pulled the skin on her face, and she had luminous brown eyes.

'Could I talk to you, please? It's about—'

'One moment.' Five-toes raised a slim arm which ran with metal bangles. 'First I must sit and gather my thoughts for only one very small moment. Then we can talk.' She walked close to the edge of the cliff and sat down cross-legged on a patch of red earth peppered with tough grass. She closed her eyes.

Alida sat opposite her and unconsciously mirrored her position. Her gaze was drawn to the other woman's feet, visible under her knees. There was the brown, dull, toeless foot, and there was the pampered foot, the toenails perfectly curved pink shells, not a speck of dust on them. This foot was so appealing that Alida couldn't take her eyes off it. Was this careful painting and jewellery designed to reinforce the contrast between left and right foot, or was it intended to distract the eye away from its misshapen partner? Either way, it was doing both for Alida. She found herself wondering what had happened to the missing toes. She imagined them rolling over the cliff like petals in the wind, or taking root and producing tiny toe plants.

Five-toes opened her eyes and gravely followed Alida's gaze. 'I am making the best of this foot of mine,' she said, wiggling it. 'When I had ten toes, I paid them little attention. These days I am careful to appreciate the ones I have left.'

'I see.' There was a brief pause. 'I wanted to talk to you about my—'

'I mourn the loss of my other toes,' continued Five-toes, 'but I do not let their loss prevent me from enjoying the remaining phalanges. I try to give them quality of life. I show them they are important to me.' She looked very serious, her nose and mouth straight lines.

'I understand.' Alida shifted position on the spiky grass, which was prickling through her sarong. 'What happened to them?'

'My brother-in-law cut them off with an axe.' She waved a hand dismissively at Alida's shocked expression. 'I do not know what he did with them after that.' She stared out over the sea. 'Fourteen bones, I have lost. I think perhaps the fish ate them.'

There was a respectful silence.

'I've lost something, too,' offered Alida when Five-toes' gaze swivelled slowly back to her. 'My daughter, Mia, is missing. She stayed here about a month ago, and I think you may have met her.' She passed her the silver-framed picture.

Five-toes took it and studied it. 'She is in a place so cold that her breath forms clouds.'

Alida jumped as if bitten. 'You know where she is?'

'No, no. In this picture, she is in a cold place. That is all I meant. Is this England?'

'Yes. Do you remember her?' She was crushing the grass in her fist.

'Of course I remember Mia. She has an excellent ear for colour, that girl. A good eye for sound. And now she is missing, you say?'

'She disappeared from a hotel in Madurai ten days ago.'

'Mia,' murmured Five-toes thoughtfully. 'Where might she have gone?' She rolled her eyes closed and became instantly immobile. Alida waited in a state of complete tension.

'Mia talked of Hampi,' said Five-toes after a while, her eyes still closed. 'There are the ruins of an ancient kingdom, a temple with musical pillars. She wanted to see and hear those things. Perhaps you will find her there.'

'Hampi. OK. But this is just a guess, isn't it?' said Alida, despair knotting her stomach.

'Of course.' She opened her eyes. 'I know no more than you do.'

Alida thought for a moment. One of the unwritten post-cards in Mia's bag might have been of a place called Hampi. Perhaps Five-toes' tip wasn't so useless. 'Is there anything you can tell me about Mia's state of mind while she was here?' she asked. 'Her concerns or preoccupations?'

Five-toes drooped forwards slightly and trained her gaze on her undecorated foot. It twitched under her regard. She appeared to be deep in thought.

'I can tell you that your daughter had some very real, conscious dreams about things past,' she said eventually, without looking up. 'I can tell you that she wrote about these things.'

'She wrote about them?' Alida leaned forwards in excitement. 'I've found myself doing something similar recently. What did she – I mean, how ...' She stopped herself. Five-toes was still looking at her foot as if it had something to tell her. 'Sorry,' Alida said, waving a hand. 'You talk.'

'She said she wrote the way one sometimes writes down a dream, as if it is happening now. This is in order to re-enter the memory more fully. I recall Mia saying that people are made from a chain of memories. She said that in order to understand who she is today, she had to connect the links of that chain.'

'I've found some collages she did just before she went missing. Perhaps they show the same memories that she wrote down.' Alida paused, the collages flashing through her mind. Could there be some deeper connection? She shook her head to clear it. 'Did you read anything she wrote?'

Five-toes looked up from her foot. 'Nothing. Not one word. She never showed her little book to anyone. But I remember her saying that her writing was leading her by any number of routes to one person. This person was hiding between every line she wrote.'

'Who was it?'

'I am sorry. I do not know the answer to that.' Five-toes shook out her T-shirt as if she had seen a fly land on it. She stood up, wobbling slightly. 'I wish you very good luck.'

Alida scrambled to her feet. 'Wait, please. Is there anything else she said or did – did she take any drugs, talk about meditation or religion? I – just anything would be useful.'

Five-toes smiled faintly. 'I do not think that Mia was taking drugs. Not every foreign traveller does, you know. Most, perhaps, but not all. She seemed very eager to follow a writing, dreaming path into herself. And she

101

talked often of Hampi. I am sorry, but that is all I know.' She began to turn away, then paused. 'Of course,' she added, 'there is a difference between state of mind and physical state, but you are more interested in the first one, I think.'

'No, no, I want to know how she was physically too,' said Alida anxiously.

'She was very well. Her centre full of life.' Five-toes laced her fingers loosely together and slipped her joined hands momentarily under the hem of her T-shirt. Her smile expanded. 'Full of life,' she repeated, her dark eyes watching Alida almost slyly.

'Good,' said Alida, but her forehead was puckered in confusion. She didn't know what to make of these strange pronunciations. Did they mean anything, or was this merely some kind of yoga talk? Five-toes had already turned away. Alida watched her walk carefully along the cliff path, the sun bright on her coil of dark hair. When Five-toes was a good fifty metres away, the meaning of her words hit Alida like a blow to the head and she burst into a dust-raising run, sliding in her flip-flops, her heart smashing against her chest.

'Stop!' she shouted on the end of a breath.

Five-toes turned, her teeth flashing white as she watched Alida approach.

Chapter Sixteen

August 2002

Mum has another boyfriend. He's big and slow and he makes me feel very small and fast, like a minnow. He's in our house today for the first time and I zoom around trailing Mum's peacock-blue evening shawl through the air behind me and seeing how many times I can make him nearly trip over me as she shows him round the house. He's called Tom, a deep name that sounds inside me like a gong. He wants to talk about car engines, mostly. Mum pretends to find this incredibly interesting, she laughs red lipstick and flashes her eyes at him and slides her hand along his forearm until I accidentally tumble into them both.

'Mia!' she exclaims (melodiously, so that he'll think she's always sweet and smiley with me). 'Do stop knocking into Tom, please. He'll go away covered in bruises at this rate.' When Tom goes to the bathroom later, she grabs my arm in a painful pinch and brings her face close to mine and my teeth feel all furry. 'Act your age, Mia,' she hisses. 'You'll be thirteen in three months' time. I happen to like Tom and I'd appreciate it if you were a bit more welcoming to him.' She releases me and my eyes burn as if she just flung grape juice into them. She stalks back into the kitchen and I rub my arm. I don't like the way she is when she has a new boyfriend. She doesn't want to show them all the black and scarlet steam inside her, so more of it spills out onto me. She isn't herself, and after a while they realise this and stop coming round. Dad's the only man who knows her inside out, and he left her. Left us.

I go upstairs and sit on my window seat with my knees drawn up to my chin and my arms wrapped around them. This is one of my favourite positions – I'm as small as I can get and soon it feels as if peas are falling softly onto the crown of my head and everything starts to taste fleecy white, like cirrus clouds, and if I close my eyes and wait for a while, a thin imprint of the winged elephant dances across the sky behind my eyelids. I can see through it a bit and it could vanish at any time but at least it's with me for a moment, shining its blue eyes onto me so that everything grows lighter.

It's been a while since I last dreamed about the elephant.

I miss having that blue gaze on me.

October 2002

It was Poppy's thirteenth birthday at the weekend and even though we all went ice-skating to celebrate, I'm staying at her house again tonight. Her house smells of Labrador and fresh lilies. The lily smell comes from her mum's anxious eyes and flimsy green voice, and I think the Labrador smell comes from her father, who sits hunched behind a newspaper on the sofa the whole evening. Poppy and me go up to her room and sit on her fluffy cream rug and soon she starts asking me about sex again because her big sister, Shannon, is going out with a boy and all they talk about is when they're going to do it.

'Is it true you can't get pregnant if you do it standing up?'

'Of course it's not true. That's like saying you can't get pregnant if you do it on your birthday. The only way not to get pregnant is not to have sex.' I'm reciting my mother's words by rote, and my voice even sounds a little like hers as I say it.

'Well, I know *that*, duh!' She kicks at me with her pink-socked foot. 'But Shannon said that Chris said—'

'The position makes no difference,' I tell her breezily. 'But if she's going to do it with Chris she should definitely make him wear a condom. He's always snogging different girls outside youth club and who knows what else he's done with them. He could have genital warts.'

'Yuk!' Poppy rolls back onto her elbows, her fair hair splashing everywhere as she laughs. 'Hey, Mia, you should bring those photos of your mum's into school again, they really spook the boys.'

'Maybe I will.' I smile, remembering how it had felt to be the star of the day, scattering glossy prints of sexually transmitted diseases across the desk and answering everyone's questions. That's how my mother must feel when she's lecturing, straight-spined and satiny bright.

'When d'you think *we'll* get boyfriends?' asks Poppy.

I shrug. 'You'll get one soon because you're so pretty. And I'll probably still be a virgin when I'm *twenty*.'

Poppy kicks out at me again. 'Don't be weird!'

I grab her pink foot and tickle it and she shrieks like an electric shock.

January 2003

I am a small girl. I am standing on a beach holding the most precious thing in the world in my two thin arms.

From nowhere, a storm blows up. Dark clouds crash in and there are all these black lines criss-crossing the sky. The lines press down on me like metal strips and there's a sound so loud and terrible that it rips my arms from my shoulders.

I have lost the most precious thing in the world and so I run, run, right into the water to find her.

But I can't swim with no arms.

I kick, kick and gulp sea water, swallow turquoise death.

Kick, kick and drown.

I'm awake.

I'm not drowning.

I'm here in my dry-air room, the darkness as purple as rotting plums.

I switch on the light beside my bed and it's like fire shooting into my eyes. I haven't had that dream for more than five years but it's as real as it ever was. If Mum came into my room now, I'd tell her the dream, tell her my feelings, tell her the whole story. But from across the hall, there's a heavy, sleeping silence.

Maybe this time I didn't scream.

Chapter Seventeen

'Sit, you are dizzy. Sit, sit.' Five-toes guided Alida off the path to the scant shade of a palm tree whose fronds waved, delicate and umbrella-like. Alida sat down, struggling to get her breath back and calm her thoughts. She felt panicked and sweat was running into her eyebrows. Five-toes crouched beside her attentively and waited for her to recover.

'So,' said Alida weakly, 'are you telling me that my daughter is pregnant?'

Five-toes closed her eyes briefly in assent.

'My God.' She tried to imagine Mia, her Mia, carrying a child. It was impossible. 'I can't believe it.' Her voice sounded parched.

'There was a life growing there when I met her,' confirmed Five-toes.

'And then?' Alida glanced at her in alarm. 'Did she lose it?'

'Oh, no, no. I do not think so. But of course I cannot say what the situation is now with your girl. When I knew her, it was very early, the baby newly discovered, nothing there to be seen.'

'You mean she only found out while she was in India?'

By way of an answer, Five-toes wobbled her head.

'Is that a yes or a no?' asked Alida in some frustration.

'It is a yes!' Five-toes patted her bun, looking mildly offended.

'My God,' repeated Alida. The mathematical function in her brain was stirring now, working through the shock, doing what it did best. She sat in silence while this efficient, unemotional part of her brain backtracked in time, subtracting days and weeks, turning back the clock. It was impossible to be precise, but if Mia had discovered the pregnancy shortly after her arrival in India, by now she could be between fourteen and sixteen weeks along. If she was still alive.

Five-toes stood up and her movement jerked Alida back to alertness.

'Wait,' said Alida. 'How did Mia feel about this whole thing? Did she mention how and when it happened, or who the father is?'

'I am sorry. All I know is what you now know. She did not seem unhappy, only looking inside herself with this dream writing. I have told you all I know.' Five-toes leaned in towards Alida and held her gaze for a long, still moment. 'Good luck.'

When Five-toes had gone, Alida sat teary-eyed, her arms gripped around her knees. Was this pregnancy the result of a fling with a boy in England, or with another backpacker during Mia's early days in India, or had she been raped? Had Mia run away from the consequences of her pregnancy, ashamed to tell her parents? Or had she run from the father, whoever he might be? An image of Taos edged into Alida's mind and she stared at it in horror. What did he do to my child? she thought, and was overcome by a despair so vicious it made her tremble. It's not him, she told herself. Taos didn't do it.

For a long while, Alida let her thoughts spool out until the images lost some of their ugliness and her emotions settled. She reminded herself of Five-toes' words. *Mia did not seem unhappy*. When the sun had eaten away her shade, she got up and with renewed energy visited every establishment along the cliff top, asking after Mia and pinning 'missing' posters to walls and doors. Nobody else recognised Mia's photograph. The sea had appeared in Mia's collages, and Alida wanted to stand close to the breaking waves and think. She walked along the cliff until she reached the path down to the beach. It was steep, and her flip-flops cut into the space between her toes as she skidded on the loose earth. The beach was curved and shining, and almost deserted. She spotted Taos immediately. He was sunbathing on his back in a pair of black swimming shorts, his hands cupped under his head. She slipped off her flip-flops and walked barefoot towards him over the sand, which collapsed in miniature landslides under her feet.

When she arrived next to his prone body, she saw that behind his sunglasses, Taos was asleep. She hesitated, looking down the length of him. He was evenly tanned, with ruffled golden body hair and long, muscular limbs. His left nipple was pierced with a small silver hoop, as was his belly button. Would Mia find him attractive enough to sleep with him? He was certainly good-looking, but was he so desirable that Mia could forgot all about sexually transmitted diseases and pregnancy? Perhaps so, conceded Alida reluctantly. Below the second silver hoop, emerging from his shorts, was a blue dragon tattoo. As Alida's eyes rested on it she experienced a thread of lust which mortified her. He might have had sex with my child, she reminded herself in disgust, forcing her eyes swiftly past the bulge in his shorts. Running all the way across the middle of his right thigh was a wide pink scar, as if someone had unzipped the flesh and left it open. He had large, square toes. Alida's gaze edged back up to his scar.

'Enjoying the view?' asked Taos suddenly.

Her eyes leaped to his face. His eyes were still closed, but two vertical lines of irritation had appeared between his eyebrows.

'Oh, I'm sorry. . . I thought you were asleep and I didn't want to disturb you.'

'So you decided to stand there ogling me until I woke up?' His voice was expressionless.

Alida forced a laugh. 'Hardly. I was only... I just saw your scar, that's all.'

'You saw more than that. I could feel your eyes on me.' He disengaged an arm from under his head, tipped his sunglasses back and squinted up at her. It was impossible to tell if he was genuinely upset or if he was just enjoying making her squirm.

'I'm sorry,' she said, flustered. 'But the tattoo, the piercings, the scar—'

'What about them?'

'Well they – your body – it reveals more about you than your words ever do. And I was just considering that.'

Taos sat up, the skin on his stomach crinkling. 'Piercings and tattoos can hide the truth just as well as words can. It's only scars that can't lie.' He looked her up and down speculatively. 'Did you bring your swimming gear?'

'No.'

'Shame.' He kept his eyes on her until she looked away, flushing. The sea dashed in, raising spray. A forgotten ball was being tossed around in the foam.

'You really do look way too young to be Mia's mother,' he observed flatly.

She half turned towards him, careful not to look at his body. 'I had her when I was only nineteen,' she said, and realised with renewed shock that if Mia had this baby, she too would become a mother at nineteen, following exactly in Alida's own footsteps. And she'd be a grandmother ... The thought made her head spin.

'Aren't you going to sit down?' he asked.

'OK.' She sat a little way from him with her knees drawn up to her chest and her arms locked around them. 'I might go to Hampi next,' she said, and related her conversation with Five-toes, carefully edited to avoid any mention of Mia's pregnancy. If it really was his business, he would know about it already, in which case why on earth hadn't he mentioned it? And if he didn't know and was in no way responsible, then why bother informing him at this stage?

'It's worth checking out Hampi if Mia said she was interested in the place,' said Taos sensibly. 'It's better than nothing. And if she did go there, even if she's not there any more, perhaps someone will be able to tell us something.'

'Hmm.' Alida sighed miserably. 'It's all so vague and undefined. It's like a wild goose chase.'

He shrugged. 'It's all you've got.'

For a time, they were silent, watching the waves. Then Alida turned back to him. 'How did you get that scar?'

Taos glanced at it and frowned. 'Motorbike crash. Last year, up in Kashmir.'

'Were you on your own?'

His eyes narrowed fractionally. 'No. My girlfriend was on the bike, too.'

'Was she OK?'

'Not really. She died of head injuries in the local hospital.'

Alida pressed her palms against her eyeballs so that the world went black. 'How horrible. I'm so sorry,' she said from the blackness. After a moment, she slid her hands slowly off her face and looked at him.

'Why did you cover your face like that?' he asked.

'I don't know. I just didn't want to see it, I suppose.'

'I wish I could see it,' he said, his voice suddenly harsh. 'I'd like to see every minute of it.' His face was tight with desperation.

Alida bit her lip. She scooped up a fistful of sand and let it drain away. When the bulk of it had gone, she rubbed her hands together and the remaining grains scattered over her sarong. Her chest hurt. She didn't know what to say to him. 'It must have been awful,' she murmured, inadequately.

111

'I've totally forgotten her, you know,' he said, staring out at the waves. 'I can't remember the way she smelled, the sound of her laugh, the things we did in bed, the things we said to each other. It's all gone and I can't get it back.' He glanced at her with flinching eyes.

Responding to the fear in his face, Alida leaned solicitously towards him. 'Perhaps it's too painful to remember at this stage?'

'No. You don't understand,' he said bleakly. 'This is going to sound bizarre, but in actual fact she's been wiped from my mind like a deleted computer file. After the accident, I woke up in Srinagar hospital with absolutely no recollection of this deceased Kirstin Callam girl who people kept coming in and talking to me about.'

'But that's crazy.' She studied his face, which was turned towards the sea again. 'How long had you known her for?'

'Fifteen months, apparently. Together with doctors and family, we worked out that I've lost at least three complete years of memories leading up to the crash and I've only got patchy memories of the four or five years before that.'

Alida stared at him. 'God, Taos, I'm so sorry. That's a huge chunk of your life.' She shook her head, fingering the folds of her sarong without noticing. 'Is it a sort of partial amnesia, then?'

'It's retrograde amnesia. All my memories of childhood and early adulthood seem intact, but it gets progressively worse leading up to the crash.' He looked stonily at his scar. 'I just feel bad for Kirstin and her family. She spent fifteen months of her life with me and I don't even remember her now that she's dead. Her brother was completely crushed by her death and I was worse than useless in helping him through his grief.' He laughed humourlessly. 'I didn't even know what my girlfriend looked like until they showed me pictures.'

To Alida's surprise, he scrambled suddenly to his feet,

inadvertently spraying her with sand. 'Anyway, let's not dwell on it,' he said, looking down at her with a half-smile. 'My scar is giving away my secrets already. It can't lie.'

She smiled sadly. 'I shouldn't have asked.'

'Don't worry about it.' He was already walking away. 'I'm going for a swim,' he said, and she watched the tall, broad shape of him as he walked towards the sea.

That afternoon Alida left Taos battling with the waves and walked inland to Temple Junction along a path punctured with yellow puddles of cow's urine, to change money and telephone Ian. She was followed by a short-tailed dog with chunks bitten from its fur who nosed along rather too close to her legs so that as she walked she tried not to think about dog bites and rabies and focus instead on the things she passed: a man high up a palm tree, gripping the tree trunk between his knees as he hacked away at coconuts; children playing a game with sticks and rubber-band balls; the rustle of shiny palm leaves against a pale and hazy sky; piles of discarded coconut shells.

The dog peeled away from her as soon as the first ramshackle buildings came into view, and Alida soon located a telephone booth. She caught Ian just as he was getting up for work, and he was pleased to hear from her. Sitting on a cracked leather stool in the air-conditioned booth, she brought him up to speed on her actions of the past few days before broaching the subject that really mattered. 'I met a woman in Varkala who remembered Mia and she told me some major news, Ian.'

He was immediately on a tightrope. 'What did she say?'

Alida felt sorry that he had to wait even a second for the information. She pushed the words out in a rush. 'She said that Mia had recently discovered that she was pregnant.'

'What?' he was instantly disbelieving. 'She's lying!'

'Ian, what could she possibly gain from lying to me?'

asked Alida gently. 'I know it's a shock but at least it gives us more of a clue as to her state of mind when she went missing.'

He wasn't listening. 'Pregnant,' he groaned. 'You don't think someone raped her, do you?'

'I'm not saying that, no. This woman said Mia didn't seem unhappy or anything. I think maybe she just had a fling with someone, perhaps here in India.'

'Then some bug-infested traveller will have given her AIDS.'

'Let's hope not.'

'Or else she's fallen into the hands of a back-street abortionist. That country's low on hygiene, you know. Disease-ridden blood transfusions, filthy needles, overdoses of anaesthetic . . .' He was ranting now, his breath uneven, his voice jarred. Alida listened sympathetically, both hands cupped around the receiver. 'Jesus, 'Lida. This is terrible news. The shock of finding out could have made her do anything, something really stupid even. All those hormones out of control. She might have gone completely off the rails. . . Why the hell didn't she come to us for help?'

'I don't know, Ian,' Alida said slowly. 'Just stay calm.'

'Some randy little bastard has knocked up my eighteen-year-old daughter, who has now disappeared off the face of the Earth, and I'm supposed to stay calm?' His voice was shaking.

Alida closed her eyes and spoke steadily, willing him to slow down and listen. 'I know it isn't good, but at least we *know* more, Ian. At least we know a bit more about what happened to her out here.'

'We don't really, though, do we? This has just opened up a thousand new unpleasant possibilities of what might have happened to the poor kid. Nothing good can come of this development, I'm telling you.' He paused briefly. 'That bloke who's travelling with you, the artist. What did he have to say about this?'

114

Alida opened her eyes. 'I haven't told him yet. Why?'

'Do you think he might have something to do with it? I mean, physically?'

'I don't think so, but I can't say for sure.' She leaned her head thoughtfully against the wall. 'I asked him once if he'd slept with Mia and he refused to answer me.'

'Refused, did he? I'll come over there and get the truth out of him,' said Ian darkly.

Alida sighed. 'I don't think he was hiding anything particularly, he just didn't like me interrogating him about his private life, that's all.'

'Well, I'd keep an eye on him anyway. Watch him closely when you tell him about it. Monitor his reactions.'

Alida smiled slightly. 'Should I shine a strong light in his face and beat him up a bit, too?'

'I'm serious, Alida. The man's under suspicion just for wanting to travel about searching for Mia with you. Why would he do that without some ulterior motive? He knows more than he's letting on, I guarantee it. Just be careful.'

'Yes, yes, I will be,' she said, impatient to move the conversation along. 'Listen, do you think there's any chance Mia might have gone off somewhere specific to have the baby?'

Ian hesitated, this new scenario seeming to provide him with some breathing space. 'Well, from what you say it's a fairly recent... event,' he said with some distaste. 'If she's decided to keep it then it's a bit early to set up camp to have it.'

'True.' The booth was so air-conditioned that Alida was starting to feel chilly. 'I don't know, I just feel this pregnancy might be a central reason for her disappearance, and perhaps also a clue to her whereabouts.'

'Who knows?' He was silent for a moment. 'Why did she ever go to that pit of a country?'

'It's got its good sides, you know,' said Alida. 'It's ... It actually grows on you.' She groped for words, wanting to

115

communicate something of her experience. 'The people – sometimes the most joyful smiles come from those who have nothing,' she said, thinking of the burned woman's daughter. 'And I've never seen anything like the temple at Madurai. All those deities – the architecture is so alive somehow.'

'Well, I'm glad you're enjoying yourself,' he snapped.

Alida rolled her eyes. 'Oh, come off it, Ian. I didn't say I was—'

'Sorry,' he was already saying, his voice echoing slightly down the line. 'I didn't mean to be sarcastic. You've done well to get this information, 'Lida.'

An apology and praise all in one sentence! marvelled Alida. This was so unlike the Ian of recent years that she softened immediately. 'Has it occurred to you yet,' she said with a smile that could be heard in her voice, 'that this baby which might or might not still be growing inside Mia is our grandchild?'

'Oh, blimey,' said Ian irritably. 'You and I haven't even hit forty yet. It's the size of a peanut, it could be the offspring of a rapist, and you're already welcoming it into the family?'

Alida shrugged. 'No. I'm just saying. And it'll be a lot bigger than a peanut by now.' She unwrapped the fingers of her left hand from the receiver and extended forefinger and thumb, estimating. 'Anyway, if we find Mia—'

'When,' he corrected.

'When we find her, we won't care about anything that's happened in between. Whatever she wants, we'll support her.'

Ian blew air down the phone. 'Yeah.'

There was a silence the consistency of wool, a rare moment of peace between them. Alida breathed it in, drawing strength.

'I'll call again when I know more,' she promised, and they rang off.

Chapter Eighteen

At the end of Alida's sixth day in India, she and Taos arrived in Hampi after dark in the middle of a monsoon storm, and the rickshaw driver had to be bribed to take them the last leg of the journey. The few steps from the rickshaw to a squat, whitewashed guest house near the river battered and soaked them. They splashed through rising puddles to the entrance and were greeted by a plump Indian woman with chipped front teeth, wearing a zinc-yellow sari with silver trimming.

'Welcome, welcome,' she said, and the bangles on her arms tinkled as she beckoned them in. 'I am Mangala and you look like two wet rats! Such a storm, tonight. Come in.'

Alida's room was spotless, her bed draped in a green mosquito net which was attached by hooks to the ceiling. It reminded her of a four-poster princess bed. The walls were painted white and had thin oblong holes cut into them at regular intervals along the tops. They were obviously there to aid ventilation, but she felt uneasy about insects fluttering into the room. She stripped, showered and changed into dry leggings and a pale-pink T-shirt belonging to Mia. Sleeping on the narrow bunks in the train had been like sleeping on a rolling log, as the train had swayed alarmingly the whole way, stopping and starting with great cracking jolts. She and Taos had stayed a further night in

117

Varkala, delaying the five hundred mile trip north to Hampi in the hope that a more solid indication of Mia's whereabouts would emerge. It hadn't. Although a stall-holder and a masseuse had recognised Mia from the photograph, they had been unable to give Alida any idea of her current whereabouts. Even those travellers who had spent a long time in Varkala couldn't help. It appeared that the people with whom Mia had talked during her stay had all moved on to other, anonymous destinations.

It was difficult to remain confident in the face of so few solid clues and Alida was glad to have Taos with her. The previous evening, they had eaten coconut curry with glistening bowls of jeera rice in one of the cliff-top restaurants and he had told her that before his crash, he had been a professional artist, with exhibitions all over Australia and Indonesia. Since the crash, he still sold the occasional portrait to finance his travels, but he was now experimenting artistically with the translation of emotions into animals such as the falling tiger, and he didn't feel ready yet to get back to the rhythm of his old life. Alida had understood. Since he had revealed the history of his scar, she had felt easier in his company. They were alike, she decided as she crawled around her bed tucking in her huge mosquito net. Both of them had been on the receiving end of momentous life blows, and both had emerged as different people, sadder, more wary. For a time, she lay star-shaped on her bed, listening to the crash of the storm and thinking of Mia.

I'm wearing her clothes, she thought. Using her stuff, trying to subsume myself in her essence so that I know what's happened to her. I'm having lucid dreams, the way Taos said she did. I'm writing again for the first time in years, and Five-toes said Mia was writing, too. It all means something, but what? All these threads and connections, what do they add up to? She reached out from under the mosquito net and brought her notepad and pen onto the bed. At first, without a lucid dream image to prod her along, there was nothing to write. Then Alida closed her eyes and thought of Mia's collages, conjured them up until they loomed colourfully before her. She began to write.

Mia lines her memories up. She runs a finger along them, feeling how the colours change beneath the sliding weight of a fingertip. Over her shoulder, I watch. She is remembering how it feels to have no arms. She can't reach out to anyone. If she falls, she cannot save herself. If others need help, she cannot save them. Mia can taste sadness, measure loss in inches and feet. I watch as she listens to the blue of those diamond eyes. I strain to hear her thoughts, although I'd recognise them in a flash because they are mine too. Her memories are a replica of my own, viewed from the other side of a mirror. A woman pregnant with death. A child feeling attacked, unloved, alone.

I watch her leave a fingerprint on the smaller of two bears. It clamours to be picked up by the larger bear which looms over it with arms flung high and wide. It is not clear whether the larger intends to sweep the smaller into an embrace, or deliver some terrible retribution. Her finger moves on, and I see that the memories have formed a circle. She stands in the centre, rotating her body slowly, breathing in their scent. As I watch, she spins faster and faster until her features blur, her hair chasing her cheeks.

I watch my daughter until she disappears.

Uncurling her limbs into a stretch in the morning, Alida noticed that the only colour in the room was the slippery green of the mosquito net. To compensate for such blanched surroundings, she got up and pulled colours from her bag, draping a yellow T-shirt on a hook on the wall and flinging Mia's sarongs over the chairs. As she did, she

119

noticed dozens of dusty handprints high on the white-washed walls. Peering more closely, she found the crumpled body of a mosquito in the centre of each print, and felt a sense of grim satisfaction. Being in India was teaching her to hate mosquitoes.

Turning away, she saw that a note in spindly, backward-slanting handwriting had been slid under the door. It was from Taos, saying he had gone into Hospet, the neighbouring town, to print out the digital photographs of Mia's collages. Alida donned her now habitual uniform of sarong, flip-flops and vest top, then slung a few essentials into a shoulder bag. It occurred to her that her 'essentials' had changed: these were no longer her house keys and driving licence, but the photograph of Mia, a full bottle of clean drinking water and mosquito spray. She put up a 'missing' poster in the guest house and explained Mia's story to Mangala, the sympathetic proprietor.

'Write my guest house name on your posters,' said Mangala firmly. 'We will find your Mia sooner than blinking.'

Last night's storm had long gone, but as Alida walked into the village centre she had to side-step large, muddy puddles and she noticed that the sky was still bruised with purple clouds. Hampi bazaar consisted of a wide main street with a temple at one end, colourless in comparison with the Meenakshi Temple, but still imposing. Cows lay about on the road chewing the cud as children carrying babies in slings on their backs kicked a ball around in the puddles. Locals were opening up their shops and a few foreigners wandered along aimlessly.

Walking through the village alone, Alida felt oddly conspicuous and self-conscious. When she noticed herself missing Taos's ambling, confident presence, she scoffed at herself. *He'll be back in a few hours, you dependent fool. Get a grip*. She left her posters taped to windows, or hanging off the edges of tables weighed down with sugar cane. She scribbled the name of her guest house in Hampi across the base of the posters, as Mangala had advised her to. The sellers were friendly, but none recognised Mia's photograph. Alida was beginning to feel she had done this a thousand times: pressed her palms together in the Hindu greeting of *namaste*, looked into a stranger's face and asked for help in simple sentences.

'My daughter is missing.'

'Please can I leave this poster here?'

Followed, always, by: 'Have you seen her before?'

She had seen it a thousand times: the short headshakes, eyes dropping away from hers in pity. Sometimes they asked her questions: 'Your daughter, how old? Long time missing?' Some didn't want to know her troubles, turning away from her as soon as they could. Most wanted to help, and couldn't. She tore Sellotape with her teeth, smiled at the sellers, admired their wares and tried not to scream at the opaqueness of this country that had swallowed Mia whole.

As she straightened up from taping a poster on a board next to a cyber café, she noticed a girl of about twenty staring at her from a few metres away. The girl looked to be Northern European and was drenched in jewellery: her face studded with piercings, her arms and neck and ankles hooped with silver and gold. She was wearing an elaborate headscarf that floated down her back in a mane of Venetian red silk, and above her sandals, unaccountably, she wore stripy leg warmers. Her eyes were unblinking and of a naked intensity, as if the lids had been peeled back too far. Alida returned her stare for a moment, then turned away.

'Hey,' said the girl. 'You look for that person?'

Alida turned back. The girl was pointing one straight, bejewelled arm at the picture of Mia.

'Yes. She's my daughter. Do you recognise her?'

The girl strode over and thrust her head forwards to stare at the poster. 'Mia,' she said. 'She is my friend. I know her well.'

121

Alida's hand flew to her throat. 'Do you know where she might be? She went missing.'

'I know to a dot, like, this small where she is.' She indicated the spiked stud protruding from her lower lip. 'What I don't know is what it is worth.'

'Sorry?'

'What is this information worth for you?'

'Knowing where she is – well, it's worth everything to me,' Alida stammered. 'I – She's my child.'

'So you will pay?'

'Well, I suppose so, but I don't see—' From the corner of her eye she saw frantic movement, and turned distractedly to see a man lost in his own hair. His straw-coloured beard flowed over his chest and stomach, coming to rest on his thighs. The curling ends of his dreadlocks touched his knees. He was gesticulating at her and mouthing something, but she couldn't read his lips.

'Ignore him, he is crazy. How much will you give me?' asked the girl, her eyes jabbing into Alida's face.

'Junkie,' coughed the hairy man, rolling his eyes.

The girl swung round viciously. 'Shut it.' Her earrings bounced.

Alida stepped backwards.

'Wait. You want to find your daughter, and I am the person you must speak with, you understand?' The girl's tone grew wheedling. 'You want to see her again, yes?'

Alida swallowed. 'Of course I do, but how can I be sure you're telling me the truth if you want money for the information?'

The girl spat on the ground. 'It is a trade. I help you, you help me. You are rich, I am poor. No money, no talking.'

The hairy man shook his head so that the bells sewn into his beard tinkled. Then he turned and walked away, leaving Alida stranded. She thought quickly.

'I'll give you five hundred rupees,' she said, 'but not for

a lie. If you've never seen Mia before, you'll get the money anyway. But I need to know the truth. Please don't mislead me.'

For a moment she saw a flicker of something in the girl's eyes. It was gone so fast she couldn't be certain whether it was contempt or comprehension. 'Money now,' said the girl.

Alida took out her purse and waved the banknotes in the air. 'Tell me the truth,' she said, and passed over the money. As soon as she had the notes in her grasp, the girl sprang backwards, her jewellery gleaming. She was about to run, that much was clear. Alida sighed. 'Do you know my daughter?'

'No! Hah!' She opened her arms wide, brandishing the money. 'So so sooorrry.' She rushed away down the street, her headscarf trailing gracefully behind her.

Alida passed her hands briefly over her face. *A thief and a liar. No friend of my daughter's.*

On foot, she followed directions to the ruins, which were two kilometres down a muddy track. As she walked, Alida felt dislocated from her surroundings. There were banana plants with shiny wet leaves and butterflies the size of wrens. She walked with a numb face.

Bitch junkie.

She said it under her breath, to calm herself.

'Junkie bitch.'

The path opened out on to great piles of shattered rocks the colour of a desert. The Vittala Temple, with its musical pillars, stood under the stained sky. Alida picked her way past a stone chariot, up crumbling steps, past columns and hundreds of carvings. She tapped the slender pillars and heard the soft tone. She saw a thick black millipede tracking up a wall. She saw a giant stone chariot. She saw green parrots fly from a courtyard in a squawking stream.

She felt exhausted.

She leaned against a large, non-musical pillar and then

slid down it until she was sitting, huddled, on the damp ground. I don't know, she thought. I don't know if I can do this any more. It's too hard.

After a time, a slight tinkling sound to her left caught her ear and she turned her head, but saw nothing. The sound continued, and she craned her neck to look around the pillar she was leaning against. Sitting several metres behind her was the hairy man. He had his back against a low wall and his bare, stringy legs were stretched out in front of him. He was fiddling with his beard and, when he saw her peering around the pillar, he smiled.

'She has cheated you?' he enquired. He had a faint German accent and eyes that were many layers of blue.

'Yes.'

'She has fallen over the edge. She can't help herself any more.'

'I know. It doesn't matter.' Something about this odd-looking person pleased Alida, and she found herself getting to her feet. The man's beard made him look a hundred years old, but the skin on his face was young. Possibly he was in his early thirties.

She stepped closer to him. 'Thanks for trying to warn me about her. I'm Alida, by the way.'

'I'm Langbart. Lang as in long. Bart as in beard.'

'An appropriate name,' she said, leaning against a nearby pillar.

'Such a long beard deserves recognition. It's shared eleven years of life with me, and it remembers things I forget. It even sings in the wind.' He picked up a piece of it and shook it to demonstrate.

Alida attempted a smile, and felt her mood lift a little. Her hand started to search in her shoulder bag and when it found the photograph of Mia she took it out and held it towards Langbart, her eyes fixed anxiously on his. 'Do you recognise my daughter?'

Langbart gazed at Mia. 'I would really very much like

to help a lost person to become found,' he said eventually. 'But I am certain I never saw this girl. I am in Hampi since two weeks, and I notice everyone, you know?'

Alida nodded. She slid the picture back into her bag. 'Thanks anyway,' she mumbled, and walked away, clutching her bag strap so tightly that her nails dug into her palm. It was always the same. Same, same, same.

It was late afternoon when Alida finally returned to the guest house, and Mangala came to greet her in a state of agitation: hot cheeks, flapping hands. She pulled Alida aside by the arm as soon as she stepped through the door, making her fear for a moment that something had happened to Taos.

'A girl has come. She has seen your child.'

'Someone has recognised Mia?'

'Yes, yes!' Mangala's eyes bulged in excitement.

'Wait – did she want money? Was she wearing a red scarf on her head?'

'No! No money, no scarf. She is here, on my rooftop. Reading, waiting.'

Alida's eyes widened. 'Thank you,' she said and, following Mangala's pointing arm, she bounded up the narrow steps to the roof.

Chapter Nineteen

February 2004

He fills me. I swim in his eyes. His scent makes me float off my feet and, when we kiss, I am a woman with curves and wet lips.

He wants more.

I have grown up with photographs of cauliflower-deformed penises and pubic lice. I have seen limbs covered in lesions. I'm not doing anything without rubber protection.

Alida comes and goes around the house and knows nothing of my secret life. She thinks what she sees is what she gets; that a quiet mood is just a teenage sulk.

I look at him all the time inside my head.

I want to know how it feels.

May 2004

At first it was like scorched steel. Now, when we do it, a sonic boom shudders through my veins and appears as an oval-shaped white cloud like a ballerina's tutu. White is all the colours of the rainbow spun together and the sonic boom happens halfway down my body, which is no longer a body but streams of hot caramel melting under Jack's golden limbs, his tireless tongue. His muscles are firm and sleek, and when he pushes himself into me the world collapses into blueberry dots and reforms into a wideness so tightly beautiful that I can barely breathe. We squeeze our love into car seats and toilet cubicles. Later, I look at my mother and smile at her unknowing. She packs up her black bag and goes off to talk to twelve-year-olds about AIDS and pregnancy, not knowing that she has supper every night with a fourteen-year-old nonvirgin.

Jack is salt and cinnamon and has deep green eyes. His voice echoes in my chest and tingles every hair root on my body. He is sixteen and writes me poems which move from pale indigo to damson, and sometimes he steals his brother's Golf during the school lunch break so that I can become Concorde in a ballerina's tutu, flying through the sonic boom.

If my parents knew, they would combust on the spot. I don't care. For once, I have something which is all my own, and they can't stop it or me.

June 2004

Alida has been spying on me. She has been into my room and she has found and read Jack's poems, which I keep hidden at the back of my underwear drawer. I find them stacked over-neatly in the corner of the drawer and anger sends my head thick. I wait until she goes out to a drum concert with her sleepy-eyed new boyfriend. Then I go into her room and violate her privacy in revenge. I search through her drawers and turn out the bottom of the wardrobe.

I find silky stockings and old photographs that I can't bear to see.

I find a bag full of hand-dyed wool, which is strange as she doesn't knit.

Under the bed, lounging in the dust, I find a notebook.

When I read her sentences, it's as if I'm pedalling a bicycle but the wheels are turning backwards instead of forwards. It's all wrong, but this is how she feels. The words are bunched up on the page, and my eyes bounce over them guiltily, recoiling from the images. It's a story, or a dream, or a waking nightmare.

The swimming pool flashes turquoise and silver in the sunshine. I notice what none of the other party guests have seen: a tiny body floating in that glistening rectangle of water.

I run across the polished green lawns, my eyes never leaving that little head. The guests see me coming and surge towards me. They want to stop me jumping in and saving the child.

'Baby in the water!' I gasp, pointing. Their hands grip my arms, their bodies hold me back from the edge.

'It's a doll,' they tell me. 'Not real, only plastic.'

I know they lie. Wild now, I shake them off with my punching fists. I take the leap and hit the water with a splash that rocks the baby back and forth. I break surface and swim to her, lift her up and out. She is wearing a sodden Babygro with tortoises printed all over it, and her eyes are empty of life. The guests are a hundred pairs of cold eyes. They ring the pool silently, their shadows falling on the water. I shout at their bland faces.

'Can't you see she's real? Plastic dolls don't have birthmarks on their wrist. They don't have lungs. They don't drown.'

I am crying now, gripping the baby to my chest. I notice Mia among the guests, watching me with the same cold impassivity. We exchange a long look, then she turns on her heel and slips away into the crowd.

I look down and the dead baby has turned into a doll.

June 2004
Alida is biding her time.

I know she knows about Jack, but she doesn't know I know she knows. We step around each other and try not to

128

confuse what we think with what we say. She is considering the best approach. All these years of playing the cool, understanding adult in London classrooms, and now she must try to do the same in her own home. I feel her eyes resting on my back as I turn in the kitchen to pour tea into a mug. I catch emotions flickering across her face when she thinks she is unobserved. Anxiety. Bitterness that I haven't chosen to confide in her. Disappointment.

There's something I want to ask her about, too, but I don't think the right time will ever come.

Chapter Twenty

The girl was Icelandic. She introduced herself as Sigga and regarded Alida from pensive pale-blue eyes.

'I'm sure your daughter is in the ashram where I was two days ago, in a remote place by the Krishna River. I didn't speak to her personally but I saw her often sitting in the garden, reading under the banyan tree or preparing vegetables for the meals.'

Alida rattled out questions and wrote down all the details in her notebook. A curving thread of honey had been spilled on the table and several ants were dying in it, their legs stuck fast. Others scrambled over Alida's wrist as she wrote but she barely noticed. The girl had hesitated when she asked if Mia had looked pregnant. 'She's not a very thin girl, and she wears loose clothing, you know?' she said.

When Alida had thanked the girl, she returned to her room with a fluttering heart to pack for the three-hour journey north-east while she waited for Taos to return from town with the developed photographs of Mia's collages. Minutes later, there was a knock on the door.

'Mangala told me you have a lead,' said Taos as soon as he was through the door. His face was flushed.

'Yes. Are you coming with me?'

'Isn't that what I'm here for?' he demanded in mock indignation.

'I don't know. Is it?' she asked.

He grinned at her but didn't answer, just handed her the envelope with the photographs in it and hurried off to pack.

Mangala, resplendent in a cerise sari with gold edging, waved them off from the door, having given them a bagful of sticky banana cakes for the journey. 'Good luck,' she called, flashing them her generous, chipped-tooth smile. 'You'll find her, I'm very sure. Come back and see me again.'

The bus crunched along with noisy determination. Small children swayed on their mothers' knees or perched on food sacks in the aisle. Opposite Alida and Taos a man was transporting a pair of beady-eyed cockerels on his lap, one thick hand clamped around each neck to keep them under control.

'Why are you travelling with me, Taos?' She asked her question loudly, to beat the noise of the bus.

'You asked me to, don't you remember?' He glanced sideways at her, the laughter lines around his eyes crinkling for a moment. It occurred to Alida that she had always liked Australian accents, especially cultivated ones like Taos's. His voice was resonant and deep, nothing nasal about it, the timbre rich and sure. There was safety in this voice, she thought.

'Yes,' she answered him, 'but that can't be the only reason.'

'Why can't it?' he asked, twisting around in his seat to look at her.

'Because people don't just unselfishly drop everything for virtual strangers.'

'You're overlooking the fact that I had nothing to drop. It's like I'm floating in space. I've nothing to keep me in any one place, not even the weight of the past.'

'What about your family in Australia?' She asked the question casually, but she was deeply curious.

131

He shrugged. 'They're fine, engaged in their art-crazy lives in Melbourne – my parents, at any rate. My dad's a sculptor and my mother's a theatre costume designer and a watercolour artist.' He gripped the top of the seat in front of him with his right hand and appeared to study the worn leather bands – as thin as the shoelaces on shiny office shoes, noticed Alida – that encircled his wrist. 'To be honest, being with my family since the crash is exhausting for me and them alike; it upsets them that I'm not the son or brother I used to be, that they can't count on me to know what they're talking about. I didn't even recall the existence of my two smallest nieces when I woke up after the accident, which must have been beyond weird for my sister. And it upsets me that I'm causing them that pain.' He glanced at her quickly. 'I came travelling again as soon as I could because that's what I was doing before the accident and you never know, it might be a way of jolting memory recovery.'

'Do memories sometimes come back to you, then?'

'Very rarely things that seem to be bits of memories appear. The strange thing is when they do I have trouble claiming them as my own. For several weeks after the accident, I had flash visions of a body lying crumpled on a road, seen from the perspective of someone who was lying on the same road. And this peculiar light and silence hanging over it all. At first it felt like an image from someone else's nightmare had been imposed onto my mind and I fought it. Then when I knew about the memory loss, I grudgingly accepted that it might be my imagination trying to recreate the crash. And now I suppose I believe it's a real memory of me looking at Kirstin where she lay dying.'

Alida found herself suddenly blinded by tears. She lowered her head mutely. Taos has lost someone he loves and he can't even grieve because he can't remember her, she thought. There must be some part of him that desperately needs to grieve her loss.

132

'The thing is,' continued Taos, unaware of Alida's rush of sadness, 'nobody can say how much will return, and I need to live my life for now, not only look backwards. I need to build up new memories. Maybe that's another reason I find myself travelling around with you.'

Alida looked up at him.

'Why are you all tearful?' he asked, looking dismayed.

'I don't know.' She wiped her eyes with the back of her hand and attempted a smile to reassure him. 'I think I'm just trying to imagine what it must feel like to know that you've forgotten all the details and knowledge and even the feelings about someone you love.'

Taos nodded sombrely. 'You know, it's questionable whether I'm still myself these days.'

'Whatever do you mean?' she asked, fishing in her bag for a tissue and steadying herself with an elbow as the bus lurched around a bend.

'People are made by their past. Past thoughts, past actions. Life-changing moments. Relationships built on shared experience. Lessons learned as we go. So where does that leave a person who has lost a sizeable wedge of their past?'

'But of course you're still you,' said Alida, pausing to blow her nose. 'Your past is stored in the cells of your body, it's part of your physical and emotional make-up. For the time being those memories are unavailable to you, but they're still there, somewhere inside you.'

He shook his head. 'They're nowhere. The amnesia is a void so clever that after swallowing the memories it sealed itself up again and I can't even find the opening.'

'Somewhere inside you, in your bones, in your soul, you remember Kirstin,' said Alida. 'I feel certain of it. Human memories can't be like computer files, capable of being irrevocably deleted from time and space. I just can't accept that.'

Taos looked pensive. He hooked his hands around the

133

top of the seat in front of him. 'I want them all back,' he said. 'Even the bad, painful memories. They define me.'

She nodded. 'I know,' she said. They fell silent. Out of the window, Alida glimpsed a toddler and his big sister standing in a ditch at the roadside, holding hands and staring solemnly at the approaching bus. As it hammered past them, they were engulfed in a cloud of dust. She turned back to Taos. 'But if there's a bright side to memory loss, it has to be the fact that the past can hurt you again and again. I have a memory from years ago that I can't escape from. It crouches on my chest like an incubus and gives me nightmares. I'd love to be able to forget all about it.'

'But this memory, whatever it is, is part of what makes you yourself.'

'Yes.' Alida tugged uneasily at a lock of her hair.

'Can't you reinvent the memory?'

'You know as well as I do that you can't change the past. It's rigid. Things happen, then they're over and it's too late.'

'Not change, reinvent. For example, you have a white object, right?' He held out his palm and they both looked at the imaginary white object on it. 'Its colour changes depending on what colour light you shine on it. Of course, really it's still white, but it looks different now.' He curled his hand around the seat in front again. 'I think you can do the same with memories. Shine a different colour light on them and watch them reinvent themselves. If the past is stored in cells in the body, as you say, then do you think you know where that bad memory is stored?'

Alida thought of Mia's collage of the skeleton foetus, and nodded.

'Want to tell me?' he asked with a hint of mischief. She looked dubious and he grinned. 'Don't worry, you don't have to. If you have an idea which part of your body might be holding it, though, then maybe that's a good start.

134

Although let's face it, I'm possibly not the best person to help others to face the past, since when I turn around and try to do it myself, there's not much there to work on.'

They shared a speculative look. 'It's a curious thing,' mused Alida. 'We're coming at this from opposite poles. You feel you have too little to face, and I sometimes feel I have too much.'

'Good luck to both of us,' he murmured.

'What's your short-term memory like?' she asked curiously.

'Perfect. Eight months of vibrant, multi-sensory short-term memory is what I have.' He looked pleased with himself. They smiled at each other and settled back in their seats, each thinking their own thoughts.

They had been going for just over two hours when there was a loud bang and the bus rolled to a jerky halt. The driver got off, grim-faced, and within minutes everyone on the bus had followed suit, including Alida and Taos. They were on an empty road surrounded by rice fields, and the sun was setting. They stood around looking at the tired bus and the red sky. The driver and a cluster of Indian men were changing a wheel, and passengers wandered off to squat in the grass at the side of the road. Taos disappeared behind a tree. There was an unreality about the scene, and Alida tipped her head back and looked at the vast, bleeding sky. She was nearly there, nearly with Mia again.

A woman with a tiny baby on her arm was standing near Alida. When their eyes met, she smiled shyly. She was slight and pretty, her long black hair threaded with wilting jasmine flowers.

Alida returned her smile. 'Hello. Nice sunset.' She nodded towards the sky.

The woman giggled, displaying bad teeth. She was young. Nineteen, perhaps. She stepped closer, eyeing Alida curiously. She pointed at Alida's hand and said something in Urdu. Alida obligingly displayed her hand,

and the woman pointed at her topaz ring and beamed, talking all the while.

'You like it? I've had it for years. I like your nose ring,' said Alida, tapping her own nose. Then the woman showed Alida her little baby, who was wearing a pink dress and had gold ear-studs.

'She's beautiful.'

Then she was holding the baby out for Alida to cuddle. Alida stepped back. 'Oh, no, I'd rather not.'

But the woman, uncomprehending, had already pushed the baby into her arms and there was nothing to do but take her. The flower-weight of her was like a gift. Her eyes were dark puddles circled with kohl. Her fingers curled around Alida's forefinger and gripped, then she pulled it to her mouth and sucked ferociously. Alida felt weak.

'Hello, little star,' she breathed. The baby's squidgy gums, the heat of her mouth, the frailty of her bones, it was too much.

The child's mother watched smilingly. She gestured to the baby, then pointed at Alida, her face open and enquiring.

Here we go, thought Alida. The question to which I have no easy answer.

Wrapped in colours, the woman waited, her sandalled feet patient in the dust.

'Two,' Alida said, withdrawing her finger reluctantly from the baby's mouth to show her on her fingers. 'I had two babies.'

The woman murmured her approval.

'One is dead, the other lost,' added Alida, and tried to smile.

There was a moment's silence as the woman hesitated, bridging the gap between Alida's foreign speech and the sadness in her eyes.

'One dead?' said Taos's voice, directly behind her.

136

Alida jumped. The baby squirmed, its face puckering. 'Don't creep up on me like that!'

'I wasn't creeping up,' he said, emerging to her right. 'I just came to find you, that's all.' He glanced distractedly at the baby, then looked into her face. 'I didn't mean to overhear.'

The young woman was watching their faces. She stretched out her arms and Alida returned the baby to her guiltily, as if she had in some way maltreated it.

'Sorry,' she said. 'I'm sorry.'

The woman nestled her baby into the crook of her arm and smiled again briefly. Then she turned and got back onto the bus.

'I didn't know Mia had lost a brother or sister,' said Taos quietly.

Alida frowned. 'It's all way in the past.' She tried to step around him but he moved, blocking her path.

'I honestly didn't mean to eavesdrop,' he said, holding his hands up in a calming gesture. 'I just happened to come up right at that moment.'

She sighed. 'It's OK. It's just that I never usually talk about it. The only reason I mentioned it to that girl is because she doesn't seem to understand English.'

'That's like only showing your artwork to the blind.'

'Well, maybe.' She hugged her arms across her chest. 'Holding that baby triggered it. I mean, obviously I've held babies since then, but I try not to . . .' She stopped talking. In the semi-darkness, she couldn't see Taos's eyes.

'Was your child a baby when he died?'

'She. Yes, she was.'

'That must have been awful.'

'It was more than awful. After it happened, I just sort of . . . unravelled.' She looked at the sky, which was filling with black and red dots as night crept in. 'It was like living without my life. It changed everything. Mia was just a little girl, but I, on one level I . . .'

'What?' prodded Taos. He was tall and shadowy against the sky.

Alida felt dizzy, as if she might sink to the ground unconscious. She bit her lip. 'On one level I ... blamed Mia.'

'For surviving?'

'No.'

'For the baby's death?' The thread of shock in his voice stung Alida.

'No. No, of course not.' Her voice was harsh. 'Look, Taos, I really can't talk about this any more. It's ...' He had become a black silhouette, and she faltered. 'It's something I never talk about and I ... just can't do it.'

'Woah, you're swaying a bit.' He took her by the shoulders. 'Want to sit down?' His hands were warm and real through her T-shirt. Their gentle pressure steadied her.

'I want to get back on the bus.'

'I'll help you.'

'No, please don't. I'm fine again now.' She pulled away from his grip and climbed carefully back onto the bus. Her head ached. She picked her way back to her seat and when she passed the woman and her baby she couldn't look at them.

Chapter Twenty-One

It was dark by the time they arrived in the village. There were no rickshaws here, it seemed, and a local woman from the bus agreed to walk with them. When they had followed her sari-clad bulk down a grassy track for about half a mile, she pointed at a square white building, accepted their thanks with a smile, and disappeared into the fields. Alida looked at the building with its infrequent rectangles of light and hoped this was the end of her search. As they approached the entrance she imagined Mia in there, sitting on floor cushions eating vegetable curry with the other guests, or lying on her narrow bed, dreaming up at the ceiling.

An Indian woman of about fifty, dressed in a simple sari, answered the carved wooden door and ushered them in. She was devoid of jewellery and make-up.

'I am Sushila, the ashram is in my care,' she said quietly. 'You are in luck – two rooms still free tonight.'

Alida showed her the photograph and explained the situation. Sushila peered at it for a moment with patient eyes. 'It was taken a while back,' said Alida pleadingly.

'Yes. I think the same girl is here, but she has braided her hair and I believe she calls herself Wesley.'

'Wesley?' Of all the nicknames Mia might choose for herself, this seemed the least likely.

'But now the ashram is sleeping, madam. You must wait until morning.'

'Oh, no, please let me see her now. You can't imagine—'

Sushila looked regretful but shook her head. 'I am sorry, but after nine thirty, the ashram rooms are not left by their inhabitants, nor entered by others. This is not a hotel, but a place of spiritual rest and recuperation. Morning yoga session begins five o'clock. Breakfast begins seven o'clock. Here is a list of the ashram rules.' She passed a hand-typed sheet of paper to each of them. 'Now I will show you to your rooms.'

Alida glanced anxiously at Taos, but he just shrugged. 'If she's here now, then she'll still be here in the morning,' he reasoned.

They were led through the building and across a large paved courtyard which was flanked by accommodation blocks. The ashram was far bigger than Alida had first thought. The occasional light glowed from a room, but the vast majority lay in darkness. Her bedroom was on the opposite side of the courtyard from Taos's. It was small but cosy, with an embroidered eiderdown on the bed and orange nylon curtains. She kicked off her sandals and lay on the bed intending to scan the ashram rules, but the light was bad and the typed lines ran together. Despite her worries that Mia might leave the ashram before she managed to locate her, she drifted off to sleep. When the only light around the ashram buildings came from the luxurious canopy of stars, Alida dreamed she was walking through a neglected garden. There was a strangulating sense of grief, and after many hours of wandering in that dark place with no way out, when the stars outside had paled into morning, she understood that she was dreaming again. As if in response, the colours brightened and the contrast sharpened. The wind rustled through the long grasses and an iguana flickered across a tree trunk.

Only six feet in front of her, camouflaged in thick stripes of shade, was the disc-headed man. He was standing motionless, watching her. She walked towards him and when she was just a foot away, she stopped. His disc was a mirror, and when she looked into it, someone else looked back. She had flat, dark eyes ringed with red welts and her hair was frizzy and unkempt. There was no kindness in her gaze, no pity, least of all for herself.

Alida recognised her and her heart banged in fear.

She scrambled upright. Her teeth ached as though she had been clamping her jaw in her sleep, and her throat and mouth were tight with dehydration. She had slept for hours, she could feel it in her muscles. She drank a litre of bottled water and stumbled out into the courtyard, clutching her toothbrush. The sun was already up. How could she have slept for so long? Panic swelled in her. What if Mia had already left the ashram?

Taos was at one of the washstands, splashing his face.

'How could we have slept so late?' asked Alida.

'It's only twenty past seven.' He squinted sideways at her through the water. 'Don't fret. We'll find her.'

The breakfast area was filled with the smell of porridge. Westerners sat at long tables, talking quietly together. Alida stood in the doorway and studied each face, standing on tiptoe to see the ones at the far end. Taos, beside her, was doing the same. Sushila, who had opened the door to them the night before, spotted them and waved.

'Try the garden,' she said, nodding towards Alida's left.

The garden was walled and had a wrought-iron gate. Inside, it was nothing like the garden in Alida's dream. It was every shade of green, but not nearly as wild and overgrown. Flowers bloomed in neat rows. Every plant had a plastic sign designating its name and origin. In the centre was a banyan tree, its arms sprawling out to the skies, its trunk decorated with strips of faded pink material. Alida's eyes slid to its base, and fell upon a smudge of blue which jutted out from the other side of the tree. It was the edge of a sari, or a sarong, fluttering in the breeze. Someone was sitting under the tree, her back resting against its trunk.

She looked round at Taos, and saw that he had seen it too.

'I'll wait here,' he said. 'You go on.'

She nodded, and walked forwards down the narrow grit path, one foot after the other, her eyes never leaving that blue.

She was only four metres away. Three. 'Mia,' she called, urgently.

The blue whisked suddenly from sight. She was scrambling to her feet.

Alida ran towards her.

Chapter Twenty-Two

July 2004

As I come out of the bathroom with a towel twisted heavily on my head, I hear the sound again: a rasping cry with a slightly tinny quality. It's one of Alida's computerised demonstration dolls. They are the size and weight of three-month-old babies and can be bottle-fed, or 'breast-fed' using a computerised clip. She sets them to go off at certain times, then lends them to her students overnight so they can see how exhausting it is to have to get up and feed and burp and change babies in the middle of the night. Ever since I read her dream or story or whatever it was, the sound of those unreal babies makes me uneasy. I stalk down the length of the corridor, then whip her bedroom door open without knocking. She is sitting on the edge of the bed with the doll perched on her lap. When I burst in, she looks up in surprise.

'Why is that doll screaming?' I demand, standing in the doorway.

'I'm trying to reset it but I think something's jammed.' She continues to fiddle with its back. I watch her for a second and the images in her writing press into my mind and suddenly I am furious, mad, sick with hurt.

'How could you keep something like that in your wardrobe?' I shout over the noise of the doll. 'You're deranged. Dee-ranged, Alida.'

143

'Mia, what on earth . . .' She stares at me. 'I need them for my job, you know that. What the hell's the matter with you this morning?'

'I hear them crying in the night. You set them, don't you? So that you have to get up and feed them. Don't deny it. I've heard you do it.'

'They go off by accident.' She silences the doll and lays it on the bed.

'Rubbish. I'm not stupid. You activate the dolls to bring them to life, don't you?'

She stands up so fast that she bruises the air around her, and suddenly I am afraid. Her eyes are on me, they see right into me. 'You know nothing,' she says. Her voice sends a blackness through my stomach. 'You understand nothing.'

There's a long, shivering pause, and I almost lose my nerve. But I have to say it. 'If . . . If you want a baby, then why don't you have one? You're not too old yet.'

She balls her fists on her hips and speaks through her teeth. 'Who do you think you are? Who are *you* to be dishing out advice? A little tart who sleeps with her boyfriend at fourteen! Don't think I don't know exactly what you're up to. Haven't you learned *anything* from me?' Her words have the warped edges of corroded metal. They scythe my chest into strips but for once I speak through them with my own power.

'What, like how to sneak through other people's possessions and read their private stuff? Yes, I have learned that, as it happens. That's how I know about your fixation with those baby dolls. You still dream her death, don't you?' As the words leave my mouth, I know I have gone too far to return. Alida's face crumples, then turns ugly.

'Get out, Mia. How *dare* you speak to me of such things?' Her splayed fingers slash the air, leaving trails of soot which stain the room with menace. She looks like a witch, or a vampire. I turn and get out of there. She strides

144

after me and I quicken my pace in alarm but she doesn't come into the corridor. Instead, the bedroom door bangs with such force that the wind flattens my dressing gown against my legs and the sound travels right through me like an X-ray, turning me for a moment into a skeleton, an unhappy tower of bones.

I sit in my room waiting for my heart to slow. Ashes drift around my face. I can taste them on my tongue. The house is horribly silent.

When my heart is calmer, I get dressed and pack a small bag. Then I write a sentence on a thin strip of yellow paper. 'I don't want to live here any more.'

I open my door with great caution. From her room comes a dead weight of silence. I can almost see her thoughts patterning the ceiling, turning it dark with crossing lines. My hair is still wet but I'm not hanging around to dry it. I leave my sentence on the kitchen table as I go. It curls up slightly at the ends like a lily-livered yellow smile.

I don't want to live with a mother who spends her nights breast-feeding plastic dolls.

I can't live with someone who still blames me for something so far in the past.

I need Jack.

August 2004
Everything has changed. Everything has gone wrong. I broke the taboo, mentioned the unmentionable, and I have lost my mother a second time.

It's her own fault.

After that fight, I went straight to Dad's and explained that Alida was being nasty to me for no good reason and that I'd be happier staying with him and Maggie. He was lovely to me, said I didn't have to go to school that day and that I'd made the right choice. He said Alida was 'unhinged' and that she had no right to shout at me. He made me scrambled

145

eggs on toast and I was allowed to watch TV all day while he worked in his study. That same evening, while Maggie was out at her Spanish class, Alida came over. She was red-eyed and white around the lips, and Dad called me his angel and said she should damn well treat me better and they started to yell at each other over my head so that the air imploded into crushed ice, cold and heartless, until two pink spots flared on Alida's cheeks and she stepped back from Dad and said, 'I presume your angel hasn't told you yet that she's having sex with a boy from school?'

Dad went crazier than I've ever seen him. He swore at Alida in a falling tower of burned knives and called her a bad mother for not keeping me on a tighter rein. He threw things at the walls and the air grew roily and rasped through my hair. He shouted an inch from my nose and it felt like tar spreading all over my face. He searched my bag and found my beautiful poems and called them pornography and started tearing them into shreds and flinging the pieces into my face like hate-filled confetti, but then he said they were evidence and that he was going to the police and that Jack would be prosecuted for corrupting a minor.

That's when I said I'd do anything he wanted.

I am not allowed to see or speak to Jack until I'm sixteen. That's fifteen months away! If I try to see him, Dad says I'll be moved to another school before I can blink twice.

I didn't want to go back to live with Alida after the way she grassed me up, and Dad said he'd do a better job of keeping an eye on me than she would, so now he and Maggie chauffeur me to and from school. I think Dad must have tracked Jack down and had a talk with him (I hope it was no more than that), because now when I smile at him in school assembly or when we pass each other in the halls, his eyes jitter away in fright. Poppy and Ellen try to cheer me up with cigarettes, but I'm terrified of Dad finding out I've started smoking, plus they make my breath smell of dog shit.

I see Alida most weekends, but everything has changed.

14 November 2004
I want to stay in darkness for ever. I can't face the colours
of my bedroom or the brightness of the air outside. I secure
the duvet around my head, leaving only the tiniest gap for
air.

'Migraine, migraine,' I say to Maggie and Dad. They
are sympathetic, but suspicious. I want to shout at them
that there's no need to be suspicious any more. Jack has
started seeing a girl in his year. She wears a black leather
jacket and her hair waterfalls over it in lines of pale silk.
She's old enough to do what she wants, old enough to do
what he wants to do with her. I turned fifteen yesterday
and all I want to do is die.

January 2005
The sky is fluffy, and the colour of cinnamon. I can smell
him on the breeze. I move towards the car park and the
Peugeot is there. As I approach I see frenetic movement,
bodies thrusting together on the back seat. I break into a
run and when I reach the car I stare inside to see who
Jack's got in there. A whirl of dark curly hair, a hand with
a topaz ring clutching at his shoulder. I bang my fists hard
on the window and they look up. It's Alida, sweaty and
triumphant. Our eyes lock, and time stands still.

I'm dreaming. I turn from them and shoot up into the
sky. It changes colour before my eyes, from cinnamon to
butterscotch to tangerine. I can taste it all, feel it ripple
over my skin. Then something nudges my hip and I look
down to see a wing tip, a laughing elephant's trunk and a
diamond bright blue eye.

For the first time in weeks, I smile with my whole heart
in it.

Somehow, sometime, everything is going to be all right.

Chapter Twenty-Three

In her haste, the tip of Alida's flip-flop caught on a tree root and she found herself tumbling to the ground in a whirl of blue. She was aware of the girl trying to catch her as she went down, her fist grabbing at her T-shirt. Then she was sprawled flat on her back, unharmed.

She blinked and the girl was Mia.

She blinked again and the girl was a stranger, bending over her in concern. Tree branches sprouted from her head and, a long way beyond that, the sun shone weakly.

'Are you all right?' A Yorkshire accent emerged from swinging dark plaits. Mia's eyebrows arched over eyes that were too dark, too wide apart.

Alida's gaze slid past the girl and settled on the sun, distant and pale under a screening of cloud. She felt she could lie where she was for ever. She felt she could stop breathing and die there. The girl who was not Mia was talking at her. Then she rose and left Alida's vision. Without the blue and the oppression of that dark head so close, the sky opened up. Out there in the sky, there was silence. There was Mia, five years old, one ear pressed to Alida's pregnant belly, her mouth speaking the baby's thoughts.

'He says he's an umbrella baby.' Umbrella was her favourite word. 'All folded up. He wants to come and play with me in the rain.' Alida stroked her hand through her daughter's curls, which were still slightly damp from bath time. They made a patch of coolness on the stretched skin of her stomach.

Voices intruded from the side somewhere. '. . . a sort of open-eyed faint . . . grey-faced and limp.'

I have not fainted, thought Alida scornfully.

The crunch of footsteps. The smell of lemon grass and tobacco. Eyes with pale green flecks, a strong nose. Taos forced himself between the sun and the ground, stopping her vision. She looked through him anyway.

'Are you hurt?' His eyes were struggling to connect with hers, his hand swiped back and forth in front of her face, hoping to break her gaze. He tried to gather her up from the ground but she resisted, stiffening. At this, his expression changed. 'What's going on? Why won't you let me help you up?' He shook her shoulder and she ignored him effortlessly. He peeled himself away from her and she sank her gaze into the sun again. Mia, seven years old, was riding her new acid-green bicycle. Her knees wobbled and she was grinning.

'My feet can't touch the ground!' she squealed to Ian as she slid to a halt beside him. Alida watched them through the French windows. She wanted to go to them but something kept her behind the glass, which misted under her breath.

Taos was back with a bottle of water. Before Alida could react, he had unscrewed the plastic lid and dashed its contents into her face.

Alida gasped. Suddenly, everything was back. Birdsong. The breeze cold on her wet face. Tree roots digging like rope into her spine.

'Now get up.' Taos seemed angry; this time his arms did not take no for an answer, and Alida was hefted into a sitting position. She stared at him mutely, water dripping off her nose and chin. He stared back. 'I'm not letting you lie there all day like the victim of a traffic accident,' he said. 'It wasn't Mia, but so what? She'll turn up. There's no need for this melodrama.'

Alida wanted to silence him with a cutting remark, but she couldn't speak. She couldn't even swallow. She wrenched herself away from him and stood up, imprints of the sun flashing in her eyes.

Standing in the path was the non-Mia, her dark eyes watching them. Moving swiftly, Alida passed her and headed for the gate.

Back inside her room with the door bolted shut, she kicked off her flip-flops and curled up on the bed, knees touching her elbows, hands clamped over her ears.

'I will never find my daughter,' she murmured, and her voice filled her head.

When the room grew so hot and stuffy that perspiration stood out on her forehead, Alida uncurled herself and switched on the fan. Cool waves extended immediately outwards, and she closed her eyes for a moment. She needed to do something to pull her from her state of morbid self-pity, so she took her notepad from the window sill and recorded last night's lucid dream, seeing again the woman staring empty-eyed from the disc-headed man's silver face. The image hung in the air like a rain cloud, then moved and changed as Alida wrote, layering back down into memories which she hadn't uncovered in a long time. She knew again how it felt to be so weary with grief that even dragging a comb through her hair seemed a waste of energy. She remembered wishing she could shrink to a vanishing point and never return. Her breathing was slow and regular. Her hand continued to push the pen across the page.

Years ago, my baby girl died. Her blood wasn't spilled; it coalesced in her veins when her heart was stopped. She left empty clothes and a lingering smell of nutmeg sweetness. I walked, ate and slept, but I forgot how to be a mother. Mia looked on from the shadows, ready to step out but never asked to. In the early days, when my breasts still wept milk and traces of the baby were lodged all over the house like shrapnel, I did some black things. I looked blindly at Mia's tears. I threw a paper-weight at Ian's heart. I rehearsed my baby's last moments until I knew, for sure, what it must have felt like to die that way.

Words were bandied around by social workers and police. Negligence. Child endangerment. I didn't care about any of that. Holding a knitted bobble hat to my face, I breathed its scent. I slept with rag books and Kizzy's tiny, bright dresses heaped around me like totems. In the end, the inquest recorded a verdict of accidental death.

The household gathered itself quietly over the next months. Sometimes I saw white strips of paper on the carpet, with arrows drawn on them. I knew where they led, but never followed them. Knowing I was hurting Mia couldn't soften me; I was too far gone in my grief. Ian tried to touch me but I was behind glass. When he rapped too hard at the surface, I lunged forwards and bared my teeth at him. Shining blue eyes followed me about the house, disappearing each time I turned to look. The wail of a baby in the supermarket cut through skin and muscle, bit into cold bone. I dreamed of death.

One day I looked up from my lap and heard Mia talking to herself about ivory smells and the woolly feel of radio static. I looked at this child of mine into whom the world seemed to plunge at all angles, and for the first time I considered her. How must it feel to be six years old with a dead sister, an often absent father and a deaf-dumb-blind mother?

I can't change what her life has become, I thought. Nothing I can do will make a difference. See – my hands have rusted into fists. But slowly, in spite of the great weight of myself, I raised my body from my chair and *took the first faltering steps towards her.*

Taos had set up his collapsible easel in the ashram garden and was sitting on a shaded section of the outer wall, painting. He was bare-chested, dressed only in a pair of sky-blue cotton trousers rolled up to the knee. Every line of his body leaned into his painting. When he saw Alida walking towards him down the grit path, he scowled and jumped off the wall in a hurry.

'Hi,' she called.

'What do you want?' he asked, starting down the path with a slightly menacing air.

She stopped, her hands floating uncertainly at her sides. 'Nothing, I just wanted to say sorry about earlier. The disappointment drained me so completely that I couldn't—'

'I'm busy working.' He was gripping a paintbrush in his left fist and he raised it unsmilingly.

'Fine,' she said, stung. 'I'll go.' She turned, and heard his footsteps crunching away from her.

Walking from the garden, Alida blinked several times to clear her vision, which had clouded with tears. *He's been following my dash across India for days now and I expect he's sick of the sight and sound of me.* She remembered what he'd said when he'd pulled her up off the ground that morning. Something about not letting her lie there like a crash victim. His girlfriend had lain on the ground and never got up. She felt a rush of shame. Selfish, she thought. All I think about is me and my loss. It's time Taos did his own thing. I have to get out of here.

Back in her room, she packed quickly and carelessly. She found herself thinking not of Taos or Mia, but of Five-toes, who had lost half her toes and decorated the ones she had left. In her place, I would have decorated the maimed foot, realised Alida as she watched her possessions fly into the bag. I would have turned it into a walking shrine, a lament to the lost. I would have neglected my remaining

152

toes, let the nails grow until they snapped off, let dirt work its way into the skin. Five-toes is wiser than me; she gives love to the living instead of squandering it on the dead. She closed Mia's bag with unnecessary force, so that the zip squealed in protest. When the baby died, I couldn't accept it. I gave her memory so much of my love that Mia had to tunnel and dig to get any for herself. Am I making a similar mistake again now, by throwing myself into finding Mia instead of accepting that she has gone for good?

As she lugged her bag down to the main building to pay for their stay, Alida saw Taos, seated on the garden wall again. His naked back was dappled with shade and he looked dark and angular, poring over his small canvas. She put her bag down in the dust. It would be unforgivable to leave without thanking him for all his help. Rather than going the long way around and entering the garden by the gate, she instead headed straight for him, walking across the sulphur-coloured ground until she was level with his back and only separated from him by a few metres. She saw that he was painting a portrait in hues of orange. As she edged closer, the brushstrokes converged to form a narrow face pulled tight with determination. The lips were generous and lifted the face into beauty. The harmony of the features was broken by a vertical frown mark between the eyebrows, yet there was a sense of the magical, of something shimmering within the woman on the canvas, radiating outwards through powerful dark eyes which were hiding a smile.

Alida stepped back, something close to fear making her heart bang inside her chest. Sensing someone's presence at his back, Taos glanced around.

He jumped when he saw her. 'What do you think you're doing?'

'You've painted me,' she said.

For a moment, he stared at her rigidly.

Alida's hand was at her throat, her fingers calming the pulse point under her jaw. 'Do you really see me like that?'

Taos took a deep breath and sighed it out. The tension left his body and suddenly he looked younger than usual, his expression opening up. 'Like what?'

'I don't know.' She squinted at the painting. 'She's so... resolute. Unstoppable. Is that how you see me?'

'Well, when you did your zombie impression this morning, I had second thoughts.' He gave her one of his rare, full-beam grins.

She smiled uncertainly, taken aback by his unexpected good humour and struck by the boyish charm of his face which was dappled in shadow with splashes of sunlight moving across it.

'I thought you'd be pretty talented at that kids' party game, though,' Taos said, twirling his paintbrush idly. 'What's it called? The one where you all have to lie down and be completely immobile and the last one to move wins.'

'Dead lions?'

'That's the one. And now I'm thinking you'd make a good spy, sneaking up and peering over walls.'

'Yes. I'm sorry. Again. I've decided to leave and thought I'd risk your anger a second time to say goodbye.'

He stared at her in dismay. 'You want to leave without me?'

'Well, no. But I don't want to exhaust you with my problems any more. I realise I've been obsessive and selfish, and I—'

'Look, I was brusque earlier because I wanted to get you as far away from this as possible.' He indicated the painting with his thumb.

'Why?'

'Why d'you think? It's going to make you... think things, isn't it?'

'Is it?'

'I don't know. Is it?'

Alida pushed a loose curl out of her face. 'Just tell me what you mean.'

'When I paint people and they find out, they always fabricate grand ideas in their heads about why I did it. Ideas to do with admiration or fascination, or some inner quality they think I've perceived in them.'

Her gaze returned to the picture. 'You mean the fact that you've spent hours focusing on their image goes to their heads?'

'It does.'

'Well, it won't go to mine,' she said solidly, although she could still feel the pulse in her throat fluttering.

He shrugged. 'Fine. So what do you think of it?'

'It's ... It's very well done, Taos, but she's quite intense, isn't she? And painfully orange.'

Taos looked quizzical. 'Painfully?'

'Did I ever tell you that Mia associates me with orangeness?'

'Really? How else does she perceive you?'

'Oh, I don't know. As some kind of vanilla-flavoured custard.' Taos made a face and Alida began to laugh. 'Imagine me as this large orange blob of custard, cooking a meal for Mia, or driving her to school.' She attempted a custard impression, with puffed out cheeks and a wobbling body, but had to stop when her laughter grew into a sob which rose in her throat. She choked to a halt. 'Sorry, I'm all over the place today.'

'I noticed.' He was watching her keenly from his twisted position on the wall.

Alida gathered herself together, folding her arms across her chest to give herself some support. She kept her eyes on Taos's face. 'I'm thinking I should stop the search.'

'You're giving up on her?'

'I'm starting to think she's gone for good. Dead, maybe.' She swallowed, aware of the sun lying on the crown of her head, ringing it with heat. 'I have to accept it.'

'You don't have to accept anything until a body turns up. And none has, has it? She could still be out there some-

155

where, and you know it.' He gestured towards the portrait. 'Would *she* give up?' he asked with a wry little smile.

'Who, the orange maniac?' Alida half smiled, half grimaced. 'Oh, I don't know. I'm not really giving up, I just don't want to delude myself.' She rubbed her forehead hard with her left fist. 'I don't know anything any more except that we're getting nowhere. All we've achieved is a morgue visit with the wrong dead body and a false trail ending in some girl in a blue sari.'

'Listen. We'll find her. Now come and sit in the garden so we can figure out what to do next.'

'I've already packed.'

He leaned back from her slightly, so that his frown seemed intensified. 'Oh come on, Alida,' he protested. 'You still want my help, right?'

'Absolutely, Taos, if you're still happy to give it. But I can't waste time. I've been in India eight days already and it's been *sixteen* days since Mia disappeared from Hotel Guru, and we're no further than we were when I arrived.'

'But where do you intend to go next?'

Alida hesitated. 'I was thinking of returning to Hampi, I suppose. But I've already plastered the town with posters, same as in Madurai.' She opened her hands in a helpless gesture. 'I actually don't know where to head next,' she admitted.

Taos tilted his head to one side, considering. 'Well, since we have Mangala's number, we could always just call her each day to see if any new leads have turned up in Hampi. But you know what I was thinking? I think we need to look at those collages properly. People create art to express something that preoccupies them, something they spiral back to in their life, their emotions. Or something that they want to explore. Get to know better . . .'

Involuntarily, Alida's eyes flickered to the orange portrait of her. When she looked back at Taos, she noticed the tinge of colour that swept up his cheeks. 'And anyway,'

156

he continued quickly, 'I remember Mia standing across the roof from me the day she started to work on her first collage – it was the winged elephant one. Her hands were full of feathers and bindis and stuff that she'd found on the streets or in the market. She had plastic bags full of materials. She told me that the collages came from powerful memory-dreams. So it's sort of like having pieces of her psyche to investigate here; the collages tell us about her state of mind before she disappeared, just the same way that a letter would do, or a phone call.'

'You're right, and since you gave me the photos yesterday, I've been waiting for an opportunity to spread them out and have a proper look at them,' said Alida. 'It's not like we've got an entire art gallery, though – just five pictures.'

'I'm used to working with very little.'

'What do you mean?'

'I've been trying to reconstruct several years of my life using images – photographs of me with Kirstin, or with my niece when she was newborn – all the stuff that's vanished.' He gestured towards the garden, which was green and shady and emanated the sound of hundreds of crickets. 'Come on, let me help you out. You can get the pictures and we'll have a brainstorming session.' When he saw her hesitate, he added, 'There's no point in setting off until we have a clear idea of where we're going.'

'All right, I'll get the photos.' She touched a hand to the top of her head. 'I think my hair's about to catch fire; I'd better get out of the sun.' She turned, then paused and looked back at him. 'Why *did* you paint me, Taos?'

'I tried to feel the emotions you carry inside you,' he said. 'And that's how you came out on canvas.'

She glanced sceptically at the painting. 'Marmalade-coloured and slightly deranged?'

''Fraid so.' He shrugged one bare shoulder disarmingly.

When she reached Mia's bag, which was squatting blue-striped on the ground, Alida's eyes were lit by a secret smile. He's painted me, she thought as she stooped to pick it up. Taos has painted me.

Twenty-Four

The banyan tree stood in the garden like a many-armed ancient woman, simultaneously stooping and stretching. Some of its aerial roots hung in grey dreadlocks which fanned out into sun-bleached split ends, while others plunged into the earth, acting as support sticks for the tree's heavy branches. Taos had leaned his easel and the painting against the trunk and was stowing his paint bag in the tree's copious shade when Alida reached him and set down Mia's bag. Crackling inside it was a large brown envelope which she tore open. Glossy colours slid into her fingers: salmon pink, daffodil, maroon. She spread them out on the ground, which was a snaking mass of banyan roots interspersed with grass and fallen leaves. There were zoom-in shots of the main images in the collages, and full shots which included the surrounding colour detail and the postcards glued to the top corner of each collage. Five memories. Memories from way back that Mia had dreamed about while here in India.

'These are the way in,' said Alida, crouching on the ground and balancing on her toes and fingertips as she leaned into the pool of images. 'The way into Mia.'

She pulled the photograph of the Klimt-style pregnant woman collage towards her, and settled herself gingerly on a tree root. The woman's belly was transparent and the skeleton baby inside it glowed whitely. This, thought

Alida, must be me with the small, dead, fourth member of our family tucked inside me. Of course, the image was incorrect. Kizzy had left the womb with kicking mottled-pink limbs and a healthy shriek and had filled the house with her presence for nine months before she died. This image might be Mia's dream of her mother pregnant with death, unaware of what was to come.

'What do you think of when you see that?' Taos asked her, leaning down into the picture, his eyes scanning the pipe-cleaner bones.

Alida shuddered slightly. In her mind's eye, she could see herself sitting in a modern church with whitewashed walls, surrounded by family, friends, flowers. The stench of lilies had pressed her into her seat and she hadn't been able to take her eyes from the tiny oak coffin just ahead and to her right. Beside her, her mother had taken hold of her hand and was pressing it over and over again, convulsively. Her skin had retained the chilled dryness of paper.

'It makes me think of Kizzy's funeral.' Her voice was barely audible, so that Taos instinctively shifted closer, moving to sit at right angles to her. 'I sat there thinking that four days before, she had been sliced open with surgical tools to see how she died even though I told them again and again.' She swallowed. 'And I remember thinking that just the night before, my baby had lain frozen and alone in the morgue, but that day we were going to incinerate her at temperatures exceeding eight hundred degrees centigrade. I couldn't stop imagining her little body being burned in a white-hot haze. Her skin melting, flesh running off the bone. The blue of her eyes vanishing in a splutter of liquid. Her fragile bones cracking to powder.'

Taos winced. His eyes were narrowed in concern, and the solidity of his large frame so close to her gave Alida the strength to carry on.

'I think the squeezing pressure of my mother's hand was the only thing that kept my heart beating throughout the service,' she continued. 'I ... Kizzy was my laughing, squealing girl, and she was going to be burned to ashes. I couldn't imagine scattering her. I felt her bones belonged together, with me—' Alida broke off. 'Oh, but this isn't helpful,' she exclaimed, close to tears. 'This tells us nothing about Mia.'

'Maybe not directly, but your reaction to the baby's death would have affected Mia profoundly,' reasoned Taos. 'And she's collaged a woman with a dead child inside her.' He leaned back on his elbows, staring at her. 'You know, you didn't mention Mia at all. Was she at the funeral?'

Alida shook her head. 'We decided it was best to leave her with Ian's sister. And to be truthful, I didn't want to see her that day.' Resolutely, she turned to the next photograph. 'There must be something in one of these other collages that will give us some clue,' she muttered. She picked up the image of the child being attacked by a winged creature and simultaneously pelted with word-sensations which couldn't be read on the photograph, as the flash had faded the letters into cobwebby lines. She leaned over the picture, brushing a few spidery-legged red ants off its edges.

'I think the words that were bombarding the child had something to do with clanging bells and chartreuse,' she said.

'The most visible colour to the human eye,' observed Taos.

'Chartreuse? Really?'

'So I've heard. In its most brilliant shade, at least.'

Alida sat back on her heels, her toes gripping the ground through the thin rubber of Mia's flip-flops. 'If it's bright to most eyes, what must it be like for Mia?' she wondered. 'She senses everything so intensely. You know, it's said that all babies probably experience synaesthesia, most of them just grow out of it after about four months, once the

161

senses have become modularised.'

'To have the world flowing into you unchecked like that for your whole life must be quite something,' mused Taos. He passed a hand briefly over his head in a gesture that Alida was starting to recognise as habitual for him, and she noticed orange paint ingrained in the folds of skin on his finger joints.

'Right. On a couple of occasions I actually saw Mia experience sensory overload, which is what this collage seems to express.' Alida squinted at Taos; the sun was whiting out the garden, turning the colours into dazzle. 'Once it happened on a sunlit afternoon when she was about eight. I'd paused to watch her through the sitting room window as she performed cartwheels across our garden in this floppy pink miniskirt with silver hexagons printed all over it. In the middle of a cartwheel, she crumpled to the ground.' Alida's finger moved tenderly over the photograph, tracing the figure of the child. 'I ran to her. She seemed to be having some kind of fit; her hands jerked through the air. Her face was closed up – eyes tightly shut, mouth clamped into a thin line. I thought for a moment of epilepsy, but when I bent over her, I saw that she seemed to be fighting off an invisible assailant. She was noiseless but absolutely frantic.'

Taos nodded when she glanced up at him. He was cross-legged, Buddha-like. The intensity of his listening was such that it compelled Alida to speak frankly. 'I lost it then,' she admitted. 'I screamed at her to stop it, to get up.' She blinked at Taos anxiously. 'Mia reacted strangely – not a sound passed her lips, and she blocked her ears with her hands and kept her eyes tightly closed, as if all she wanted was silence. That's when I saw the wasp. It was zooming in aggressive yellow zigzags above her head and I swiped it viciously away. I was suddenly so furious that a mere wasp had reduced Mia to this. I wanted to crush it to death, watch its guts ooze into the grass. I realised then that I had to wait in silence for Mia to cut through the overload and return.'

'How long did it take?' Taos spoke quietly, as if he didn't want to disturb her thoughts.

Alida swept her wrist across her forehead to clear the film of perspiration that had gathered there. 'Long enough for me to count back through the years and the days, letting my thoughts settle into a pattern of numbers.'

'What pattern of numbers?'

'Oh, you know.' Alida bit her lip, feeling a little embarrassed. She had never told anyone about the numbers. 'I sat and worked it all out, as I sometimes do. That day I would have come up with a pattern of numbers something like this—' Here, she thought hard for a moment, doing the maths. 'Two, six, three, four . . . nine hundred and thirty-seven.' She looked away from Taos's perplexed gaze, focusing instead on a jungly bush in a corner of the garden, her eyes slit against the glare. 'Which means that on that day, when Mia was about eight and a half, I would have sat there and said to myself something like: "Two years, six months, three weeks and four days ago, Kizzy was still alive. Now, that time will stretch and stretch until I die. From now on, every day that I live will mean one more day that she's been dead. It has been nine hundred and thirty-seven days now since I last saw her alive."'

Taos leaned forwards in agitation, losing his Buddha pose. 'What? Do you really do that?'

Alida stared at him apprehensively, wishing she hadn't tried to explain.

He rushed on. 'Alida, that's such a dark way of seeing things. Every day you live means one more day that she's been dead – I mean, what *is* that?' He seemed angered by her, or perhaps incredulous that she encouraged such dire ideas to flourish inside her head. Alida shifted her gaze to the photograph for a moment, uncertain of how to respond

163

but feeling the need to defend herself. Taos waited, leaning forwards tensely with his fingers splayed on the ground in front of him.

'The numbers help me to stop seeing limp, blue-eyed images of death,' she said, too quickly to check the words.

Taos's shoulders sagged, and what might have been anger was replaced with a sadness which Alida sensed was not just for her, but for Taos himself, haunted by a death he could not remember.

'I always know to within a few days just how long it's been since Kizzy's death,' Alida said softly. She needed him to understand. 'Counting and checking the numbers calms me; it reduces the horror of the event to simple mathematics – a date fixed in the safety of time, growing ever more distant as life carries me forwards. I'm proficient at adding in multiples of three hundred and sixty-five,' she said, despair shadowing her face. 'It's been thirteen years now since I last saw her alive. That's almost too many days to count. And now I'm marking off the days that I haven't seen Mia.' She raised her hands to cover her eyes. 'Where will it end?'

Taos reached across and grasped both her hands in his own, pulling them away from her face and holding them so tightly that Alida's topaz ring dug painfully into her finger. 'We'll find Mia,' he assured her.

She looked into his eyes which were so sure, with the sun pushing light into them even here in the shade, turning them a brilliant hazel. She wriggled her fingers slightly to make him loosen his grip, which he did, easing the pressure off her ring. He didn't let go of her, though, and Alida was glad.

'Mia is findable,' she murmured, answering his nod of conviction. It had to be true – Mia was out there in the world, in India, in a town nearby. And they would meet again.

Their hands were already slippery with sweat from the

contact. The shade was no real protection from the heat which shimmered from every corner of the garden and wafted in on the wind along with the smell of singed grasses and baked earth. After a moment, Taos released Alida's fingers with a brief smile. He offered her his water bottle and she took a deep draught. When he had drunk too, he picked up the picture of the armless child on a beach and propped it against a root directly in front of them.

'We'll just keep looking at these and talking,' he said. 'Something might come up – a connection, a memory.'

This picture hurt Alida; it pushed a physical weight under her ribs and made her ache. Dark, rolling waves under a dark, rolling sky. An arm, disappearing beneath a wave.

'Mia's armless nightmares,' she began heavily, 'happened at that time when I used to reach out in the darkness three or four times a night to check that the baby was beside me. There was no warmth any more, of course, not a breath of life. Only a small stone urn on the bedside table, a few powdered bones. Ian didn't want the baby to share our bedroom with us in her new, processed state. I was terrified that I'd arrive home one day to find the urn gone. I knew it was excessively paranoid of me, but the presence and safe contents of the urn were the first things I used to check when I got in.'

She shot a look at Taos, wondering whether she should be this honest. But he returned her gaze with a steady look of understanding, and it felt so freeing to talk about these untouchable parts of herself. Alida settled herself more comfortably on the bumpy roots, tucking her knees beneath her.

'I knew that one day it would have to end, that things would have to change. In the meantime, I tried to dream of Kizzy, alive and well. But in my dreams, I was always half a minute too late, and she always died. Across the hall, Mia would scream and drum her feet in the night and explain in an incoherent sweat about huge masses of water and having no arms. I was filled with dread and guilt when I saw her like that, but I couldn't get the right words out; they simply wouldn't come. I let Ian say them to her instead – *It's all right. Not your fault. We love you.*' Alida paused to rub an ant off her ankle. 'It was a bad time and I knew it had to be got through but there were many times when it would have been so much simpler and somehow cleaner to give up.' Blades of grass as spiky as cacti were reaching up between the roots and prickling through her thin sarong so that she had to shift a little to one side. Her preoccupation with her physical comfort made her speak without thinking.

'In my darker moments I used to imagine opening up my veins with a fish knife and gradually, beautifully, vanishing into a tiny point of light.' She pressed her lips together, realising what she had said.

'I thought you said you weren't the suicide type.' Taos looked baffled, as if Alida's words had shown him something incomprehensible.

'And I'm not,' she said firmly. 'I never cut myself, or took an overdose. I just thought about it at times, that's all. And while I thought, I kept on breathing.' She hesitated. 'Taos, if what I'm saying is too much for you, just tell me. I know it's heavy stuff ...'

He straightened his spine. 'I want to know,' he insisted. 'I want to know you.'

Despite his half-naked state, his nipple and belly-button piercings and the starred length of his eyelashes – or perhaps because of these things – Alida felt his friendship as a tangible thing, something shiny and muscular encircling her. He's very sweet, she thought, and immediately erased the thought. She looked away, towards the scattered photographs, and saw something that she didn't immediately understand. It was a creature with a flexing tail at one end and a pair of feebly twitching legs at the other.

'Oh no, Taos, what's that?' she asked, pointing.

He looked. 'It's a lizard eating – or trying to swallow, at any rate – something.'

'A giant grasshopper,' Alida said in consternation. 'It's only got the head in so far. Do you think they'll both die?'

He shrugged. 'I think the grasshopper's already pretty much dead.'

'It's moving onto one of the photos!' objected Alida as the lizard and its oversized meal staggered onto the glossy surface. She stood up in a hurry. 'Can we just take the pictures and go somewhere else? I really can't watch this.'

They gathered the photos, shaking off ants, Alida skirting determinedly around the lizard so that Taos was the one who had to extract the photograph from underneath it. It toppled into a patch of grass between two roots and lay there like a failed python with the grasshopper – now motionless – protruding from its mouth. Taos collected his easel and picture and the two of them walked away as swiftly as the heat would allow, Alida's shoulders erupting in little shudders.

'Let's get a cold drink and sit in the ashram courtyard,' suggested Taos.

On the way out of the garden they passed a yoga class taking place on a large wooden platform with a marquee-style roof that had seen better days, parts of it dangling in torn triangles which flapped in the wind. The students were doing the sun salutation at varying speeds and the effect was shambolic, with some stretching to the sky while others bent double. Their efforts made the wooden boards bang, and Alida slowed to watch. It looked exhausting in such heat. Perhaps this wasn't a proper class, but just a pre-lunch, metabolism-speeding practice session. There was no sign of a teacher.

Armed with two 1.5 litre bottles of refrigerated spring water which they'd bought at the reception, they found a shady corner in the ashram courtyard and settled themselves at a round table made of a roughly hewn granite slab and encircled by a granite bench. The stone was wonderfully cool and Alida rested her forearms gratefully on the tabletop. There were ants, as always, but these were smaller, black ones which didn't bite vindictively as the red ones did. Twenty-five metres away, at the far end of the courtyard, two girls in bright headscarves were carrying coloured paper lanterns out from a doorway and lining them up against the wall. Alida watched them absent-mindedly for a moment and then spread out the photographs and studied the fleecy wings and crystalline blue eyes of the winged elephant, which was clearly no nightmare. She waited a moment to see whether a memory or association would emerge – had Mia ever had a soft-toy elephant? Had she ever mentioned dreaming about elephants? – but there was nothing except for a fleeting thought of the disc-headed man, some deep wish suspended behind that blinding silver face.

'Anything?' prompted Taos.

Alida shook her head, pushing it into the middle of the table. 'It's the only one that seems unconnected from the rest.' She pulled a close-up of the final picture, with the two bears, towards her. To her this one felt ambiguous; the little bear was clamouring, raising its arms for solace, but the big one's body language was harder to interpret. Were its arms flung wide in love, or were they preparing to annihilate? 'If you had to summarise the feeling in this image in one word, which word would you choose?' she asked Taos.

Taos pored over the picture, then sat back suddenly. 'Which word would *you* choose?'

'I don't know – it makes me feel anxious, so it can't be positive... Maybe "retribution",' replied Alida haltingly.

'I know it's not just one word, but I was going to say "mother love".'

They looked at each other. 'Well, that's just it,' said Alida. 'It could go either way, and there's no title to help us out. Did Mia mention the meaning of any of the collages?'

He shook his head regretfully. 'All she said was that they were dream-memories, and after that all we really talked about was her technique, the perspective, the background colours and so on.'

'Maybe the secret lies in the spaces around the images, rather than in the images themselves,' suggested Alida, still looking at the picture. 'You know, like that black-and-white optical illusion where depending on how the eye falls either a vase is seen or two faces.'

Taos rooted around on the table and pulled out the photograph that showed the entire collage. 'Any help?' he asked.

Alida propped her chin in her hands and looked until the shapes lost their colour and form. She refocused her eyes as if looking at a three-dimensional image on a two-dimensional page. She blinked and stared, but found nothing.

I am the mother bear, and Mia is the cub, she thought. The thought, once it appeared, seemed obvious to the point of banality. Alida frowned, frustrated. Come on, there's more, there's more, she urged herself. She had that tip-of-the-tongue feeling: two wires in her brain waiting to brush each other and spark the memory or thought, or whatever it would turn out to be. Alida squinted and tried to imagine the image moving. She heard the roar of rage, the slashing claws and the death scream of the smaller figure – and superimposed onto this image, simultaneous with it, came the rumble of affection, warm bear limbs wrapping, lifting, forgiving.

'Sometimes,' she said slowly, more to herself than to Taos, 'I'd get cross with Mia. About silly things, you know – her experiments with red paint on the sitting room curtains, a refusal to get dressed, pinching the baby. Even without the arrows, which spun around in currents of air like offset compasses, even without them, I knew where to find her.'

'What arrows?' Taos leaned an elbow on the table and looked at her, but she continued to stare at the two bears.

'Well, sometimes Mia would sulk for a while and then continue to play, but at other times her silence would be followed by a string of arrows scribbled in crayon on scraps of paper. *Come and find me*, the arrows would plead, turning forgiveness into a game of hide-and-seek.' Alida rubbed her skull distractedly with both hands. 'I used to wonder, as I followed those arrows, what was going on in Mia's head as she lay hidden. She was only five.' She looked around into Taos's eyes. 'Do you think she stopped thinking while she crouched at the bottom of the wardrobe? Or did she hallucinate bright, scary images in the darkness?' She touched her fingertips to the photograph, frowning at it. 'I used to wonder what would happen to her if I didn't come. I'd imagine her draining to alabaster white and fracturing into thousands of pieces. I'd quicken my pace. She would be curled up at the end of the last arrow – usually in my wardrobe – in a foetal position, her eyes blinking in the sudden light, fearful and lonely.' Alida sighed, looking out over the courtyard now, at the twenty or so paper lanterns lined up against the end wall. The girls who had brought them out had disappeared, and the lanterns made splashes of colour which eased her eyes.

'And what would you do then?' asked Taos.

'Oh, I'd bend down and pull her into my arms, tell her I wasn't cross any more, and Mia would hug me as if she never wanted to let go. "You've saved me again," she'd say. "I can't save you from yourself, my sweet," I used to tell her, but she'd always say, "You can, you can".'

Alida stared at the paper lanterns, blurred now by tears which filled her eyes but didn't fall. 'Once,' she said, 'after the baby died, I saw the arrows but didn't follow

170

them. Ian found Mia hours later, soaked in urine. She lay there wondering if I would come. Wondering whether I would still be angry, or if I would forgive her. Wondering until the pain in her bladder got too much and she wet herself.' She placed her right hand squarely in the middle of the two bears picture. 'I think this image is what she saw while waiting in the wardrobe for me to find her. She wanted my forgiveness but was expecting retribution. She knew I blamed her.'

Taos was nodding. 'Makes sense,' he said. 'The two of you have really been through a lot, hey?'

But Alida wasn't listening. The postcard in the top corner of the two bears image had caught her eye, and now she switched her gaze to the images that lay across the table in disarray, corners overlapping, colours clashing. In the centre was the winged elephant. It stared at her from its diamond blue eye and suddenly everything clicked into place.

She finally knew what had happened to Mia.

Chapter Twenty-Five

5 December 1994

I've been five for three weeks now. Being five tastes as shiny as new conkers and it feels sparkly, like the glow-in-the-dark stars on my bedroom ceiling that I count with Mummy before I go to sleep. All Mummy wants to do at the moment is lie down with the baby-belly pointing up to the sky. The baby is like the wind – invisible, but it makes movements that can be seen; it sends ripples across the taut surface of Mummy's skin, or it makes hillocks pop up for a moment as it stretches its legs. Today it made the air around it gnash together and grow stiff, and Mummy made a deep noise which reached from her chest to mine. After that, a lot of things happened. Mummy spoke in jagged lime-green lines on the telephone, and Grandma and Daddy arrived together looking as tall as giants because I was lying on the carpet with my arms hooked around Mummy's ankles. They were more interested in Mummy than in me and their voices jangled importantly above my head.

She laced her hand through my hair and gave me a vanilla kiss which melted on my cheek and said she was going to go off with Daddy and that when they came back the baby would be with them, not on the inside any more but outside with us. Daddy was twiddling his car keys and his eyes looked at Mummy all the time, except when he blew me a disappearing kiss which landed on my forehead with fairy feet. Grandma said she and I would bake camel-shaped biscuits and eat them in my tent in the garden. Then Daddy closed the door behind him and Mummy in a puff of air and I sat very still and felt their warmth leave my skin as the car rolled away.

Christmas 1994

My baby sister smells of strawberries and sour milk. Her name is Kizzy and she is soft and floppy and has a big crimson mouth and when she screams you can see the veins turn deep purple all across her head. She makes faces that only I can understand. She tips her face back and her lips shape words and wishes that she's too young to speak. I tell Mummy what she wants but she never agrees with me. Kizzy says she wants me to give her piggybacks. She says she wishes she wasn't bald and red. She wants to eat my mince pies and be draped in tinsel from the Christmas tree. She wishes Mummy would let me look after her more. She snuffles and sneezes and when her fingers clutch at mine her nails are sharp and they leave tiny marks on me.

Kizzy has a boiled cabbage face with twin sapphires so blue that it hurts me a little to look at them. Her name is like a kiss on the mouth and she gets kisses all the time, especially from Mummy. I think some of the kisses Mummy normally saves for me end up on Kizzy's nose and forehead.

I've started to watch and count, just to be sure.

Easter 1995

Everything is turned towards her. She is where the music is. Although she does nothing except vacuum-suck fingers and turn lollipop red, she is in the middle. Sometimes I don't mind. Since Kizzy came, the burned-onion taste of my parents' shouting has drifted from the house. Their fingers overlap when they pass their floppy baby to each other over my head, and for those few seconds it's all soft golden light.

I want her to need me. Sometimes I pinch her when no one is in the room, just so that I can cuddle her and make her stop crying. But Mummy always rushes in and pulls her away from me and says why did she suddenly start screaming like that, what did you do to her? I've tried pinching her more slowly and that sort of works but even if Mummy doesn't tell me off, she still looks at me with stones in her eyes. I hate that look. It makes the air go speckled grey and I know what it means: she's starting to like the baby better than she likes me.

June 1995

The slow pinch didn't work this time. I think Kizzy knows now when I want to make her cry. She started to scream like kicking buckets the second I went for her cheek, and I ended up scratching her face.

I back away quickly because I can hear footsteps running from the kitchen and the vibration is sending painful dark lines up through my feet. There's a swirl of orange and Mummy snatches up the baby, exclaiming over the mark on her face. Her words lash me with heat and everything smells of asparagus. Then Daddy's there too, and I edge towards him because he's never normally around when I hurt Kizzy so he might be on my side. He rests his hand on the crown of my head and turns to Mummy.

'Calm down, Alida,' he says, and I want to add my voice to his but am too scared to speak because the baby has turned into an uncontrollable red devil, forking the air with her shrieks, and Mummy looks like a pyramid that's about to burst open.

'She's done it again!' she shouts. 'I can't deal with this.'

'Mia,' says Daddy. 'Go and play in your room. I'll come and see you in a minute.'

His hand leaves my head and I feel cold all over but I have to go. I run out into the hall and bang up a few steps to fool them, and then I sneak back down and stand against the wall to listen through the sound of the baby wailing. I can hear my father talking.

'You favour the baby.'

'I do not!'

'You favour her, Alida. You barely give poor Mia the time of day any more. She may look like a big girl compared to Kizzy but she still needs her mum.'

'What are you talking about? You see nothing of my day. You have no idea what I do or don't do. Mia is so jealous, she barely lets me touch Kizzy. It's ridiculous at her age. She'll be six in November!' The air is sandpapery. It rasps against the skin on my arms, pressing me against the wall.

'Then let her do more with Kizzy, let her get involved.'

'How can I, when I can't trust her alone with her for five minutes? Our six-month-old baby is screaming and she has red marks on her skin where her sister has hurt her. Why can't you take it more seriously?' The baby stops crying suddenly, as if she's waiting for an answer. I picture the three of them staring unhappily at each other.

'All I'm saying is, give Mia some responsibility – just little things, like helping to dress Kizzy or change her nappy. She's jealous because she feels excluded. If I can see it, I don't know why you can't. You're her mother.' He fires out the last sentence and it lands on my mother with a thud. There's a wavering silence and I open my eyes wider to understand it but there are no more clues.

After a long time, she speaks. 'I'm just so exhausted.'

His voice rumbles something and I think they must be hugging, the baby caught between them like a jewel-eyed fish in a net.

I creep down the length of the hall to the telephone table, take a pair of scissors from the drawer and tear a piece of paper from the notepad. They are nestled together without me in the sitting room, and none of them seem to care.

With a fat, dragon-green pen, I draw arrows on the paper and then cut rectangles around each one. This is the trail I'll leave behind me when I go. When Mummy stops being angry with me, she'll follow it and I'll know that she still loves me. I gather the paper arrows in my hands and lie down flat on my stomach with my head turned to one side. The ear that the hall carpet tickles into is listening.

I can hear the tigery growl of a lawnmower. I can hear my father's baked potato voice. I can hear the slow beat of my heart. It thumps in my chest and through my ears and into the carpet, which is all around me. I know what's going to happen next, although it's different every time. I watch without blinking as the carpet shifts under my body, blue cropped wool flattening and crunching down to the walnut brown of thousands of broken twigs that glisten wetly. The banisters push upwards, their bases thickening and growing gigantic spidery roots. The forest floor is soft and crackling, and I am surrounded by trees. My yellow Frisbee is lying at the end of a leafy avenue and, when I see it, it rises slowly into the air and becomes a gilded sun. I lie still and wait. I can feel the next stage starting: a pale itching of my face and neck. My skin tightens and suddenly I am rushing downwards and inwards, shrinking so fast that for a moment I fear I might not stop until I disappear completely.

But I'm still here. Smaller, and magicked into another world, but here. I stand up and the trees tilt towards me with chattering leaves. I let an arrow fall to the ground, and begin to walk through the forest. The sounds I heard before the forest appeared are now only almost-sounds. As I walk past where the sitting room used to be, I know that even if Mummy walks out right this second, she won't see me.

I let another arrow fall.

My feet sink into the forest floor with every step. I can feel beetles scurrying under leaves, and on my tongue I can taste the pungent wetness of bark. The ground rises steeply and I am clambering over moss-covered boulders laid out in steps. I work my way upwards, arrows fluttering from my fingers. I'm nearly at the cave; just a few steps across the grassy landing and I can see it looming before me. I leave an arrow floating on a puddle of silk and push aside the entrance flap, which is hung with vines and criss-crossed with snail trails. I climb inside and the vines swing closed behind me. The cave is dark and lonely but there's a smell of birdsong on the air.

I curl up on the hard floor with the last of my arrows crumpled in my fist and wait for her to come and break the spell.

After a rimless black space, light falls on me, and there she is.

Chapter Twenty-Six

Alida grabbed her shoulder bag and got up so rapidly that she grazed her hip bone on the edge of the stone table.

'Could we have a break for a minute?' she asked Taos tensely.

He threw a quick sideways glance at her and nodded, and she left him stretching his long legs out under the table and drinking from his water bottle. At the reception, she discovered it was possible to make international calls at an extortionate rate using the main ashram telephone: a rotary dial one with a chewed-looking black cord. There was no chair, and Sushila remained standing a few feet away from the phone, filling out some forms, so that for some semblance of privacy, Alida turned to face the peeling white wall and its array of photographs of smiling gurus and people practising yoga postures in clean white outfits.

'Any news?' asked Ian as soon as he heard her voice.

'Not on a concrete level. I mean, I followed a false trail and found the wrong girl, but the thing is, I've finally realised—'

'Sorry,' he interrupted. 'You followed a what?'

'A false trail. To an ashram. But Mia isn't here, just a girl who looks a bit like her.'

There was silence for a long moment. Alida leaned into it, wondering. Was he merely disappointed, or was there something else? The faintest hint of a sneer?

'She has similar eyebrows,' she said to test the water, and heard him mumble something under his breath.

'We have to face the facts here, 'Lida,' he said. 'You're not getting very far with this search, and I think it's time for a change of tactics.'

'What's that supposed to mean?' she snapped. 'That I should hire a helicopter and do a James Bond?' Out of loyalty, she had intended to share with Ian her realisation about what had happened to Mia before telling Taos, but now she was having second thoughts. Ian would undermine her idea, she knew he would. She wondered bitterly why she had bothered to phone him.

'No, it just means that I'm arriving in India on Thursday the thirty-first,' Ian announced grandly.

'You're *what*?'

'I get in to Madurai around seven in the morning, local time.'

Alida gripped the telephone hard. 'But today's the twenty-seventh. That's just four days away. Ian, this is my thing. *I'm* doing this. If I can't find her, what makes you think you can?'

'It isn't "your" thing, is it? It's our thing. And I'm ... Well, I'll make sure I go about things in a methodical way.'

'Oh, like I don't?' Alida stared wide-eyed at the wall. For a moment, she wished she had him before her so that he could see how furious she felt. 'For God's sake, Ian,' she said, her voice low and uneven. 'Why don't you just come out and say it. In your eyes I'm completely incapable, aren't I? I've been wasting everybody's time, haven't I? I might as well have stayed at home and twiddled my thumbs.'

'Actually, yes, that would have been helpful,' he said with a hint of aggression. 'It was crazily irresponsible of you to leave your flat and telephone unattended. What if she's left a dozen messages on your answerphone?'

179

Alida's anger deserted her in a rush and was replaced by a cold sensation which gripped her stomach. 'She hasn't,' she said faintly. 'I asked Mrs Anderson to check and she'll email me if Mia calls.'

'Well then, what if Mia phoned and got the answerphone every time and didn't want to leave a message?'

Alida bit the tip of her forefinger hard just below the nail, so that the bone hurt.

''Lida? Have you thought of that?'

Alida narrowed her eyes. She didn't want to think of that. She took her finger from her mouth and looked at it. The two dents which her incisors had left in the skin reminded her of the underside of a staple. 'I'm not the only one with a phone,' she said then. 'And she's more likely to call you than me.'

Ian sighed the sigh of a man who is trying to rise above the situation. 'Well, whatever. I'm not going to get into this kind of senseless wrangle with you. I'll be there in three days and, when I arrive, you'll fly back so that if our daughter rings you'll be there to answer the phone.'

'I'm not leaving until I find her,' said Alida flatly.

Ian made a noise between a groan and a sigh. 'Alida, just understand me for once. I can't sit here feeling useless any more. I can't lose two children ...' His voice tailed off and for a moment they both listened to the gap of silent space between them. Alida pictured Ian standing half sorrowfully, half angrily in the hall of his house, longing for Mia. She knew by heart the old pain scored in horizontal lines across his forehead, lines his flopping blond hair tried to hide. 'I can't let it happen,' he continued.

Alida twisted the telephone cord around her fingers. 'All right,' she said. 'I suppose I'll see you on Thursday. I can bring you fully up to speed then.'

'What was the name of the hotel you stayed in when you first arrived?'

'Hotel Raj.'

'I'll go straight there and check in, so if you meet me there at eight thirty we can compare notes, and then you'll fly back to hold the fort, right?'

She swallowed. 'Maybe.'

'Alida,' he said warningly. 'You're of more use back in England than you are out there.'

'Don't you condescend to me like that,' she said, furious again. 'You have no idea how bloody hard it is. It's like trying to sprint blindfolded through thigh-high water.'

'I know it must be hard. You've done your best, and now I'll see if I can do better.'

'It's not a competition.'

'Oh, for crying out loud, just leave it, will you? You twist everything I say. You always did.'

'What a shame, I've run out of money,' remarked Alida sarcastically. 'Bye, Ian.' She hung up the phone, and was shocked to discover that she was shaking. She paid Sushila, who was studiously pretending that she hadn't heard Alida's side of the conversation. Then she stepped out into the heat of the fields in front of the ashram.

He's coming and I haven't found her yet, she thought. This can't be happening. He'll ruin it all.

She stood still for a moment, trying to empty her mind. Tinny Indian temple music wailed from somewhere within the depths of the ashram. Alida found herself smelling the air. There was rain in it now, heavy and damp. Across the field, two cows had been rubbed all over with purple dye and were tethered to a post. Beside them stood two slight men dressed in turbans and lungis who seemed to be having a heated discussion about the animals. She tried to imagine their conversation. Were they arguing about the colour of the dye, or were they debating the bondage of holy creatures?

I'm not going home, she thought. If I do, I'll be impossibly far away from Mia. Here, I see what she has seen. The same warmth surrounds our bodies, drawing out the

181

sweat, making our skin prickle and slide. Her face is in my bag, laughing up at me when I dip my hand in for a tissue or a sweet. I can draw her into my lungs along with this rainy air. And now Ian's trying to bully me off her trail. She squinted a little, still watching the men and the cows. Things seemed to be settling down: one man had lit up a thin cigarette and was resting against the post, while the other had backed off slightly. The cows stood purple and passive, their horns framing pieces of green foliage. Alida tried to imagine Ian navigating India, his clothes rumpling in the heat, stubble shadowing his jaw unchecked as he organised a grand-scale search party. He would be fine, she decided. He was always fine.

She hoisted her bag so that it sat more comfortably on her shoulder, and walked with slow steps back to Taos, who was where she had left him, with his easel and the orange painting propped against the courtyard wall and Mia's indigo and turquoise striped bag lying on the flagstones in partial shade, the photographs scattered brightly across the table. It was a colourful vision, and Taos was lounging in the middle of it, smoking contentedly with his sunglasses on. She was reminded of the first time they'd met: his irritation with her, his defiant smoke rings. They had known each other little more than a week, but he was already so familiar. As she sat down next to him on the stone bench which ringed the table, he looked at her expectantly, blowing a thin stream of smoke out of the corner of his mouth.

'Want to keep looking at the pictures, or have you had enough for one day?' he asked sympathetically.

Alida turned in her seat a little and looked at him, her eyes dark and serious. 'I think I know exactly what happened to Mia.'

He froze in the act of raising his cigarette to his mouth. 'Good or bad?'

She shrugged. 'That depends on us, I think.'

'Don't get mysterious on me, Alida,' he said, stubbing his cigarette out on the ground with a rapid gesture and turning to face her fully so that their knees bumped. 'Spit it out.'

'I will,' she assured him. 'But first, could you tell me where you think the postcards Mia stuck in the top corner of each collage might be from?'

Taos frowned impatiently, but turned to sift through the full-view photographs. He identified each of the locations on the postcards with impressive speed; despite their reduced size they were clearly visible, thanks to his high-pixel digital camera. 'That one's obviously the Vittala Temple in Hampi,' he said, and Alida nodded her agreement. 'This one shows the elephant statue at the Five Rathas complex in Mamallapuram, which is down the coast from Chennai,' he continued. 'This is the Sri Meenakshi Temple at Madurai, that looks like a cliff-top view of Varkala Beach, and I reckon this one has to be the Bull Temple in Bangalore.' He looked at her keenly. 'So, what's the story?'

'Well, I've realised ... I've realised a few things.' Alida took a deep breath and picked up the winged elephant collage. 'This is a representation of Kizzy. See the colour of its eye? That's the very bright blue of Ian's eyes – and of Kizzy's. It's the colour Mia always referred to as "favourite blue" after she died. As you know, all of these images, except maybe the synaesthesia-overload one, relate back to Kizzy dying and the ways in which her death affected Mia and me.'

Taos nodded. The fingers of his right hand were curled on the tabletop and he was flexing them slightly as he listened.

Alida touched another photograph. 'This image of the two bears made me remember the paper-arrow treasure-hunt trails she used to leave for me as a child.' She looked at Taos, who was frowning slightly. 'Kizzy's death is at

183

the root of Mia's behaviour.'

'What are you saying?'

Alida's eyes flashed with something between fear and excitement. 'I'm saying it's a treasure hunt.'

'What is?'

'Mia has set up a treasure hunt for me.' Alida patted the photograph nearest to her. 'And these collages are the clues.' She sat back as though she had finished her explanation.

Taos passed a hand over his scalp. 'Keep talking,' he prodded.

'Well—' Alida leaned forwards again. '—she's done the same thing that she used to do as a child when I was cross with her, but this time it's on a far larger scale. She wants to know that I've finally forgiven her for the baby's death, so she's set up a trail. Only instead of paper arrows, she's left me collages which focus on the loss of Kizzy, and picture postcards of different places in India.' Alida's eyes shone now, deep and beautiful, as she willed him to understand. 'She's alive, Taos. Mia's alive and she's waiting for me to come and find her.'

Taos tilted his head back and stared into the blueness of sky, which was being rapidly eaten away by a black-bottomed cumulonimbus cloud that was sailing in from the east. 'Well,' he said eventually, looking around at her, 'it's great to see you making connections with the collages, Alida.' He hesitated, pushing his sunglasses up onto his forehead. 'I don't want to suggest that you're not right about this, but I have a couple of ... considerations.'

Alida met his gaze unflinchingly. She knew she was right.

'First of all,' he said, counting off the considerations on his fingers, 'it's highly unlikely that Mia would do such a selfish and irresponsible thing, causing her family extreme anxiety and grief and placing your life in danger by making you race around India on local buses.'

'But if she felt despairing, hopeless—'

'Wait, Alida. Secondly, she could have no way of knowing whether it would be you or her father who would fly out to search for her.'

'My address was written in her passport. Obviously the police—'

'Just let me finish, will you?' His forehead creased in irritation. 'The third thing is that I don't get why Mia didn't drop more hints to me or someone else at Hotel Guru if she really created the collages for this purpose. From what little I know of her, I can't imagine she would want you and the police to fear for her life the entire time. The only significant thing I can recall her saying was that she wanted to show her artwork to her mother someday.'

'Perhaps she didn't know why she was doing them until one day it hit her – and maybe her saying she wanted me to see the collages *was* a hint.'

Taos let his hand fall onto his leg in a gesture of hopelessness. 'I'm not dismissing your idea out of hand, but it sounds a bit desperate, Alida.' He waited for her to speak, but Alida averted her eyes and sat stiffly for a moment. The temperature in their small patch of shade seemed to be rising every second as the storm clouds grew closer, even her ankles were sweating.

'Are you sure you're not just . . .' Taos began.

'Making it all up?' She eyed him resentfully.

'Don't put words into my mouth,' he said, a slight growl of annoyance edging into his voice. 'What I wanted to ask is, are you sure you're not just following the lines of your own longing?'

Alida raked her hair back with both hands. 'Oh, how do I know?' she asked. 'I don't know. It might all be conjecture and fantasy and longing, but what else have I got? Mia's disappeared without physical trace and all I have are these collages.' Her eyes pleaded with his. 'But it's Kizzy too. She's everywhere in these images. She's the link.

185

Every memory I've shared with you today leads straight back to her. And all the writing I've done since I've been in India does the same.'

'And that's not just your own preoccupations colouring things?'

Alida didn't reply. She watched her fingers twisting together on her lap. Taos stretched out an arm and touched her lightly on the shoulder to get her to look at him. When she turned, he left his hand there so that they were linked by the suntanned length of his arm.

'Any creative work is coloured by the perception of the artist,' he said. 'If I'm angry while I paint, even if the subject is unrelated to my feelings, some part of my emotion will still be transmitted onto the canvas.' His eyes flickered as he searched for an example. 'Maybe I'll choose harsher contrasts or my brushstrokes will be tighter, crueller. It must be the same when you write – the mind makes you circle back, again and again, to the source of your strongest emotion, until you liberate it by bringing it to life on the page.'

She was aware of his paint–tobacco–lemon grass scent rolling off him in pleasant waves. She looked into his eyes, which were steady and sincere, and saw that he didn't want to undermine her theory; he wanted to test her certitude. His hand rested reassuringly on her shoulder.

'All right,' she said. 'But it all fits together, Taos. Our estrangement, her disappearance, these images, the memories that I keep unearthing through writing about my lucid dreams and through talking to you. Everything leads back to the unresolved trauma surrounding Kizzy's death. I blamed Mia, and she knew it. I never told her any of the things she needed to know. In the crucial months after Kizzy died, those big words like love and forgiveness never left my mouth.' She looked at him, wondering how to convince him. 'I think she's testing me one last time.'

'Why did you blame Mia?'

Alida stiffened involuntarily, and she shook her head.

Taos's hand left her shoulder. 'All right, let's see if there's any logical pattern to the postcards.'

'We've already visited three of the places that they show.' She leaned eagerly over the photographs. 'Where shall we go next? Mamallapuram or Bangalore?'

'Well, it's easier from here to get to Bangalore, I'd say. But do you really think that's what these postcards are there for? To tell you where to look?' Taos was sceptical. 'There doesn't seem to be any obvious connection between these places.'

'You know,' said Alida, 'there were some unwritten postcards in Mia's luggage and I'm almost certain they were of the same places. I brought them with me. Wait.' She got up and went to Mia's bag, and after several minutes of rummaging through it she found what she was looking for in one of the side pockets. She had tucked the postcards inside a book, and when she fanned them out on the table they saw that they were indeed identical to the places that featured on the collages. 'Look, Taos. This is it. It's like a double clue – a repeated one, do you see?' she said. 'Mia would do that, just to make sure I got the message.'

Taos was nodding thoughtfully. 'Maybe so.'

He seemed more convinced now, and Alida was relieved. Taos glanced up at the sky, which was darkening visibly, the black cloud gaining speed and power. Alida followed his gaze. It was clear that another monsoon storm was about to break, and its imminence reminded her of the passing of minutes and hours and days, and the necessity of reaching Mia. 'We need to act fast,' she said, a note of anxiety entering her voice. 'We have limited time. Hotel Guru didn't even notify the police of Mia's disappearance until a week after she vanished. Who knows what state of mind she could be in now? And on this grand-scale treasure hunt, what might she do to herself if I don't turn up in time?'

'What would she do? If your theory is right, she'll be somewhere safe and warm, waiting,' reasoned Taos. He shifted on his seat. 'So you really think she's hiding out in one of the five places on the postcards?'

'Frankly, I don't know, Taos, but we've got nothing else to go on and with Ian arriving any day now I can't just sit here and do nothing.'

'You what?' Taos gave her a disbelieving look. 'Your ex-husband's coming to India?'

'Yes.' She looked at him, taking in his consternation with a smile. 'I know, I was pretty shocked, too. I forgot to mention it before. He'll be here on Thursday.'

Taos stood up abruptly. 'And once he's here, I suppose you won't be needing my help any more.'

Alida blinked. 'Of course I will.' She craned her head to look at his face, trying to gauge his mood. 'Although actually Ian wants me to go back to England as soon as he sets foot on Indian soil.'

Taos scooped up his lighter and tobacco and stuffed them into his pocket. He was red in the face. 'And you're going to do as he says?'

'Not necessarily, no.' She stood up, suppressing a sudden urge to laugh. 'Taos, you're not leaving because Ian's coming, are you? He won't be in the country for another four days yet!'

He looked at her stonily. 'I would have appreciated you telling me this before. Right at the start, perhaps.'

She stared at him, uncomprehending. 'I'm sorry. I suppose I was just preoccupied with my treasure-hunt theory.'

'I don't mean at the start of this afternoon, Alida,' he said, coldly sarcastic. 'I mean at the start of you being in India.'

'But I had no idea. Ian only told me when I telephoned him a quarter of an hour ago.'

Taos bit his lip. 'Ah.' It was the first time she had seen

him looking unsure of himself.

'I'm as surprised as you are,' she said soothingly. 'And that's another reason why I'm so keen to get moving. I want to find Mia before he comes here complicating things, and these postcards are the only clue I have.'

'Well,' said Taos, recovering his cool. 'If that's the way it is, then I guess you should get out your guidebook so we can plan our next move.'

But as he finished his sentence, the first drops of rain began to plummet from the sky, as large as ten-pence pieces, so that the two of them leaped in different directions – Alida to save the photographs, and Taos to protect the portrait he had done of her. The wind blew in and the sky surrendered its last blue corner. At the far end of the courtyard, four girls raced out and began snatching up the paper lanterns. Alida and Taos rushed to collect their own possessions, Alida's hair wild around her head, her eyes watering from the gusts of wind and, as the courtyard flagstones were spattered dark grey with rain, they ran together into the cool spaces of the ashram.

Twenty-Seven

Calls to Mangala in Hampi, Warren at Hotel Guru in Madurai and Five-toes at the Blue Sunrise Guest House in Varkala had revealed no fresh leads. Following the postcard clues, Alida's hopes were pinned on Bangalore and failing that Mamallapuram. During their tiring day of travel between the remote ashram and the nearest train station on the Bangalore line, they had researched Bangalore in Alida's guidebook. Taos felt he must have visited the city in the past but he had no memory of doing so; the place belonged to the twilight area of his amnesia, shady and unreachable. Alida understood now why tension emanated from Taos when people approached him unexpectedly – he didn't know whether or not he perhaps knew them but had lost his memories of them. It was an unsettling way to live. As Bangalore was a vast, busy city, their search strategy would be to show Mia's photograph around at the Bull Temple, since it featured on the postcard, and put up missing posters in the city's main backpacker areas in the hope of attracting a positive identification.

They had waited four frustrating hours for the overnight express train to arrive, and Alida had passed the time by eating samosas with a red chilli kick and reorganising her bag. Amongst her things, she'd found again the little soapstone elephant with its blue stuck-on eyes, and had sat for a while turning it in her hands, thinking of Mia. She'd tried to visualise her in a guest house tucked beside the Bull Temple. It would have the sort of name that appealed to Mia: the Velvet Hammock Guest House, or the Purple Peacock Hotel. Alida had imagined their reunion, playing and replaying it in her mind as a source of comfort while the life of the station had coursed around her, people lugging giant bags tied with string, or having picnics on the platform. Her nostrils had filled with the scent of cooked dhal and engine fuel. Now they were asleep inside the jolting steel casing of the Bangalore night train, breathing in its smells of stale curtains, chai and warm bodies.

With both hands placed under her cheek to make a pillow, palms sealed together as if she were engaged in prayer, Alida dreamed she was balancing high above India on an arrow made of polished steel. It was as big as an aeroplane wing and glittered white-gold in the sunshine. She looked down at rivers laid out like curling whips between the hills and wondered where Mia was hiding. The arrow started to tip downwards and she slid the length of it, fearing the fall but then realising with a flash of joy that she was dreaming again. She came to rest before a lake the colour of lapis lazuli. Floating cross-legged on the water was the disc-headed man, full of love for her. In his lap was the sequinned treasure chest Mia had made for her all those years ago. He gestured to the centre of the lake, where a pink blanket bobbed on the water, and Alida waded in to fish it out. The water came to chest level and chilled her through and through. The moment she touched the blanket, it became a shrunken corpse no bigger than a nine-month-old baby. It had Mia's face, the eyes shrivelled to the size of raisins. A moan rose in Alida's throat and she tried to stretch out the limbs but they responded like rubber, bouncing back into position with surprising energy. She stroked the head, with its desiccated skin and seaweed hair. Tears started to fall from her eyes.

Then the world rocked sideways and she was ejected

from the scene like a kicked stone. Her body was flung forwards, then back again, and she was struggling under the crumpled scarlet sarong she had used as a bed sheet. The train had lurched to a sudden halt, almost tipping her from her bed. She pushed the sarong off her head and sat up in the half-light. Voices carried from outside, and wheels rattled along concrete. They had stopped at another station. Alida was wide awake, her dream emblazoned across her mind. Parting the pleated curtain that ran along the length of her bed, she peered out into the compartment. There was no sign of life; everyone else seemed to have slept through the halt. Taos was in the bunk below hers and she leaned down, hoping that by some freakish coincidence he would open his curtains at that precise moment and want to talk to her. But the curtains didn't stir.

She switched on the light at the head of her bed, then rummaged around in the luggage rack beside her head until she found her pen and pad. She recorded her lucid dream and then lay back, thinking. Did the dream mean that she was right about the treasure-hunt trail, but that it would end in Mia's death? She wished she hadn't woken up in the middle of it. Why had the disc-headed man shown her the little corpse in the lake? She thought of the look of love he had given her.

I love him, she thought, ridiculously. I barely know him, but he's part of me. Tears sprang to her eyes and she hugged her notepad to her chest.

God, I'm ludicrous, she thought. My thirty-eighth birthday is hovering around the next bend in the road and all I've managed to do with these long years of life is lose my two daughters. And now I'm harbouring feelings of love for a faceless man in my dreams. She wriggled onto her side and pressed her feet against the coolness of the wall. An invisible mosquito whined around her head and she swatted at it ineffectually. She found herself wondering what Taos was dreaming of. She considered his long body

192

lying below her own and imagined herself sinking down through the mattress and coming to rest beside him. He had gone to sleep feeling resentful of her, she knew. Once they had boarded the train, he had asked her with his habitual abruptness how Kizzy had died. Caught by surprise, Alida hadn't been willing to answer him.

'I'm not ready to talk about that with you,' she had said gracelessly, and he had nodded and withdrawn into himself, staring grimly out of the window. She had felt bad, but what could she say? Who could know for sure what had occurred in that short period of inattention that had resulted in the loss of Kizzy's life? The little corpse from her lucid dream materialised again, dragging other images behind it which emerged in her mind dripping wet and distressingly vivid. Alida frowned. 'Go away, just go,' she murmured, but they stayed and she knew what she had to do. It was a simple choice: either she could drop back into sleep and suffer the lost baby nightmare again, or she could try to write it out of her system. She retrieved her pen and pad, then propped herself up on one elbow and described what she saw.

The bathroom is a particularly beautiful one that we inherited when we moved into the house. The previous owners went to the trouble of installing a right-angled bath decorated inside and out with inch-high mosaic tiles in shades of turquoise and blue. When the bath is filled, turquoise light refracts up through the water so that it scintillates in an inviting, swimming-pool-in-the-sun sort of way. Kizzy is sitting solidly upright in the shallow water, its brilliance reflected in her blue eyes.

Kizzy's bath time is always a loud occasion. We switch the radio on and she crashes her fists up and down to make turquoise splashes, her eyelashes stuck together in dark blonde triangles. Mia kneels on the bath mat in her yellow dungarees with her arms hanging over the rim of the bath and makes the plastic dolphin do jumps and tickles Kizzy's toes until she squeals with glee. I stride in and out of the bathroom, opening the window wide to let the September sunshine in, stacking clean towels in the cupboard on the landing, clearing toys out of the way with a sweep of my bare foot.

The doorbell chimes.

'Oh, who on earth is that?' I grumble. I hurry into the bathroom, meaning to lift Kizzy out and wrap her in a towel before answering the door with her perched fluffy and damp on one arm. But Mia looks around beseechingly.

'I'll watch her, Mummy. We're playing,' she protests.

My eyes flick over to my splashing baby and I hesitate, but they're playing so nicely and Ian is always harping on about giving Mia more responsibility with Kizzy. 'All right,' I say. 'But don't take your eyes off her for a single second, Mia.'

'I won't!' Shining with pleasure, she turns back to Kizzy and I run down the stairs. The doorbell goes again just before I reach the front door, and this irritates me. Who is this impatient caller?

I open the door and look into a stranger's face. He is my height and has a crew cut and watery green eyes. The smell of cheap aftershave wafts off him.

'Alida Salter?' he asks, and I see that he is holding a clipboard. On the path just behind him is a large box which I assume must be the laptop computer Ian ordered over the internet recently.

(Upstairs, Kizzy has already slipped backwards – or been pushed. Her mouth gulps down water.)

'Yes?'

'Delivery for you. I'll need a signature, please.'

'Fine.' He hands me a pen and the clipboard, and tells me where to sign. The blasted pen doesn't work. It's a ballpoint pen, and the ball is jammed solid so that it won't run across the page. 'It doesn't work,' I tell him, holding it out impatiently. Upstairs, the radio is chattering away.

(Water is filling Kizzy's small lungs at an alarming rate. Her arms and legs punch the surface of the water but her head remains under.)

'Oh, I'm sorry about that.' He accepts it back from me and frowns down at it, as if just looking at it will make the ink flow. 'It worked a minute ago,' he says, perplexed. 'I think I have another one in the van.'

'No, wait, that's fine, I've got one right here,' I say hastily, and duck into the hall to snatch one off the telephone table. I glance up the stairs as I return. A Louis Armstrong song is playing now and I wish I'd turned the radio off before coming down here, in case Mia calls me.

(Kizzy's eyes bulge. The water is hurting her, turning to fire in her lungs. Her consciousness is fading.)

The man watches as my hand flies across the dotted line. There's a feeling jumping inside me, a feeling in my stomach that the seconds are ticking past far faster than I think.

'Thank you very much,' says the green-eyed man. He takes the clipboard and pen from me and slides them into his bag before stooping to pick up the box and hand it to me.

'Thanks,' I say, stepping backwards into the house.

'Oh, wait,' he laughs as I'm about to close the door with my foot, 'I took your pen, didn't I. Hold on.' He fishes in his bag for an agonisingly long moment.

(Kizzy has been without oxygen for one hundred and thirty seconds. She is not struggling any more.)

'Oh, just keep it.'

'No, no, here it is.' He pops it on top of the box.

'Bye,' I say, and practically kick the door shut in his face. Something isn't right. I spin around, dump the box on the carpet and rush up the stairs.

'. . . I see trees of green . . .' the radio sings lazily as my feet hit the stairs one after another.

'. . . Skies of blue . . .' I burst into the bathroom,

195

wanting to see my two girls playing and laughing. But Mia is prone on the floor beside the bath, trembling with her hands clamped over her head, and the baby ... I can't see the baby. I slew into a painful skid on my knees, cracking into the side of the bath and not feeling it. The baby is on her back in the bath staring motionless from beneath the water with her blue mirrored eyes. My arms stretch out so fast that it's a blur. Her hair floats around her head like golden seaweed. I snatch her up, screaming, screaming.

'. . . And I think to myself . . .' *the voice croons.*

Her body a wet fish, heavy in my arms.

I lay her out on the floor and start mouth-to-mouth.

'. . . What a wonderful world . . .'

The slackness of her tiny mouth, my breath making her chest rise and fall, water spewing from her throat.

Pressing on her chest is like squeezing a soaked sponge

where's the heartbeat

come back baby come back to me

'. . . Yeah, I think to myself . . .'

her eyes don't change no matter what I do

staring blue

I am breathing into a corpse

she's not there any more

'. . . What a wonderful world . . .'

Kizzy's gone.

In the morning, Alida heard Taos stir and then open his bottle of water and take a long drink. She lay in silence, absorbing the cries of chai-sellers and the rustling of other passengers dressing behind their curtains. Then she reached for her notebook and ripped from it the pages describing Kizzy's death. She dragged her curtain aside and leaned down to Taos's bunk. Without a word, she pushed the pages through the gap in his curtain and held them there, waiting to be noticed. In a couple of seconds, she felt them being taken out of her hand. She withdrew her arm and lay curled up on her mattress again, listening to the crackle of paper and waiting.

After a few minutes there was a loud creak as Taos climbed out of bed. Alida lay very still. His creased morning face appeared beside her bunk, and neither of them spoke. Taos reached out and laid his hand, large and warm, on the side of her head. His eyes were very soft. Alida put her hand over his and they remained like that for a while, watching each other peaceably.

'It only takes a matter of minutes for a baby to drown,' said Alida, staring at him clear-eyed.

Taos nodded.

'I sometimes still wonder how many seconds I spent talking to that fool whose pen didn't work. Two hundred? One hundred and eighty?'

He grimaced. 'It makes no odds.'

She shrugged as well as she could in her curled-up position.

'And Mia?' he asked, his voice reaching her ear through the muscle and bone of his hand.

'We never got a coherent story out of her. She was physically unhurt but completely traumatised. She saw me trying to revive the baby, you know. She kept making circling movements above her head and crying about grains of sand. It meant nothing. Everyone, including the police, thought it possible that she had pushed Kizzy under the water in a fit of jealousy. She had hurt her in the past, you know, the typical sibling jealousy thing, a pinch here, a slap on the head there, but she had been so much better in the months leading up to Kizzy's death.'

'What do you think happened?'

Alida sighed and slid her hand off his. Taos took his hand off her head and transferred it to the edge of her bed, and she sat up, pulling the sarong-sheet around her. 'I don't know. She seemed to feel so remorseful, but at the same time she couldn't explain what had happened and after a few weeks she appeared to have completely forgotten that two- or three-minute slot of time. Ian tried to get her to talk about it at times, especially after her nightmares, but she couldn't. Or didn't want to.'

Slowly, Taos nodded. 'Well, thanks for telling me.'

Alida closed her eyes for a brief moment, and then she smiled at him sadly.

Alida sat in a spacious refrigerator of a cyber café which they had located as soon as they arrived in Bangalore. Taos was sitting a few chairs along, already typing furiously. Alida's computer was inexplicably slower than his; it was taking her an eternity to get into her account. Finally, the pages shifted and she was in. She scanned her inbox: several friends and her mother had written back to her last message. Email was such a convenient way of keeping everyone up to date on the search, avoiding the tensions and misunderstandings of telephone calls. Ian had written, presumably to pass on his flight information and nag her again about returning to London. There was an email from a sender she didn't recognise, but her full name was written on the title line. She clicked on it.

> *Dear Mrs Salter, you are advised that Madurai City Morgue has the following: Caucasian female estimated nineteen years of age, no identification marks, brown-haired, post-mortem revealed strangulation cause of death. Respectfully, A. Prakash.*

Shocked, Alida glanced at the date. The email had been sent the previous afternoon. She looked over at Taos but he was intent on his screen. The cyber café hummed around her and a swarm of tiny black dots appeared at the sides of her vision. She clicked out of the message, then changed her mind and clicked into it again. She would

198

forward it to Ian, just so that he knew. She added a message above it to the effect that she was sorry that she had been short with him on the phone, and went on to explain in two sentences her theory about Mia's collages. 'I've just arrived in Bangalore and I don't know what to do about this message below,' she wrote. 'Should I go? Might it be her? What shall I do?'

Feeling dizzy, she sent it off and then called over to Taos. He glanced at her sharply, saved the message he was writing and hurried over.

'Everything all right? You look a bit white.'

'Look,' she said, and showed him the message.

He leaned over it anxiously, his hand gripping the back of her chair. 'Oh, Jesus.'

'Strangulation,' she said, staring blankly at the screen. 'I'm sure it's not her.'

'We'll have to go and find out,' said Taos.

There was a long pause. Alida fiddled with the mouse, sending the cursor whirring in zigzags across the screen.

'It's not Mia,' she said finally.

Taos sighed. 'We have to check, though.'

'No.' She signed out of her account and stood up shakily. 'I'm not going.'

'Alida, they won't be able to store the body indefinitely. We should go down there and check, and then we can continue with the search.'

'No.' She headed for the exit. 'I'll wait for you in the doorway,' she said over her shoulder. 'And then we can find a hotel. I'm sure she's in Bangalore somewhere.'

'Alida—'

She swung around, suddenly furious. 'Don't insist, Taos. She's my daughter, not yours. And I know she's not dead.' She stared at him, her eyes hard and bright. 'This is my choice.'

Turning on her heel, she walked away.

199

Chapter Twenty-Eight

8 September 1995
ashes
there are ashes
everywhere
choking
the whole world

November 1995
Whenever I blink, I see Kizzy. I can smell her on the furniture, hear her laughter echoing in the empty spaces she has left behind. I turn to look and she's almost there, an outline, a transparent shape who disappears as soon as I turn my head to see. Mummy doesn't want to look at me any more. She wishes it was me who went away, not Kizzy. She loved her more, and it's my fault that she's gone.

I can hear the tinkling of cutlery being sluiced in the kitchen sink. I can feel the weight of my body on the ground. I have a stack of arrows in my hand. Thick, gristly black lines, unmissable. They shout with a strong voice. But will she come?

My eyes swim in water, swim until there's too much water and they start to drown. Water pools on the carpet, flowing faster until the entire room is a fast-filling lake. I wait to see whether I will drown or float. I feel the changes begin; my body growing compact and powerful, feathers pushing out of every pore. My face narrows and shrinks and reforms.

I am a slow bird, a swan, gliding over a lake, up a waterfall, into my cave. The arrows bob on the water behind me.

I settle myself down to wait.

I need a wee.

Will she ever come? I picture her flying towards me on a magic carpet, or sitting astride a unicorn. She sweeps up my arrows with one long soft arm as she goes.

It's starting to smell of dandelions in here and I'm afraid I'll wet myself. But I have to wait. If she doesn't find me, it might mean she doesn't love me at all. And if she doesn't love me, nothing can ever be the same again.

I imagine the way it will be: a sudden shock of light and warm vanilla custard spreading around me in rings. She'll scoop me up into her arms and I'll feel the stretch of her smile on my cheek.

'Hello, silly,' she'll say, and I'll lock my arms tightly around her neck and never let go.

What if she comes, but she shouts and cries? She cries so much, her eyes turning red from the inside out. When she isn't crying she is a statue with unseeing eyes. There's a fire in my belly and I have to keep my legs crossed to stop it coming out. I hug myself and feel the way that my stomach has ballooned up.

Then suddenly, it happens. I can't stop it any more. Hot liquid all down my leg, and the stench of dandelions hurting my nostrils. Liquid runs from my eyes too. I am drowning in myself, shivering in spite of the heat. Now I'll be in even more trouble. I imagine her wrenching open the cave door and attacking, nails scratching me, tearing me to shreds. I curl myself into a soaking wet ball of clothes and cry myself to sleep.

Then there's light.

I squint upwards and it's baked potatoes, not vanilla custard. In a way I am relieved because Daddy's love doesn't have power cuts; it's always there, shining on me. His voice crashes over me and he pulls me up and out, exclaiming at my wetness, holding me close, surrounding me with the warm vibrations of his voice and heartbeat. I dive into him. My hair is plastered to my face with a paste made from sweat and dried tears. For a long stretching moment that I hope will never have to end, he holds me still and strong, pouring love into me so that I know I am safe.

Then he takes a big breath that crushes me and howls out a name, 'Aleeedaah!'

Footsteps come running up the stairs and she bursts into the room. Draped over Daddy's shoulder, my face pressed into his neck, I can't see her but the air shivers with fractured orange shapes. 'What? What is it?' she demands, sounding shocked.

'You have to wake up,' he shouts at full volume, and I cling to him in terror. 'Look what I found, lying in the bottom of your wardrobe in a puddle of her own piss! This is your daughter, Alida. Things have gone too far.' He swings around abruptly so that she can see my face. We stare at each other mutely. She is frizzy and pale, her eyes skull-holes.

'Mia,' she says helplessly, but doesn't move even the tiniest part of her body in my direction.

'I've had it, Alida,' he cries, swinging around again so that she is lost from my sight. 'You have to climb out of this hole you've dug for yourself. We're all suffering, not just you. Stop thinking about yourself every fucking minute of the day and pay attention to your six-year-old child who has lost her sister and is wasting away from grief.' His voice cracks and suddenly we're all crying, all three of us, walls and walls of ugly black sobs which connect us in a triangle. She comes to us and holds us and at the centre of

202

the ugliness is a feeling that tastes of lemon soda, a cleansing freshness that we are trying to touch.

When everything lightens to a drab grey, we disentangle ourselves and Daddy inspects his suit, which is all smelly with wee. I turn to Mummy hoping for something: a touch or a word.

'Mia,' she sighs, wiping her cheeks with a thin white arm. 'Promise me that you'll never hide in my wardrobe again.' She waits, and I say nothing. She ought to know that my promises mean less than nothing.

I'll watch her, Mummy.

'Come on.' She attempts a smile. 'Let's get you washed and changed and then I'll make you a cup of hot chocolate.' And that's all. I don't know what it is that I want her to say, but it isn't that. I need something that will fill the dark space in my chest.

Slowly, on trembling legs, I follow her out of the room.

Twenty-Nine

The Bull Temple in Bangalore hummed with the combined sounds of musicians, tourists and prayer. There were so many colours that Alida felt invaded; where could she start looking for traces of Mia among this distraction of flowers, cum-cum powder, saris and shrines? She frowned through the crowds, incapable of appreciating what she saw. Taos was ambling beside her, his height enabling him to see easily over people's heads. Alida felt envious; he must always have a sense of space and perspective even in the most crowded place. They had checked into a large hotel in the town centre and had spent the morning putting up 'missing' posters in traveller cafés and guest houses, asking around without the slightest whiff of success. Taking Mia's photograph from her bag, Alida pushed her way to a stall selling coconut slices and incense. She was beginning to hate this routine – pantomiming her loss to an interested crowd like a one-woman Punch and Judy show.

'Lost,' she repeated wearily to the man, her hands flying to the sky. 'Gone.'

The coconut man jabbed a finger at the picture and said something in Kannada.

Alida sighed. 'Just. . . Just tell me, do you recognise her? Have you seen her before?' She tried not to sound shrill. This man had the sweetest smile, yet she couldn't bring herself to smile back. When they had established that he had never set eyes on Mia before in his life, Taos, standing next to her, did the smiling and thanking for her. The man waved them towards the temple, speaking kind words which rumbled from him peacefully. Alida wavered, caught between an extreme sense of frustration and the need to respond to this man's goodwill. Almost reluctantly, she turned back to him and bought a jasmine string and a coconut slice. Grasping the solid rope of flowers in her fist made her feel a little brighter, as if some of the fragrance could infiltrate her skin and cool her blood, but as she followed Taos into the temple she couldn't free herself of the image of a dead girl with strangulation marks around her neck.

Was the face Mia's?

When they came to the temple's namesake, an imposing granite Nandi, she arranged her flowers and coconut on the nearest shrine, sending her thoughts out to a reunion with a living, happy Mia.

'Why don't you sit down for a bit and let me show the photograph around,' suggested Taos. 'You look pale and exhausted and I think you need a break.'

She looked at him sorrowfully. She knew it was true. 'I just feel there's no way forward any more,' she said. 'If that morgue girl is her ...'

'Don't think about it,' he said, shaking his head. 'You said earlier you were sure Mia is still alive, and I think you're right that we need to continue searching. If we waste time returning to Madurai at this stage, we might miss some vital clue.'

Alida looked at the ludicrously large bull in front of her and began to laugh weakly. 'Yes, and this place is really swarming with clues.' She blinked back tears. '*Swarming* with them!'

Taos looked at her, his face grave. 'Don't do that laughing–crying thing, Alida, it's unsettling,' he said. 'Just give me the photograph and I'll be back in half an hour. Try to think about something beautiful.'

When he had gone, Alida sank to the floor and sat staring at people's bare feet as they walked around and past her. Decorated feet, undecorated feet. Feet always made her think of Five-toes now, and Five-toes made her think of Mia's baby. She sat and thought unbeautiful thoughts about how the baby might have come into existence.

They had discovered nothing at the Bull Temple, nor at any of the other places they had visited around the city. Zero clues: not one person had even thought that they might possibly have seen Mia. Bangalore seemed a dead end, and Alida was beginning to wonder whether her treasure-hunt theory was just wishful thinking.

The hotel they were staying at was equipped with running hot water, one of the rare few since the upmarket hotel in Madurai where she had spent her first few nights in India. She stripped off her clothes and stretched and turned under the stream of heat, rubbing soap all over her skin to dissolve the ingrained dust which seemed to be lodged into every pore. This was luxury, pure physical pampering which made her feel ten times stronger.

She noticed that her hip bones were jutting slightly more than usual and that her stomach was taut and flat. She had always been naturally slender, but even after just ten days in India, the constant sweating and lack of snacking, combined with her worry about Mia, was having an effect on her body. Alida washed her hair, shaved her legs and generally groomed herself as well as she could. When she had finished, it didn't matter that she began to perspire again the moment she stepped back into her room; she was cleaner than she had been in days. She changed into her cream trousers and a pale-green vest top – the first time she had worn her own clothes rather than Mia's since she had arrived in India. It's like I want to become Mia, or at least throw off my usual self, she thought as she found a melting eyeliner and applied it as best she could. Wearing her clothes, studying her collages, writing out my memories, dreaming the way she dreams, these are my ways of reaching out to her, tuning in to her.

The picture of Mia had half slid out of her bag where it lay on the pillow and, as she saw it inverted in the mirror, Alida tried to remember what Mia had said to her while she had snapped pictures of her breathing white clouds in the cold air. Was it something about holding her breath until she started breathing in colour? Yes, because Alida had made some jokey remark ('You mean as opposed to breathing in black and white?') and for once the adolescent Mia hadn't minded being teased. She had told Alida about the feeling that went with this coloured breathing: was it a feeling of being exceptionally alive? It was hard to remember all of Mia's frequent and sometimes astonishing sensory revelations, but these, too, were the key to her daughter, Alida felt. She imagined Mia waiting hopefully for her somewhere out there. I'm on my way, Mia, she promised. I'm coming for you. She ran a comb through her wet hair and looked at herself solemnly in the mirror before going out to meet Taos. Tonight she would tell him about Mia's pregnancy.

They had just settled themselves into seats inside a pizzeria across the road from the hotel. Looking around, Alida saw that the ceiling was strung with fairy lights and that there was a Shiva shrine just along from the cutlery tray. Taos was wearing a white cotton shirt which accentuated his deep tan, and he looked as clean as Alida felt, although she noted that he hadn't bothered to shave. Perhaps he had decided to grow his stubble into a beard.

He grinned across the table at her. 'The showers are good, huh?'

'Better than good,' she said. 'I think that shower and general spruce up just saved my life.' Taos felt very accessible; she was ready to tell him about Mia. A waiter with a gold wrist chain and long fingernails came up with menus which he laid politely on the table for them. Taos picked his up and opened it.

'I haven't told you this yet,' said Alida casually, 'but I thought you might be interested to hear that Mia's expecting a baby. If she's still pregnant – which of course I don't know for sure – then I should think she's anything up to about four months along by now.'

Motionless, Taos stared at her over the menu. 'Mia's pregnant?'

She lowered her eyes and nodded. She was trying to formulate her next question so that it didn't come out sounding too accusatory. Did you sleep with Mia? Might you be the father of this baby? Taos's stillness across the table unnerved her and she found herself unable to look up.

'How come you never mentioned that before, Alida?' His voice was ominously low. She risked a look at him and was struck by the coldness in his eyes.

'I only found out when we were in Varkala.'

'That doesn't answer my question.'

Alida swallowed. 'Look, it's my decision who I tell,' she said defensively. 'Why are you acting so angry?'

'I'm not acting.'

She sighed. 'Taos—'

'You don't trust me.' He blinked rapidly. 'You actually don't trust me, even though I'm working side by side with you every day to help you get to the bottom of your daughter's disappearance.'

'I *do* trust you.'

'What's this all about, Alida?' he asked, slapping his menu down on the table. 'Do you think I'm some untrustworthy crackpot because of my memory loss?' He waved away her protest and leaned in over the table, glaring at her. 'In that case it wouldn't surprise you to learn that my friends look at me as if I'm a frame with no picture in it. They think Taos has stepped out of this' – he indicated his body with a brusque gesture – 'and left some vacant goon in his place. Is that what you think, too? That there's nothing in here worth trusting?'

Alida stared at him, horrified. 'No, Taos, that's not it at all.' She pressed her fingers briefly to her temples, trying to clarify her thoughts. 'I suppose the thing is that I can't trust what I don't know, and I don't know whether . . .' she faltered. 'You still haven't told me whether or not there was anything sexual between you and Mia.'

Taos gave her a sharp, questioning look.

'You think I got her pregnant?' he asked flatly.

'You were so cagey when I asked you right at the start if you'd slept together,' said Alida. 'What was I supposed to think?'

He shook his head disgustedly. 'I can't believe some of the things that go on in your head. All I did with Mia was talk about lucid dreams and art. She's not my type, I'm not hers. If you leaped to the wrong conclusion, that's hardly my fault, and I don't think it justifies you hiding what could be a valuable clue from me.'

'Fine,' said Alida, feeling both relieved and annoyed. 'But you have to see that refusing to answer me when I asked you about this outright did made you look fairly guilty.'

'The reason I refused to answer you, Alida,' he said sharply, 'was because you rubbed me up the wrong way with your bossy, intrusive questions and your assumption that I'd have to tell you every detail of my private life just because your daughter had done a runner.'

'Well, I'm sorry if I came across that way but I was exhausted and terrified for Mia's safety. I couldn't—'

'Whatever.' Taos stood abruptly, scooping up his tobacco pouch and lighter. 'I've lost my appetite.'

'Oh, don't go!' Alida leaped to her feet, almost knocking her chair over. Grabbing behind her to right it, she saw the waiter watching them in round-eyed wonder. She snatched her bag from the table and hurried after Taos. When they were outside, lit up by the glare of passing yellow headlights, Taos turned on her.

'You're quite two-faced, aren't you? Being all nice with me and yet thinking all along that I'm some unprincipled fool who shagged your daughter and got her into trouble. I thought you were more real than that, Alida.'

'That's not fair. If you had a daughter you'd know how I feel.' She was shouting above the street noise, oblivious to the curious gaze of traders and passers-by. 'I wasn't just being nice for nothing, Taos. I liked you *in spite* of my concerns.'

'Am I supposed to be flattered by that?' He loomed over her, tension wired through every muscle.

'Yes, actually you are.' Alida stared at him, her eyes challenging. 'Even though I didn't know if there was anything between you and Mia, I couldn't help ... liking you.'

For a long moment, nothing was said. The two kept up their positions. Then, to Alida's surprise, Taos reached out and caught hold of her chin in the circle of his thumb and forefinger.

'Don't point your chin at me like that,' he said with an unreadable look in his eyes.

'Let go of my chin,' demanded Alida. It was hard to sound authoritative with someone holding on to part of her face. She put her hand on his wrist but he wouldn't budge. 'What are you playing at?' she mumbled, wondering at the tenderness she saw in his face.

'I've been wanting to see how it feels to grab this chin,' he said, shaking it a little.

'And how does it feel?' she asked to humour him.

'Satisfying,' he said, and turned his grip into a caress which ran the length of her jaw and sent tiny shivers of pleasure down her neck. His thumb moved gently across the contours of her lips. Alida stood, shocked and moved almost to tears.

'Alida?' he asked, and she had no words but found herself nodding, in agreement or approval, and then he was so close that she could feel the scent of him diffusing into her skin and a fraction of a second later his lips were pressed warm against her own. Alida stretched up and into him, feeling his hand on the back of her neck, his tongue soft and dark in her mouth. For a moment the presence of the busy street was reduced to nothing but muffled sounds and a distant pressure under the balls of her feet. Then her head was buzzing and she was pulling away.

'We shouldn't be doing this on an Indian street,' she said shakily. 'The locals won't like it.'

'Bangalore's a pretty liberal city,' said Taos, deftly hooking his arms around her waist before she could separate herself from him any further. 'But I have to agree that they might not like it if they knew what I'd like to do with you next.'

'Which is?' asked Alida, taken aback by how fast things seemed to be moving.

'I'm not saying,' said Taos. 'But if you come back to the hotel with me, you might well find out.'

'Are you propositioning me?' she asked in disbelief.

'Yes,' he said firmly.

'But Taos—' she floundered. 'A minute ago you were accusing me of being two-faced and now you're kissing me and inviting me to indulge in God knows what in a hotel room.'

'So?'

'So it's a little surprising and I don't know, I feel ... surprised.'

He smiled. The solid warmth of his arms around her felt good. 'I'm surprised too,' he said. 'If you knew how much I'd been hankering after you, you'd understand my impatience.'

'*Hankering?*' She smiled at him, a hint of mischief in her eyes. 'I like the idea of you *hankering*.'

'Don't push your luck, Alida,' he warned. 'Come on, let's get some supplies of whiskey and warm coke from one of those general stores and go back and turn up the air con until you're begging me to warm you up.'

'Oh, is that your terribly original master plan of seduction?'

'Mmm.' He looked at her, suddenly meek. 'Think it'll work?'

She laughed. 'Of course it won't. You're forgetting that I haven't been cold in days. Coldness is my mirage, my oasis, and once I get there I'll sit pretty and spend the rest of the night counting my goosebumps.'

As Alida spoke, an image of the six-year-old Mia curled up shivering in the wardrobe, soiled and miserable, came to her with an unexpected rush of pain. Her teasing demeanour vanished instantly. She couldn't do this. Mia was sitting alone somewhere, waiting for her. Alida's attention had to be fixed on her night and day; if she broke their tenuous connection by focusing on Taos, it felt as though she might lose Mia completely. I should be wearing her clothes, not mine, she thought illogically. This is no time for romance. She loosened Taos's arms from around her waist. Sensing her abrupt change of mood, he reluctantly stepped back.

'Being serious now, I need to concentrate on Mia,' she said gently. 'This is just not the right time... I'm sorry.'

Taos said nothing. His face was closed, his expression impenetrable. She could feel the heaviness in him but didn't know how to ease it. Beside them, the road swept past, motor rickshaws sounded their high, nasal horns, and the air was hot with fumes and dust. Alida pressed a hand to her forehead, disbelieving. She was Mia's mother, but she was also a woman standing close to a man with beauty in the touch of his hands. Yet Mia was lost; she needed her mother. And here her mother was, allowing herself to be kissed by this tall Australian who tasted of lemon grass and had surprisingly gentle lips. It was all wrong, and she felt a fierce urge to weep.

Life never stops, she thought. It has the roaring momentum of a waterfall and, when you least expect it, when you're drowning in grief or wishing you were dead, or feeling as though the last bit of hope has slid through a crack in the Earth's crust and you are ready to give up, something of great beauty is thrown your way. A life raft, a friend, a lover. But I can't say yes to Taos. Not when Mia could be lying somewhere, dead.

She took another step back from Taos, almost knocking into a broad woman in a green sari who was hurrying along the pavement laden with shopping bags, her husband striding beside her with a screaming infant in his arms. There were too many people here, too much action.

'Shall we go back into the restaurant?' she asked Taos, trying to sound more normal than she felt, as if there was no lump constricting her throat when she spoke, as if kissing him had not brought her into a state of violent guilt and longing.

'I told you I'd lost my appetite,' he answered dully. He ran both hands over his head in a weary gesture which made him suddenly seem vulnerable, even a little lost. 'I'll see you in the morning.'

He turned his back on her to cross the street and Alida watched with intense sadness as he walked away.

Chapter Thirty

In her dream, Alida was sitting on a cliff edge, watching the waves roll in. The sea was dark and swollen and the waves were growing ever higher, dark-blue walls of water bearing in at speed. She could barely drag her eyes from the sight, but something further along the cliff was calling her like an ache. With an effort of will, she turned her head and saw a bronze and silver mannequin standing on a piece of land which jutted far out into the sea. It was the disc-headed man and Alida got to her feet because seeing him meant that she was dreaming. His hands were behind his back, pulling his shoulders taut. His disc was blindingly beautiful. With great care and concentration, he started to pull his arms from behind his back. She began to move towards him but as she did a monstrous wave roared up over the cliff and she was borne away by it.

Alida woke up gasping for breath, her arms tangled in the sheet. For a moment she saw nothing but blue water swirling around her as she struggled to open her eyes. Drowning as Kizzy did, she thought. Faced by waves as Mia was in those nightmares. What was the disc-headed man about to pull out from behind his back? She squinted around her room, trying to wake up fully. She saw the ubiquitous rust-coloured smears on the walls where previous occupants had swatted blood-filled mosquitoes. The fan was spinning on rotation level one, slow and calming.

Alida's hair was plastered to the sides of her head with sweat. She tugged free a section of her mosquito net and crawled out onto the floor. Her head was banging, and as she headed for the shower she kept seeing the disc-headed man pulling his arms slowly – too slowly – from behind his back. She had the sickening sensation that somewhere, for someone, time was running out.

The shower refreshed and calmed her. She combed her wet hair and tied it back from her face before dressing in a green and white sarong of Mia's and a white vest top. Still, she felt unsettled by her reaction to Taos's kiss the night before, and had to steel herself before going to knock on his door, hoping wildly that he hadn't decided to run out on her. Friends is enough, she thought. Being friends is all I can do at the moment. There was a strange feeling, though, in the pit of her stomach. A churned-up feeling, as though she were walking too close to an impossibly deep drop, a feeling of vertigo and longing. Who would have thought that I would meet such a person? she thought. Taos had something very true about him, no pretence.

A crease of irritation or perhaps embarrassment was jammed between Taos's eyebrows when he opened his bedroom door at her knock. He was already dressed, in a long-sleeved white top featuring the goddess Lakshmi slow-dancing on a lotus, and his sky-blue cotton trousers.

'Sleep OK?' asked Alida, attempting cheerfulness although she could already see that he wasn't in the mood for pleasantries.

'Not really,' he said flatly. 'You?'

'I just woke up from a nightmare,' she offered, hoping for clemency.

'Oh really?' His face remained hard and frowning. 'I hope my unwelcome kiss wasn't responsible?'

She felt a flash of annoyance. 'Don't be ridiculous.'

Taos shrugged and made to close the door, but Alida moved forwards hastily, holding a hand out as if to stop him. He paused. 'Taos,' she said. 'Your kiss wasn't unwelcome, all right? I was just taken aback and I felt overwhelmed. There's so much happening at the moment, with Mia and morgues and Ian on his way—'

'Yes,' he said, seeming to relent. 'I know. I have the worst timing.' He shook his head regretfully. 'Let's forget it now.' Relief flooded Alida, and she stood patiently while he stretched to his full height and yawned. 'So what's the plan today, then?' he asked, looking alert. 'Bangalore galore, or off to Mamallapuram?'

Alida smiled wanly. 'I've had it with Bangalore,' she admitted. 'I know we only got here yesterday, but let's face it, we've achieved zilch apart from putting up the posters and sitting in front of that bull statue for hours on end. And Ian arrives in India the day after tomorrow . . .' She tailed off because the thought of the curved, elephantine lines of the bull statue had made her think of the stone elephant Mia had left among the discarded possessions in her travel bag, the one with the stuck-on blue eyes, an echo of the collage of the winged elephant. Was it a double clue?

'Right,' said Taos, looking grim. 'You've promised to meet him in Madurai, and you'll need to take a look at that body in the morgue, so I guess heading back down that way is the logical next step.'

Alida shook her head, still sifting through elephant imagery. 'Actually,' she said, 'I think we should get to Mamallapuram.'

Taos shifted with a hint of impatience. 'Logically—' he began.

'The Mamallapuram postcard showed an elephant,' she murmured. 'It's all about Kizzy, and the elephants represent her. This is the way Mia thinks.'

'What are you saying?' asked Taos. He was leaning towards her a little, his goddess top releasing the light scent of him.

'I'm saying we have a triple repeated clue, Taos.' Alida

ticked the clues off on the fingers of her right hand. 'The winged elephant collage, a stone elephant with eyes the colour of Kizzy's that Mia left at Hotel Guru and the post-card of the elephant statue at the Five Rathas in Mamallapuram. We have to go to Mamallapuram.'

He looked at her speculatively. 'Fine by me, Alida, but are you sure you're not just trying to find a way to avoid Madurai morgue? It'd be understandable if you were,' he added.

'This is Mia's treasure-hunt trail,' she said definitely. 'We're being pointed very strongly towards Mama-llapuram—' She paused, then slapped her hand to her fore-head. 'Mama!' she exclaimed. 'Mamallapuram – Mama! Mum! Of course it's the trail!'

For a second, he stared at her as if she were insane. Then he caught on. 'Alida,' he began, rubbing his cheek tiredly. 'I think you're oversimplifying a bit here. Don't pin your hopes on a bit of wordplay, OK?'

'Why not?' she demanded.

'Because there's no point in inflicting unnecessary damage on yourself through hoping for the improbable, that's why.'

'But I can't afford to do otherwise,' she said. 'Let's go. Come on, Taos, she's there, she must be.' Her knees were jiggling with impatience. 'Let's go.'

Taos nodded unsmilingly, his eyes fixed on hers. 'All right,' he said.

Their telephone enquiries led them to discover that the next train was fully booked. Alida was in a state of nervous excitement, her pupils dilated. 'I can't wait,' she said. 'We'll just have to hire a car. This hotel has rental cars, I remember seeing an advert down at reception.'

'It must be a good three hundred and fifty miles away,' said Taos. 'And I won't be able to help you out with the driving. You remember, I told you – since the bike crash I don't drive any more.'

217

'I do remember, and that's fine,' she said. 'You can map read if necessary. Shall we make tracks?'

By the time they had sorted out the paperwork for the car and crawled out of Bangalore's clogged streets, it was after eleven. The hire car was an old black Ford with black leather seats, a dark sun magnet. Alida's back was slithery with sweat. As she drove, at first she kept leaning forwards and flapping her top about with one hand to let some air onto her spine, but as they progressed, she remained slumped in her seat, squinting at the road ahead. This part of India – or at least this road – all looked the same. Banana trees fringed the asphalt, their drooping leaves coated in dry yellow dust. Small dwellings with chickens and children were positioned randomly at the roadside, often seeming to serve a purpose as cafés or a place to buy meat in the form of goat carcasses and other unidentifiable corpses strung up from the roof. The traffic was a mixture of thundering, colourful Tata trucks, ox carts, which limped along getting in the way, and buses, which overtook on blind bends, on a road surface studded with potholes which everyone veered to avoid. Alida's face felt as if it was setting like clay into fine lines of strain as she looked ahead and ahead, watching the miles squeeze themselves awkwardly underneath the wheels of the car. Her mouth was parched and the taste of yellow dust was on her tongue.

Taos had been uncommunicative all morning as they travelled, and was now a hulking shape to her left, thoughtful and withdrawn behind his sunglasses. Despite their truce that morning, Alida was still worried that she had been too brusque with him after they had kissed. She licked her lips, remembering again the tobacco and lemon-grass warmth of his mouth on hers. That kiss had caused her to disappear for a moment and fly on tiptoe into pure physicality. Part of her longed to go back to that vanishing point and remain suspended there, in Taos's arms. She'd had her share of boyfriends over the years, but it had been a long time since she had felt this way, as if her solar plexus was secured to his by a block of energy, so that she felt full and vertiginous when he was near her, and smaller, strained when he was elsewhere. He has never been with Mia, she thought, and was glad. He said he's been hankering after me. Her heart beat faster, her foot pressed harder on the accelerator and the road sang beneath her wheels.

During their first refreshment stop at one of the roadside cafés, they drank chai in a strained silence which Alida tried from time to time to fill, while a two-year-old boy a few feet away from them conscientiously rounded up hens with a stick. When they returned to the car, which Alida had managed to park in the shade, Taos seemed to throw off his pensiveness the moment she started the engine.

'Had any more lucid dreams lately?' he enquired, pausing in the buckling of his seatbelt.

'A few, yes.' As she eased the car back on to the road, Alida searched quickly for something more to add to this. She didn't want to miss the opportunity of returning to conversational normality. 'When I write down my lucid dream images, I slip into a sort of trance and I often end up writing about the past.'

'What's it like for you, this trance?'

Alida considered. 'Well, if it could be described in terms of texture and colour, it would be a foamy lilac mist,' she said. 'With pictures emerging from it like photographs being developed in a darkroom.'

Taos laughed. 'That sounds like something Mia would say, attributing textures to states of consciousness. What colour would normal waking reality have, in your opinion?'

'Oh, who knows.' She smiled, then immediately winced as a Tata truck overtook her in a storm of dust and filthy exhaust. 'I keep forgetting how rubbish the acceleration on this thing is,' she muttered. 'I'm not even up to forty yet. Um, blue, I suppose, like the sky in the morning. Yes, a very clear-edged blue.'

'You're making my fingers itch,' said Taos. 'They want to paint a tiny, pixilated Alida sliding between these different states. What colour would lucid dreaming be?'

She laughed. 'This is like a sort of invisible I-spy for aspiring synaesthetes, isn't it? I think lucid dreaming would definitely have to be a wide, bold sunshine yellow. And non-lucid dreaming is for me a viscous, drifting orangeness.'

'Mmm,' agreed Taos, with a smile in his voice. 'You know,' he continued, 'one of the things I liked about Mia while we were hanging out at Hotel Guru is the way her multi-sensory comments about mundane objects made me think more broadly. I mingle dimensions of taste, scent and texture while I'm painting but that wider form of perception rarely comes into more conscious thought processes, such as the language I choose to use. She reminded me to be more aware, even when I'm not in a lilacy-foamy trance.'

Alida smiled, happy that he was complimenting Mia and inexplicably pleased that he had taken her wacky definition and used it for himself. She felt a strong pull to him which made her lean slightly sideways in her seat. She wanted to look at him but the road was demanding her attention: an oncoming bus was overtaking a rickshaw and was charging towards her on her side of the road. She slowed down and the bus swerved erratically back on to its own side at the last minute. 'Sometimes these buses just bounce along normally,' she observed, 'and other times they seem to be driven by kamikaze maniacs. It's unnerving.'

'You're remarkably cool about it,' said Taos. 'You seem to be taking it all in your stride.'

'There's not much else I can do,' she said.

Her hands were slippery on the wheel. One after the other, she wiped them on her trousers.

The drive was taking for ever. The roads were badly

surfaced and the presence of slow-moving vehicles, such as rickshaws, bullock carts and trucks piled with stones, meant that their own pace was frustratingly slow. The intense heat had obliged them to make several stops for coconut juice or tepid Sprite. It was coming up for half past four and Alida was beginning to lose hope that they would arrive at Mamallapuram to find the Five Rathas temple complex still open. For the past forty-five minutes, while Taos slept with his head nodding against the window, Alida had succumbed to a feeling of general despair. It felt as though a stone was pressed up beneath her ribcage, hampering her breathing, pulling her down into misery.

She was driving them along a curving stretch of road with little traffic on it. Fields of crops rose at her side of the road and she watched the greenness of the landscape unfold with a vague disquiet. This was a vast country, vast, and Mia was less than a pinprick on its humongous surface, less than a microscopic dot. Something that small was so easy to lose. The car was bowling along tirelessly and Alida barely felt that she was driving it any more. It seemed to be driving itself, affably taking the curves while she sat and watched through the insect-smeared wind-screen. She was beginning to feel floaty; she seemed to rise slightly in her seat as the car flowed along beside the greenness. I need to take a break and eat something soon, she thought. This is starting to feel like a dream; I must be getting tired. There was nowhere to stop, no place to pull over. No matter; something would come along soon.

She wished she had a sweet to suck.

Her attention receded from the dust-caked road and the surrounding greenness as she climbed through a tangle of thoughts and images: her putting up posters, the taste of sticky tape in her mouth; Mia huddled in a wardrobe or a dingy room, retching because she was pregnant and alone; Kizzy, small and for ever dead; the impossible beauty of Mia's face – its youth, its subtle reflections of Ian and

221

herself, and those strong eyebrows; Kizzy, her blue eyes stained red with the harshness of bathwater and the terrible effort of dying.

It has always been this way, realised Alida, and it was as if a door opened inside her head. Images of Kizzy's dead body had always superseded loving thoughts of Mia, as if in silent reproach. We have no right to be happy, with her dead, she thought now as the road was swallowed up by the sheer blackness of the car as it pressed forwards, and she knew that she had lived by this maxim since the day she had tried to breathe life into her daughter and failed. *She lies between Mia and me not like an eternal baby, but like an axe stained with our own blood; something brutal which we've always felt is better left unexamined. It's not the fact of kissing or not kissing Taos that stands in the way of me finding Mia. It is – and always has been – Kizzy.*

For thirteen years I have loved my dead daughter more than the living one.

Alida's face crumpled, tears blinded her momentarily, and now here was something hard to comprehend, a Land Rover blaring towards her, square and demonic and with something odd about its positioning; surely it hadn't overtaken on a bend that sharp, or maybe it was Alida who had veered on to the wrong side, but here it was in front of her and no time to do anything but slam her foot on the brake and wrench the wheel around to the left and hope there was some road there to carry them through all the noise and screeching dust clouds.

Chapter Thirty-One

Wednesday, 30 April 2008
Mario is a Portuguese pirate, bone strong and beautiful.

He has the body of a dancer and moves with silken, aggressive grace.

He has platinum-hard black eyes and a rough ponytail and when he looks at me I get goosebumps all up my left leg, from toes to thigh.

He has been travelling around the world for thirteen months and twenty days.

He smells of Nag Champa incense and freshly ground pepper.

He says I make his heart turn upside down, and he kisses my goosebumps away.

He says no one has eyes brighter than mine, and his arms link around my waist, sinewy hard.

He says he wants to be my boyfriend and take me to the magic places in India.

I've known Mario less than a week and already I'm falling for him.

Saturday, 10 May 2008
On Monday night, my fifteenth night in India, we slept together and it was just as I had hoped: crunching and luminous and real.

Afterwards, I lay awake smiling.

In the morning, Mario was just an indentation on the pillow beside mine and three tightly curling ebony pubic hairs which I found when I pulled the covers back.

I've been waiting, but it's Saturday afternoon now and he still hasn't come back yet. Why do people go through life lying and constructing gaps between their words, gaps so wide and silent that I don't even see them until I've fallen right through? If his stupid pubic hairs were still contaminating my bed, I'd dissolve them with hydrochloric acid.

Sunday, 25 May 2008

I've been having strong, alive dreams. In these dreams, I know that I am dreaming. Watching these dreams unfold, I see my deepest thoughts being translated directly into images. I want to draw the images but I can't draw. So instead I've been writing the diary I never wrote when I was younger. I've been writing out the memories I've seen in the dreams. It's a strange and satisfying thing to do. I take the memory-image and let it float in my mind, gathering colours and sensations. When it begins to move and change like a multi-sensory filmstrip, I write it all down, speaking as the child I used to be. Doing this retrospective diary is making me see more clearly. Alida is there, and Dad, and Kizzy. I feel I have unfinished business with them all.

My period is late.

It's all the travelling I'm doing, the hot Indian air, these astonishing dreams.

Chapter Thirty-Two

There *was* enough road, and Alida found herself shooting in slow motion past an impossibly close Land Rover with two Indian men up front – she glimpsed clipped moustaches, soundlessly shouting mouths, gelled hair, brown eyes cinematic in their terror. As her hands and feet automatically controlled the heavy steering wheel and spongy, squealing brakes, keeping the Ford on the tarmac despite her violent swerve to the left, Alida's vision was bright, as though there was too much light in everything. There was a startlingly green field to her left, flimsy grasses bending in the breeze. From one corner of her eye she registered that Taos had woken up and that he was leaning forwards as they braked, checked by his seat-belt, his suntanned hands braced on the dashboard. Alida kept pressing on the brakes until they skidded to a halt at the side of the road, and then she yanked the hand-brake on and leaned over the steering wheel, breathing in uneven bursts.

'What the hell happened there?' Taos's voice was sharp with alarm. 'Are you all right?' he asked her urgently, his hand hot on her knee, which he shook a little.

Alida sat up and looked straight at him. In his dilated pupils she could almost see the rapid thump of his heart.

'I'm so sorry,' she began. 'You're OK, aren't you?' It occurred to her that she could have killed all four of them

– the two Indian men, Taos and herself. She switched the hazard lights on, glancing distractedly in the wing mirror. There was no sign of the Land Rover, and no other traffic emerging behind them yet, but her car was badly positioned. She would have to drive on, or ease off the rough-edged tarmac and into the shallow ditch, but at that moment she couldn't envisage moving an inch. Her mind was flashing with ugly possibilities: crushed metal, bloodied faces, broken spines. Taos was speaking, assuring her that he was fine. His hand had gone from her knee and his voice sounded strange to her, muffled, as if he was speaking through layers of material.

'What happened?' he demanded again. 'I was asleep, I think. Didn't see that coming.'

Alida stared through the windscreen. There was an eerie emptiness about the green field. 'I was thinking about Mia and Kizzy, seeing them in my head,' she said slowly. 'Wasn't concentrating on the driving at all. I think I might have veered onto the wrong side of the road for a moment. A Land Rover came from nowhere, right in front of me.' Tears of dismay welled in her eyes, blurring her vision so that greenness bled off the grass and into everything around it. 'I looked straight into the faces of these two Indian men sitting in the front, I could see the comb marks their gel had left in their hair, and the one on the right had a squint, something asymmetrical about his eyes, I saw every detail. And they screamed back at me in this awful slow-motion silence,' she said, twisting around so that she could see Taos properly. 'I scared the life out of them – we were so close, it could have been a serious smash. I nearly killed us all.'

Taos was shaken. He ran a hand nervously over the top of his head. 'You're under too much stress, Alida. We should have just taken a train.'

'Those two men are probably going to stop at the nearest roadside shrine to offer thanks that they're still alive,'

Alida murmured. The two of them fell silent for a moment. A few inches, she thought, and we could have all been crippled, or died outright. And what's the point in living so close to death – as we all do – if you can't look back and say, when I was happy I laughed, when I loved someone I told them so, when life offered me something wonderful, I accepted it with thanks. I've been living like a fool, allowing the past to fester in me too long, too deep.

A shiny silver car overtook them, beeping in annoyance or solidarity, Alida couldn't tell which. Either way, it was a reminder that they had to move the car out of the way.

'How are you feeling?' she asked Taos, wondering at his silence.

He looked at her in mild surprise. 'You know, it's funny, but I feel fine. I was just thinking that in my motorbike crash, I was wide awake when it happened, and the crash knocked me into unconsciousness, into amnesia, and this time I started off asleep and was woken up by a near miss.' He smiled at her confused expression. 'This way is much better, on every level. How are *you* feeling?'

She shook her head. 'I ache, everything looks weird … I'm not great, basically.'

Taos eyed her in concern. 'You know,' he said, 'we have to drive on. We're sort of blocking the road, parked up here like this, and I'd guess we're only forty miles or so from Mamallapuram. Are you up for it?'

Alida felt vague and disconnected, her neck was stiffening from the tension of swerving and braking, and the curious light lay over everything. 'I don't know,' she said. 'I feel … dizzy.'

'Well, you could close your eyes,' he suggested.

'Drive with my eyes closed?' She looked at him suspiciously. Was this a dig at her earlier lack of attention?

A flicker of amusement crossed Taos's face. 'No. I'd be driving.'

'I thought you'd vowed never to drive again?'

'I did, but it's a pretty impractical vow. Will you be OK just relaxing in the passenger seat?'

'Yes, yes, of course.'

Taos was very concentrated when he drove, and didn't like to talk. They continued on to Mamallapuram in virtual silence, and Alida discovered that she was too unsettled by the near miss to close her eyes for more than a few seconds at a time. The intense light slowly dissipated from her vision, and she began to feel more normal, but her mind never stopped turning, reliving those moments of near tragedy, seeing again the fright in the eyes of the Indian men and, superimposed over them, the faces of her children: one dead, one missing. Something was shifting inside her, and she was waiting to find out where the shift would lead her.

Taos drove carefully into Mamallapuram along streets bright with movement and filled with salty air from the Bay of Bengal. Alida looked out at the people who were walking on zinc-yellow dust and sand – Indian tourists, Western backpackers, locals selling cheap plastic watches, henna tattoos, silk skirts. Goats were tethered here and there, and cows stood about, long-lashed and flicking their tails lazily. Squatting on their heels against the low buildings, women were frying food in blackened pans which released thick smoke. Would she even see Mia, if she were wandering in this crowd? They drove straight through the little coastal town towards the Five Rathas site in the hope that they could find the elephant statue that had appeared in the postcard on Mia's two bears collage. But as Alida had feared, they arrived too late. Standing near the site was a young Indian woman with sticking-out ears and a glinting nose stud who they asked about opening times. She told them, 'Opening early, every day early,' but couldn't elaborate more than that, and they could see no times written up. Through her intense disappointment, Alida realised how exhausted she was; her body ached.

'Let's find a hotel and have a quick wash, then put some posters up around the town and do the rounds with Mia's photograph,' she suggested.

The hotel they found was a popular backpacker's choice, with individually painted rooms and elaborate tiles around the skirting boards and window frames. Alida's room was apple green and looked out on to the main street. As she swiftly unpacked, she found her eyes drawn again to the crowds, searching for Mia's face. After showering and changing into a red scoop-necked T-shirt of Mia's, she joined Taos, who had put on a clean blue cotton shirt and black trousers, and they went through the town leaving posters in every likely public place – cafés, guest houses, even the local hospital. There were no positive identifications, and Alida tried to swallow her panic as they went through the same motions she had been repeating for the past eleven days.

'We need food,' announced Taos eventually, noticing the strain on her face.

They headed back into the main street and soon found a busy restaurant with burgundy chair cushions and white tablecloths where they ordered butter chicken with naan bread and a bottle of what turned out to be rather rough red wine which the waiters had to serve from a teapot into small white teacups because they had no alcohol licence. Taos said he'd drunk Kingfisher beer in the same way in Kerala.

'It doesn't taste quite the same when it comes out of a teapot,' he conceded as they finished their first cup. 'But it's interesting, and we deserve a drink after that hair-raising drive.'

Alida clutched her head briefly in her hands, grimacing. 'I should have stopped the car when I started feeling floaty. To be honest, I think it was low blood sugar that did it. All

I could see were my two girls. I should have just pulled over.'

He grinned at her across the table. 'Well, you did pull over, just from the wrong side of the road and rather too rapidly.'

'True.'

'I should have offered to share the driving,' he said, suddenly contrite. 'I was so immersed in my "I'll never drive again" mindset that I let you do all the work while I nodded off. What a terrible driver's mate I was.'

'Please don't apologise. I'm the one who should be apologising.' She looked at him, concern shining from her eyes. 'I would never have forgiven myself—'

'Forget it, Alida. We're fine, and we have wine, even though it's disguised as tea.' He took the teapot by its handle and waggled it. 'More?'

'Why not?' The wine was relaxing her; she could feel it go straight to her head. A tingling feeling was curling upwards from the base of her spine. Taos watched her as he poured the wine out of the teapot, and she found the brick-like feeling of anxiety easing from her chest as she responded to the laughter deep in his eyes.

By the end of the evening, the conversation had moved from Mia's possible whereabouts and the treasure-hunt trail to Taos's memory loss and how it had affected his artwork. He had offered to show Alida the difference between his pre-crash and post-crash drawings. Knowing that they would have no time to do this the next day, since they aimed to be at the Five Rathas temple complex as soon as it opened, she popped into his indigo-painted room with him when they arrived back at their hotel. There were discarded boxer shorts and a towel next to his bathroom door, and his rucksack lay squarely on the bed, spilling its guts over the white sheets. He rushed around clearing up, then the two of them sat on the bed and he brought out his sketch pad and flipped it to a drawing of a whale lying on the summit of a mountain.

'Like I said,' he began, 'I've been working in a new way since the bike crash, using animals to represent emotions. This whale stemmed from the way I felt about my memory loss. I felt like a whale whose sea had suddenly shrunk away so that it flopped about pathetically on the sand. In the sketch, I wanted to put the whale in a situation it can only free itself from through falling to its death or flying to freedom.'

Alida looked at him in surprise. 'That's a bit harsh, especially since whales are possibly the least likely creatures to take flight.'

He shrugged. 'I wanted the whale to achieve the impossible.'

'And will it?' Alida looked doubtfully at the whale, perched vertiginously high in the sky.

Taos slid the sketchbook across so that it was resting on Alida's lap. He flicked the page over and there again was the whale, soaring down towards the ocean using its pectoral fins as wings. 'It will,' he said, with grim satisfaction.

There were sketches on almost every page of the book, rendered in grey pencil and bursting with life. There was beauty here, and something more, especially in the most recent pictures – an affirmation, thought Alida. As if they were saying yes to life.

'You know what,' she said suddenly.

'What?' He stopped turning the pages.

'Since Kizzy's death, I haven't believed that I have a right to happiness.' She swallowed with difficulty. 'That might sound silly—' she began.

'It doesn't.' Taos was very still, looking at her with that way he had, as if the world had stopped and she was the only moving, speaking person and so naturally commanded his complete attention. He smelled of wine and male body.

'And I just thought, just now, while looking at your sketches, that if life has the generosity to offer you something beautiful, you don't protest that you don't deserve it, or that it isn't the right time. You don't turn your back on it.' She glanced down at her fingers, which were curled around Taos's sketchbook.

'So what do you do?' he asked her, his voice warm.

She raised her head and looked at him. 'You say yes.' She thought for a moment. 'And then you accept the gift, whatever it is, and you say thank you.'

'See, that's why I get you, Alida,' Taos said, sighing a little. 'Because you know how it feels. After the bike crash, I didn't believe I had a right to *life*, let alone the right to happiness. I thought I should have died instead of Kirstin.' He shrugged his shoulders and in the fragility of the gesture, Alida glimpsed the broken parts of him. 'But I'm realising that living as if you don't have the right to live is no kind of life. My artwork has helped me to work that much out. That, and travelling with you.' He nudged her gently with his shoulder. 'We're here, alive in this world, so we have to make the best of it, right?'

'That's it exactly.' It was so easy to talk to Taos; there was no need to dissimulate or beat about the bush. Alida smiled to herself as they continued to look through his sketches, and the more she looked, the more of him she recognised in them. Then her eye fell on a sketch of a man stretched out in repose on a beach. A woman was standing over him, looking at his body with undisguised interest.

'Taos,' she exclaimed, half laughing, half indignant. 'I can't believe you drew that!'

'Why not? It was an erotically charged moment, for me at least.'

His eyes glittered as he looked at her, and the moment stretched deliciously. It was happening again: they had fallen into each other's eyes, looking deep. Unconsciously, Alida moistened her lips with the tip of her tongue, and suddenly they were kissing.

Alida closed her eyes, winding her arms around his neck

232

and opening her mouth to his. Without interrupting the kiss, Taos moved the sketchbook out of their way and pulled her fully onto his lap, half-lifting and then settling her as if he was a thousand times familiar with the shape and weight of her body. Something in the curve of his mouth, the heat and scent of his skin, was like the edge of a cliff calling Alida to fling her limbs wide and jump, star-shaped, into the unknown. Returning his kiss, she felt that she was accepting an offer of beauty.

His kisses tasted of salt and tobacco and wine and much more: moments of understanding, shared smiles, desire. His hand, on the back of her head, moved through her hair so that her scalp tingled.

'Are you warm enough?' he murmured after a while.

Alida smiled without separating her lips from his. 'I'm fine,' she whispered. She realised that for once her skin was quite chilly. Taos must have turned the air condition-ing up to maximum freeze. She pulled away from him and gave him a quizzical look. 'It *is* freezing in your room, though,' she said. 'Are you doing that master plan of seduction you mentioned the other night?'

He looked sheepish. 'Would it be so bad if I was?'

Alida looked at his familiar face, which seemed so differ-ent this close up. She noticed the tiny freckles that lay on top of his suntanned skin, and the isosceles-shaped flecks of green in his hazel eyes. 'No, it wouldn't be bad,' she said, and kissed him quickly on the lips. 'So,' she said then with a hint of audacity, 'is this the bit where I'm supposed to beg you to warm me up?'

'Are you cold?' he asked considerately.

'Yes.'

'Then lie down with me.' He rolled them both back-wards and for a second Alida knew what it would be like to sleep with him: like being in bed with a playful tiger, all muscle and velvet stealth and a caressing tongue. As if he could hear her thoughts, Taos bent his head to her left nipple, which was visible through her top, and closed his mouth over it.

Alida gasped audibly, and was lost.

Chapter Thirty-Three

Sunday, 1 June 2008

I'm pregnant. But he wore a condom. I keep seeing it, translucent and smelling of rubber, his hands rolling it rapidly down to the base of his cock. Silver rings on his fingers, like a pirate, or my grandmother. Could one of those rings have pierced it? When we'd finished, we lay together for a while and eventually he went to the bathroom to squeeze it off him and dispose of it. Did he notice a rupture in the rubber, sperm dripping in all directions? Did he panic? Is that why he ran from me? What am I going to do? I'm eighteen and a half years old and alone in India, and a weird little Mario-monster is dividing away inside me. My head aches and everything tastes of vomity burps. I lie very still on my bed in Hampi and try to calm my mind.

A decision. I have to make a decision. Go home to England and cold-eyed parents and blood-red abortion, or grow these cells into a real-life baby, a second sister.

I'm so scared. What do I do now?

What do I do?

Tuesday, 17 June 2008

I've been staying in different guest houses by the sea for several weeks, but the Blue Sunrise is my favourite. Rereading my memories is like observing the hatching of a chrysalis or an egg. There are moments in my life that I can't stop looking at now. Again and again I take them out and turn them around in my hands, hold them up to the light like glass beads. These are the moments that altered my course. You can go anywhere with writing, from any starting point. I don't choose to return to those moments; they pull at my pen, take me from the here and now deep into the there and then. Here on the mustard and grit Varkala cliffs, I carry the smell of home in a phial of vanilla essence. I walk flat in my flip-flops, close to the earth but not grounded. Not yet.

I've realised one very important thing: Kizzy, my eternal baby sister, is the gap between the words. Everything I write spirals back to her; she is the emptiness I must face.

I'm going to let this baby grow.

Thursday, 26 June 2008

The tests I've been waiting for came back from the clinic in Trivandrum today. I am HIV negative and have no sexually transmitted diseases. This is a day for celebration. I wonder whether to call my parents. Something stops me, though, some clogged-up ball in my chest. I'll call them soon, just not today. Today I'm going to buy a baby-sized sequinned sari, if such a thing exists. And some alcohol-free beer.

And strawberry ice cream.

And walnuts.

Saturday, 5 July 2008

The day I arrived at Hotel Guru, I got talking about my alive dreams to a man painting at an easel on the hotel roof here and he said, 'Those sound like lucid dreams to me, why don't you collage them?' Since then, everything has begun to fall into place. India is not nearly as overwhelming these days; it has calmed into a vertical hum with

236

spherical shapes bulging from it. I can go out in this hum and keep my thoughts together. I collect scraps of material from the floors of sari shops, walk around town with a plastic bag picking up feathers and any non-decomposable thing that catches my eye. Pen lids, the broken casing of a mobile phone. Indians and foreigners alike look at me in undisguised amazement when I scavenge in this way. I buy bindis, glossy magazines, paints and paintbrushes, pipe cleaners, glue, scissors.

Something important is happening, but I don't know what, nor where it might end. I feel like Icarus, launching into a daring new reality on a pair of home-made wings.

Monday, 7 July 2008

The rooftop artist, Taos, is introducing me to colours with names so sensual and compelling that I want to inject them into my veins like heroin. Vermillion, aquamarine, woad, coral. He's intrigued by the sensations I attribute to them. He asks me all the time, does that have a particular taste for you? Can you feel this colour on your skin? It reminds me of my long-ago interview with the doctor who diagnosed my synaesthesia. I feel like a star pupil. Taos can be sullen and stand-offish at times, which is slightly absurd in a man of his age, but he's helping me to get these vital parts of myself out onto the canvas. As I slap paint around and manipulate pipe cleaners, I think about the events which conspired to make me the person I am. I wonder, when your life is ruptured by terrible events, whether free will can exist, because these events take an axe to your edges until the shape of you is barely recognisable. How can you then keep strolling along your envisaged path as though nothing has changed? I used to think that suicide was an act of selfish abandon, but now I'm certain that for some people it's the ultimate act of free will, a way of controlling what appears to be uncontrollable.

I look at the complicated relationship I have with words

237

– they dazzle me, I want to lick them like candyfloss, stash them in my pockets for a rainy day, but I also mistrust them to the point of distress. I have always known that words are flighty and unreliable compared with actions. Actions don't have gaps the way words do. They are themselves, clear for all to see. Mario said he wanted to be my boyfriend, but his actions proved that he did not. My mother has said that she loves me, but her actions have shown that she does not.

One way or the other, I need to take charge of my life.

Chapter Thirty-Four

Alida dreamed of a deadly explosion. When the noise had rumbled into silence, a tiny hand landed in front of her feet with a light thump. How she wanted to pick it up! Pumping blood from the wrist, but still it would be warm, almost alive. The skin still ever so soft. Kizzy's little curved fingers. But with a flash of lucidity, Alida saw that this was just a variation of the nightmare she had dreamed a thousand times, and she stepped bravely past the hand. Sitting cross-legged on the ground under a clump of trees was the disc-headed man. He was more beautiful than ever; coppery and radiant. He drew his arms slowly out from behind his back and held them out straight in front of him, the fists closed. Alida knew this game.

'I want both, but I must choose only one.' She nodded at him sadly. 'It's hard to let go of the dead.'

He sat motionless, but she knew that behind the disc, tears were sliding. She remembered when she had first laid eyes on him in the desert, the night she had heard about Mia's disappearance. She recalled what each of his hands had held, left and right. She stepped forwards and touched his right fist. He bowed slightly in acknowledgement, but then opened his left hand. Inside was a dead baby, chalk-faced and beautiful, carved from white clay. As Alida looked, she bloomed. Colour rushed to her cheeks, she grew with astounding speed, became alive. When she was her full nine-month self, she opened her eyes. Blue stars. Alida stretched her arms out and here was her solid, shining Kizzy, her chuckle which Alida had almost forgotten but which resonated through her now. She held her close, breathed in nutmeg and milk. Kizzy's heart fluttered against Alida's breast as they laughed together, eyes inside eyes.

Then Kizzy shrank away so fast that Alida could barely follow the movement with her eyes, and she was curled up again in the disc-headed man's fist. He opened his other hand to reveal a treasure chest studded with sequins which glimmered and called. This time, the lid was open. Alida leaned forwards and there was Mia. She was herself at all ages. She was a baby wrapped in vanilla love. She was a woman with full, shining eyes, smiling up at her mother. Carefully, Alida took the treasure chest in her hands and as soon as it left the big, sinewy hand of the disc-headed man, she started to float backwards.

'I'm waking up,' she said, hugging the treasure chest to her heart. Mia was standing jauntily inside it, keeping her balance with outstretched arms, a miniature surfer. The disc-headed man watched Alida, straight-backed and calm. When her eyes fluttered open, she could still see the glint of the sun on his silver disc.

Alida lay curled on her side. She was very still, wondering what was different. In the grey dawn light, the glinting silver disc had become the round reflective surface of a shaving mirror that she didn't own. Something thick and heavy lay across her waist. There was a smell of lemongrass sweat. She looked down at herself and saw Taos's arm, very brown against the white sheet and wrapped firmly around her. Memories of last night returned to her like floating jigsaw pieces: acidic red wine in her mouth, goosebumps on her arms, a blue dragon tattoo the length of which she had traced with her tongue. The horrendous squeaking of the bed as they rolled around on it had made

240

them both laugh and they hadn't tried to be any quieter, but had revelled in their noisiness.

Today was Thursday, 31 July. One year, two months, and eighteen days, Alida calculated. That was how long it had been since she had been in bed with a man. She hoped that Taos hadn't been able to tell. She felt a deep sense of peace, as though a broken circle inside her had become whole again. It was the near miss on the road to Mamallapuram, the sexual release, the disc-headed man and his choice of treasures. Alida knew that in this remarkable state of peaceful alertness, she could do anything, could find Mia, could resolve their problems, could construct for them a beautiful future. She had to write her dream down, so she prised the dead weight of Taos's arm off her, hoping not to wake him. He stirred, but slept on. She slid from the bed, saw that she was naked and hastily gathered her clothes from around the floor. Once she was partially dressed, she ducked across the hall to her own room, got out her writing materials and wrote down every second of her lucid dream. As soon as she had finished, there was a knock at the door.

'Alida?' called Taos, sounding aggrieved.

'Wait, I'm coming,' she called, and hurried to open the door, notebook in hand.

Taos was standing there in his red cotton boxer shorts. 'I woke up and you were gone,' he said flatly.

'I had to write down a lucid dream about the disc-headed man,' she explained, waving the notebook at him.

Taos rubbed his face and looked unimpressed. Alida considered him with her head on one side. 'What are you so gloomy about this morning?'

He shrugged. 'Nothing. I guess I just felt a flash of dismay when I saw you'd scarpered.'

'I didn't scarper, I just didn't want to wake you.'

'Well,' he said, looking mollified, 'since we're both up so early, shall we go down to the beach and watch the sunrise before we check out the Five Rathas? The site won't open for at least another hour, I should imagine.'

'OK,' said Alida, balancing on one foot in the door jamb so that she could scratch her right knee with her toe.

Taos leaned forwards slightly and for a moment she thought he would kiss her, but then he swung away. 'See you in five minutes, then,' he said over his shoulder.

At just after six in the morning, Mamallapuram Beach was deserted apart from a few fishermen and stray dogs, with the sun inching up from the horizon and the shore temple's two triangular spires lit pink while the waves foamed and tugged at the sand. Alida felt clean and clear-headed. She was dressed in a long-sleeved pale-lemon top that she had brought with her from London, and a pink sarong of Mia's crossed with diagonal bands of darker pink and decorated with silver embroidery thread. The two of them walked barefoot through the curving edges of the waves, their flip-flops dangling from their hands. Alida was relieved that there seemed to be no awkwardness between them aside from Taos's brief panic that morning. Maybe it was because they had spent such an intensive period of time together over the past twelve days, she thought, or perhaps because somehow sleeping together had seemed less like getting to know a brand new lover, and more like redis-covering an old one. As she walked along the sand noticing tiny coloured shells which twirled into points like whipped cream, her thoughts turned again to Mia and Kizzy.

'You're very thoughtful this morning,' remarked Taos after a time.

Alida acknowledged the truth of this with a shrug. 'You know,' she said, turning to him as they walked. 'Since I've been in India, I've been opening my eyes, millimetre by millimetre, to all these old emotions. It may sound crazy, but it feels as if I'm negotiating with the dead and buried. And I don't just mean dead human beings like Kizzy, I mean all the attendant emotions. Do you realise that in all these years since she died I have been avoiding my over-whelming feelings of guilt and regret and blame?'

She looked at him intently to be sure that he understood. Taos was watching her face, walking close beside her in his easy way.

'It's been a full-time job and it cost me my marriage and fractured my relationship with Mia. Last night I became lucid in my recurring nightmare of Kizzy's death and for once I took a different path, walking away from the night-mare instead of wallowing in it. And there was the disc-headed man, waiting for me. He held out two hands, one with Kizzy in it and the other with Mia, and I chose Mia.'

She stopped walking and turned to face the sea. Taos stood beside her and they watched the waves for a while in silence. Far away, almost on the horizon, was a fishing boat. Alida could see the yellow flash of its prow. After a while she glanced at Taos and saw that he was smiling.

'Why are you smiling?' she asked.

He looked down at her, warm-eyed. 'Because you chose Mia.'

'If I want to have the slightest chance of finding her, I have to choose her above anything else from my past,' said Alida, her eyes moving back to the waves again. 'That's what I was on the brink of realising when I nearly crashed the car. I've been looking backwards for over thirteen years and it's time to look at what I've got right now, in the present. If Mia is still alive, I want to enjoy every moment that we spend together.'

Taos nodded. He reached out and took her flip-flops from her hand, holding them along with his own. Then his other hand clasped hers.

'I'm all for living in the present,' he said. 'Have I told you yet that the only time I transcend that depressing tip-of-the-tongue almost-memory feeling is either when I'm

243

painting or when I'm hanging out with you?'

'You hadn't mentioned it, no,' she said, smiling at him. 'But I'm glad you did.'

'So have you worked out yet why you keep seeing this disc-headed man in your dreams?' asked Taos. The intricacy of the design on his white T-shirt reminded Alida of the ceiling mandalas she had seen in the Meenakshi Temple. She shifted her gaze to the sky, remembering that morning's dream.

'I don't know,' she said. 'He's like this nature being, and he's somehow a deep part of myself. I didn't know he cared so much, but he does.' She was suddenly close to tears, and swallowed before continuing. 'He's part of me, communicating with the other part of me about the things that matter most, only not in words, but through images, and his presence in my dreams is giving me the courage to free myself of the past so that I can find Mia.' She glanced down at the sand, at her feet and Taos's feet lined up wet and shining before the sea.

'So for you,' said Taos, wriggling his toes under her gaze, 'freeing yourself from the past and finding Mia are linked?'

'Oh yes. Inextricably,' she said, nodding. 'I never used to think so, but yes.' She paused. 'And to think Mia's known it all along, with her treasure-hunt trail and her need for forgiveness.'

Taos looked worried. 'It makes my heart go cold every time you talk about the treasure-hunt theory,' he admitted. 'I'm really hoping that you're right about it because I'm so afraid of what might happen to you if it doesn't work out the way you think it will.'

Alida was immediately on the defensive. 'Every passing day, I feel more certain about this, Taos, so stop doubting. Doubting isn't going to help anyone, is it? We just have to go on the best we can.'

'You're right, but what will happen if she's undiscoverable?' Taos narrowed his eyes at the horizon as though trying to see beyond the curve of the earth.

'I don't know, Taos.' Alida twisted her hand from his and turned from the sea, her forehead puckered. 'I just don't know.'

'Hey.' He reached out for her.

'The Five Rathas might be open by now,' she said, ignoring his arm. There was a feeling of rising fright in her chest. 'I'm sorry, but can we just drop this subject and concentrate on finding Mia, please?'

Taos passed her flip-flops to her without speaking, and they walked in silence back towards the town. Alida was tense and fearful, wondering whether the Five Rathas – monolithic rock temples – would offer up a clue as to Mia's whereabouts. This is pretty much our last hope, she realised. This is the final postcard. They returned to the road that led out of the village, and several small children up early with nothing much to do accosted them.

'Sweet, sweet!'

'One rupee!'

'Pen!'

Alida was aware that giving in to their demands would encourage them to get into the bad habit of begging but her sudden, uncontrollable fear that Mia would be 'undiscoverable' made her feel tempted to empty out her pockets and give these children anything, everything, only to see their faces light up. Taos smiled at them without breaking his stride and seemed happy to let them caper around him, but clearly had no intention of giving them anything. Still, one little girl of about five had such big, dancing eyes and tugged so winningly on Alida's sleeve that she pressed a Werther's Original into her hand, and then of course she had to give the others something too, all the while walking briskly onwards. At the point where the road swung sharply to the right, the children hung back in a line as if stopped by a glass wall and waved goodbye, evidently respecting a limit their parents had set.

Despite the early hour, there were hammering noises coming from all around them: clanging and clinking and tapping. They passed stone carvers sitting outside their workshops, chiselling everything from garden ornaments to finely worked statues of Hindu gods. When they reached the entrance to the Five Rathas, the ticket man looked deeply unhappy to see such early visitors. He had eyebrows as thick as a moustache, which hung down over his eyes, and black rings beneath them, and he seemed to be struggling to remain awake. He passed them their tickets with bad grace and sank back into his seat again.

'Oh dear,' muttered Alida when they were out of earshot. 'I suppose I'd better ask him about Mia on the way out; he might have woken up by then.' She glanced at Taos, but he didn't respond. 'I'm sorry I turned from you earlier,' she said, laying her hand on his arm. 'Your words terrified me. I can't bear to think of other possibilities, you see.'

He stopped walking and looked at her, frowning slightly. 'I just want you to be realistic,' he said. 'I don't know if the treasure-hunt theory is getting us anywhere concrete. I don't mean to discourage you.' He sighed. 'I'm just concerned.'

'I can't help chasing whatever I have,' she said, holding his gaze, clear-eyed. 'No matter how slight and insubstantial it may seem to you, because apart from the strangled girl in the morgue, it's all I have.'

'Are you at least going to look at that body?' he asked her gently.

She chewed her top lip, avoiding his eyes now. 'Maybe,' she said eventually. 'Now, where's that elephant from the postcard?'

The elephant stood amongst the sand-coloured temples. It was bigger than Alida had expected; life-sized, it looked to be carved from one piece of rock. A skinny young man with one leg amputated at the knee was leaning against its round belly. He was dressed only in a lungi and one of his hands held a rough stick which served as a crutch. Alida's hand went automatically to her bag and she pulled out the photograph.

'Hello.' She smiled. 'Do you know this girl? My daughter.'

The man peered, then looked up in excitement, speaking in rapid Tamil. He began a charade which they followed in bewilderment. He pointed to the ground, then looked up at the elephant with wide eyes, then held out his left hand, palm open, while his other hand, the fingers meeting together at the tips, zigzagged over it. He repeated these gestures in the same order as if he was engaged in a surreal one-man theatre act.

'Mia was here, drawing,' said Taos.

'Or writing,' said Alida. Her heart was thumping. 'When?' she asked the man, pointing to her watch. 'When?'

He talked on in an unintelligible stream and drew two lines in the dust with his stick. 'Two days ago?' Alida asked urgently.

'Or two weeks?' asked Taos, and drew six lines next to each of the two lines, then circled them to represent two blocks of time.

The man wobbled his head in agreement.

'Two weeks,' said Alida. 'That's a long time.' She looked intently at the man. 'And – happy? Was she happy? Or sad?'

The man smiled in acknowledgement of the mimed emotions that accompanied these questions, then a slight frown appeared on his forehead and his eyes became grave. He explained to them all the while in Tamil, pointing to his face with his free hand.

'Serious,' said Taos. 'She looked serious?'

He wobbled his head again, his expression clearing.

247

Alida opened her purse and handed him a few hundred rupees; she didn't count how many. 'Thank you,' she said.

His face lit up and he murmured as he took the notes gently between his long fingers. He raised them to his forehead, sending blessings with his eyes.

'Let's check his story with that sleepy ticket-seller,' said Taos. He seemed tense.

As they moved away from the young man, Alida asked, 'Don't you think he was telling the truth? I'm convinced he was – the details about her writing stuff can't be made up.'

'No, I believe that was probably a correct identification,' said Taos. 'When did you get that morgue email?'

'Only two days ago, I think.' Alida was pale. 'It could well still be her, is that what you're saying?'

'I'm not saying that. I just want to see what this other guy has to say.' They strode purposely up to the ticket office, where the man looked just as disgusted to see them as he had earlier.

Alida nudged Taos aside. 'Let me,' she whispered, and gave the official her sweetest smile. He looked unimpressed, and when she held the photograph up his eyes barely moved. Quietly, in very clear English, Alida explained the story to him, and he began to rouse himself, interested in spite of himself. He held out a hand for the picture and she passed it over.

'I know this girl,' he said in English so beautifully modulated that it was at odds with his slovenly appearance. 'She was staying at the Sunshine Guest House, and when she left I remember her saying that she would visit their other establishment, on Mandipur Hill.' He passed the photo back and relaxed into his seat again, looking pleased with himself.

'So – she's gone from here but she said where she was going next?' Alida summarised anxiously.

'Yes, she did.' He smiled and looked almost handsome.

'When was she last here?' asked Taos.

'Oh, perhaps a fortnight ago. Perhaps a little more.'

'And where is the Sunshine Guest House?' asked Alida. 'We can get the details about the other place from them,' she added.

'Go back down the street and take the first left.'

When they had thanked him effusively, they walked away, Alida holding the photograph with both hands. She felt the way she had felt in her lucid dream when she had held the treasure chest in her hands. Even the floating feeling was there. Taos, perhaps sensing her light-headedness, put his arm around her shoulder and the weight of it grounded her.

'We're nearly there,' said Alida, staring around at the road which was stark and detailed, like a painting under bright light.

'First left,' she said a moment later. 'There it is.'

Chapter Thirty-Five

August 1995

Everything is good. My sister has shining star eyes which laugh up at me, pulling me across the room towards her. I play with her all day and Mummy leaves me in charge so that she can do other things around the house. Kizzy needs me now. I'm the first to notice when her bouncy chair needs to be moved out of the sunlight because she's squinting and sneezing, or when she starts to squirm and her mouth turns down because her nappy is full. I can read her mind and she mine. She tugs at my hair, my clothes, my face, wanting to bring me closer. Her blue eyes smile the smile of the deep. All I have to do is bend close, my hair bouncing lightly across her face, and she squeals and clutches, her whole body tensing in delight as if it's all the magic she needs in her life.

Kizzy is eight months old and for the past two months she has been able to sit up all by herself. At first she used to wobble and collapse but now she is solid and regal.

She never falls backwards any more.

She crawls across the carpet after balls and toys and Mummy says she'll be walking before we know it and that she's just like me. I took my first steps at ten months and was walking steadily before my first birthday. Kizzy's body is a warm parcel of life and I want her near me all the time. She feels the same way about me. Sometimes, when I leave the room, she even cries.

8 September 1995

Kizzy's bath time is blue splashes and strawberry laughter. We switch the radio on and she's a plump water baby sitting prettily on her own in the water while I kneel on the bath mat with my arms hanging over the rim of the bath and make the plastic dolphin do jumps and bump into her toes and squirt warm water over her shoulders to make her squeal. Mummy comes in and out of the bathroom, sometimes talking, sometimes not, but Kizzy and me are in our own world and I barely hear her.

The doorbell chimes and she grumbles something, then hurries over to us. I know she means to lift Kizzy out before answering the door and I can't bear the idea that our playing must stop even for a moment.

'I'll watch her, Mummy. We're playing,' I plead.

She hesitates and I hold my breath and say please again with my eyes.

'All right, but don't take your eyes off her for a single second, Mia,' she says sternly.

'I won't!'

I turn back to Kizzy, my heart expanding with love and pride. I hear Mummy running quickly down the stairs. Just before she reaches the front door, the bell sounds again. At that very instant, a prickly black and yellow ball flies in through the open bathroom window, straight towards my head. It makes a thick vibrating sound that burns my head and its wings whiz and silver hammers tap me all over my skin.

The world changes.

Everything is happening now, popping chartreuse-coloured sand grains squeezing into my face, making me shut my eyes and nose and mouth and cover my ears. The thing bristles and panics around the room in crazed circles. It's trying to get inside me. If I open my mouth to scream it will fly inside me and crack me into pieces with its battering wings and its urgent humming. The air is crowded and sandy and stinks of vomit and I try not to breathe it in, can feel myself curling up small on the bath mat, trying to disappear.

Time stops.

I am somewhere far inside myself, tight and alone.

The sounds batter me even though my ears are blocked with my hands. Whirring wings making bells clamour black and menacing in my head, the radio singing huskily, voices talking at the front door. Kizzy, splashing in the water. And below and beyond it all a deep, aching gap of silence, the silence of something going away from me, slipping into a shadow, becoming nothingness.

A scream makes me shudder through and through.

I open my eyes and Mummy has the baby in her arms dripping water all over the room only she's not moving and then she is laid out on the floor like a white jelly and Mummy is pushing at her chest and giving her wide-mouthed kisses and every time she raises her head to look at Kizzy's eyes she whimpers in strange half-screams which cut the air to ribbons. The sizzling flying shape has gone.

I sit up, holding my head.

Something dreadful is happening to Kizzy and I don't know why Mummy is pressing so hard at her chest, she must be hurting her. From all around, ashes are falling on us, curling downwards and filling my throat with soot.

The air is grey and terrible, eating up the light.

The man on the radio sings on and on and another man comes on and talks about high pressure zones and occasional showers.

It goes on for ever, Mummy bending and puffing and wailing over the jellified white doll who looks so unlike Kizzy now that I turn and peer into the bath to find my sister.

There's no one there.

October 1995

It's night time and I wake up so fast that colours from my dreams hang in the air before me in ugly patches of gun-metal grey and khaki. There's a sound, wet limbs rubbing on the tiled insides of a bath, water being agitated into whirlpool splashes.

I hear the crashing noise again and sit bolt upright. Under my white nightdress my heart is rolling and bucking.

'Open this door now!' Daddy shouts.

I slip from the bed to my door, which is open just enough that a slim triangle of light from the corridor slices into my bedroom all night long. I stand in the light and see Daddy leaning face forward against the bathroom door in his red dressing gown, his arms raised like candlesticks, solid fists at each tip. He speaks through the door again.

'If you don't open up this minute, Alida, I will break the door down.' Tentacles twine over and under his voice like seaweed; I can see the dark-green slime of them. He crashes his fists into the door again, making me jump.

There's a sound like a bucket of water being emptied and then the door opens with a rapid click. There is my mermaid mother, half drowned, her hair plastered to her face, two brown buttons wobbling on her bare chest. Daddy clutches her upper arms, hard.

'What are you trying to do to yourself, to us?' he asks in his strangled voice.

Grief and madness are overlapping on my mother's face as she tells him hoarsely, 'I just want to feel what she felt.'

'You can't! And even if you could, what good ...? She's gone. It's all over, Alida. All over now.'

Then she's crying, rusty sobs from deep within her chest which feel like a row of pebbles being pushed up through my veins.

'From now on,' says Daddy, holding her naked and slippery in his arms, 'there'll be no more drownings in this

253

family, real or simulated, and there'll be no lock on this bathroom door. From now on, you will not take baths any more, 'Lida. Do you hear me? You'll take showers instead.' She is deep in her tears and he shakes her a little, so that water droplets from her hair fly out and hit the door. 'Promise me,' he says urgently.

'I promise,' she chokes, and he encloses her in a hug.

Gradually, her noise slows and stops and the pebbles in my veins disintegrate. All that can be heard now is Daddy's warm potato murmur. I want that murmur on me but I'm scared that if I go to them they'll tell me to go away. I shrink away from the light and lie for ever in my bed, my eyes burned wide open. Mummy's trying to die because she doesn't love me any more, I think. When they finally go into their bedroom, they don't look in on me on their way, or even just call goodnight through my door. Do they really think I'm fast asleep? I am lying as stiff as cardboard, thinking of the way that Mummy's eyes slip off me like soap bubbles off a wet knee. My mummy's trying to die, I think. I think it again and again until it becomes a nonsensical chant that takes me into a shadow-filled sleep.

Chapter Thirty-Six

The Sunshine Guest House was in a side street which echoed with the tapping sounds of the stoneworkers. Taos asked one of these men where to go, and they followed his pointing chisel down a narrow alley with irrigation canals at the edges and a surface of compressed mud and rotten wooden planks. The guest house was enclosed by peeling whitewashed walls and to enter the courtyard they had to step first over an open drain and then over the sleeping body of a gammy-furred dog which opened a lazy eye at them as they passed. Inside, the yard was freshly swept and welcoming. Simple huts stood in a row to the right and through the open door of one of them Alida saw a female shape bunched up on a bed: a backpacker with braided hair. It wasn't Mia – this girl was tiny and blonde. She scanned the other huts carefully as they walked towards the main building but was unable to get a glimpse of the occupants.

They were met at the far side of the courtyard by the owner, a matronly woman in a burnt-umber sari with dozens of gold bangles lining her arms from elbow to wrist. She took the photograph of Mia in her worn hands and squinted away from it.

'Wait. My spectacles.' They were gold-rimmed and hung on a cord around her neck. When she had put them on she looked again. 'I have not seen this girl,' she announced.

255

Alida stepped back in dismay. 'Can you be absolutely certain?' she insisted.

The woman peered at her imperiously, eyebrows raised. 'I have not seen her,' she repeated.

Taos shifted impatiently. 'Are you the only person who deals with guests here?' he asked.

'No.' She shook her head. 'My husband also works with me, only he is away on family business and will not return for one month. I am working, doing everything, since last Friday and already I am tired from it!' She laughed, displaying teeth of startling whiteness and regularity.

'Last Friday,' said Taos to Alida. 'This lady's husband might have booked Mia in.' He turned back to the owner. 'We were told by the Five Rathas ticket man that my friend's daughter stayed here and that she left up to two weeks ago for your other establishment.'

'Oh yes, Mandipur Hill. It's very popular. It is about thirty miles inland. She might be there, yes.'

'Could we telephone them and check?'

'No telephone there, only in Sunshine General Stores nearby,' the woman said, raising her eyebrows as she spoke as if Alida's suggestion was slightly ridiculous. 'Also, we are not always writing down details of our guests,' she added with a dismissive wave of her hand.

'Isn't that illegal?' Alida asked Taos under her breath.

He shrugged. 'Probably, but with little places tucked out of the way like this, I guess nobody cares.'

'We'll just have to drive over there,' said Alida, feeling anxious and strangely deflated. 'It's not far.'

They wrote down detailed journey instructions, thanked the woman, and left to collect their belongings from their hotel.

'What if the Five Rathas man was wrong?' asked Alida as they walked back past the stoneworkers. 'That woman had clearly never seen Mia before. What if this is another false trail?'

256

Taos opened his hands in a gesture that said he had no answers. 'We've got the car, so we might as well check it out,' he said. 'Although ... I hate to remind you of this, Alida, but it's Thursday. Aren't you supposed to be meeting Ian today?'

Alida started. It was the first time she was aware of Taos using Ian's name, and hearing it spoken so matter-of-factly made her realise that Ian was not just a voice on a long-distance telephone line any more, but a solid presence in India, and that he wanted her to return to London and revert to a wholly passive role. 'He wanted me to meet him at Hotel Raj at eight thirty,' she said distractedly. She wasn't ready to return; in fact she had no intention of doing so. She would remain in India until she found Mia. She would remain with Taos.

'Well, it's coming up for eight fifteen,' said Taos, 'and I don't like to point this out, but we're a couple of hundred miles from Madurai.'

'I'll phone him, then.' The euphoria Alida had briefly experienced at the Five Rathas had changed to a strong sense of disquiet. Ian's arrival seemed to herald the final grains of sand slipping from the hourglass; she had a strong sensation of time running out. They found an international telephone shop on the main street and went in together, as Taos needed to place a call about a money transfer.

Ian sounded rough, but pleased to have arrived.

'This hotel's good value for money, isn't it?' he said. 'Which room are you in?'

'Um, actually I'm in Mamallapuram, on the east coast.'

It took him a couple of seconds. 'You didn't come to Madurai to meet me?'

'No. I've been following the trail I told you about, the one I think Mia left for me to follow, you know, like when she used to hide in the wardrobe as a kid.'

He was silent for a moment. When he spoke again, his

257

voice had an impatient edge to it. 'The dream-collage trail? And has it got you anywhere?'

'Well, we've just had a positive identification from a ticket-seller, but that was almost immediately followed by a negative identification from the owner of the guest house where he said she had been staying, so we're not sure—'

'"We"? You're still travelling with the artist, then?' He sounded disapproving.

'Yes, and he's fine, Ian. You'll like him.' Her voice was infected by the smile that ghosted across her face as she thought of Taos.

'Will I?' he muttered, before returning to the case in hand. 'So you've got conflicting statements from the people of Mallap—'

'Mamallapuram.'

'Right. And I take it you haven't been to view this body at Madurai morgue?'

'No, I . . . I felt I was needed more here.'

'So that's been left for me to do alone, has it?' he demanded. 'My first task when I'm crushed by jetlag and have just arrived in a country about which I know sod all apart from the fact that it has swallowed up my daughter, is to go and view a strangled girl who might be Mia?'

'I'm so sorry, Ian,' she said sincerely. 'I know it's a terrible thing to have to do. I had to do the same when I first got here, you know. But I'm certain it's not her.'

He sighed heavily. Both of them, Alida was sure, were imagining the girl laid out under the sheet, ugly marks encircling her throat. Whose face did she have? 'You'd better give me a contact number, then,' he said tiredly. 'I'll view it – her – this morning if I can, and then I'll phone you to . . . let you know.'

'All right, Ian,' said Alida sympathetically. 'Although I'm going off now to look at this place Mia might be lodging at, Mandipur Hill. I don't know how you can call me there, as there's no direct phone line.' She stopped and thought for a moment.

'Hasn't the artist guy got a mobile?'

'Taos? I'm not sure, I've never seen him with one. Hold on.' Through the glass partition, Alida could see Taos swinging his booth open, his wallet in his hand. She opened her own door. 'Taos? Do you have a mobile number I could give Ian? He's going to the morgue and wants to ring me afterwards.'

Taos hesitated, then nodded. 'I'll have to charge it up, but it should still work,' he said. 'I hardly ever use it.' He scribbled the number down for her. 'I'll see you back at the hotel,' he said, and left.

When Ian had taken down Taos's number he said, 'So you don't intend to return to London?'

'Not until I've done all I can to find my daughter,' she said firmly, anticipating strong resistance.

'I can't say I'm surprised,' was all he said. There was another pause between them.

'Good luck this morning,' Alida said eventually. Memories of the cool silence of the morgue and the dead face she had seen assailed her momentarily, making her feel dizzy. 'Be strong,' she murmured. 'Try not to faint.'

'Christ,' said Ian thickly. 'What if it's actually her?'

Alida's head started to buzz. 'It won't be, Ian,' she said, trying to sound sure, but her voice seemed very far away. 'Surely life wouldn't do that to us twice.'

'Once in a lifetime is already too much to bear,' he agreed, and paused for a moment. Alida closed her eyes briefly, nodding although he couldn't see her. 'I was thinking about Mia being pregnant,' he said then. 'Do you think—' He broke off.

'What?'

'Do you remember how when you were pregnant you used to get that look on your face as if you were listening to someone whispering a secret in your ear?'

259

'I remember you commenting on it, yes.'

'I used to watch you and try to follow your gaze; it was like trying to make out the exact spot where a rainbow meets the ground.' He paused. 'I've been trying to imagine Mia with that look on her face. She'd be beautiful.'

'Yes I suppose she would,' she agreed, and found herself smiling slightly as she pictured an awake-but-dreaming Mia.

'Well,' Ian said simply. 'We'll talk later.'

'Good luck,' she said again, and felt a rush of sympathy for him.

'You too, 'Lida.'

Chapter Thirty-Seven

Friday, 30 May 2008

I am writing a memory about hiding in the wardrobe and it makes me cry, big, heaving sobs that hurt like water pushing into lungs, burning me so that I drop my pen and double up on the floor. It was the time she didn't find me. When Dad got me out I was a mess, and at first all she did was look at me from those unlit holes that used to be her eyes. Writing the memory makes me scream and burn, hot metal dripping down my throat, the smell of dandelions making me die inside, the taste of ashes smothering me again. She should have found me, it would have made everything better. And suddenly I see myself as I am now, bulky, unnimble, crouching down on the floor of my hotel room in Varkala, feeling just as hurt as I did almost thirteen years ago, wanting to squeeze myself into a small space and tolerate the agony of waiting in order to experience the joy of being found and forgiven.

The idea comes to me in a great yellow-fringed gasp. I'll perform a vanishing act, a call for action just like old times. Actions speak louder than words; if she comes, if she follows me across the world and doesn't stop until she finds me, it must be love. The plan cobbles itself together in the space of seconds, but so far it is just a fantasy, another flimsy dream of regaining my place in her life.

Thursday, 10 July 2008

I'm in Madurai, at Hotel Guru, which is tall and filled with incense which tastes like burned flowers on my tongue. I've collaged my most major lucid dreams now, with Taos's artistic advice helping me out now and then. At first, I did it just for me, but as the plan grew, I realised I was doing it for her, too. My one chance to speak to my mother in images! My one chance to speak to my mother, full stop.

The plan has started to take shape: I'll put postcards on the collages, big arrows pointing to my hiding place. I'll leave one of the collages in my room, the one that asks whether or not she can forgive me. I'll drop a hint to Taos that I'd like to show these images to my mother one day so that if she's interested enough to ask around, she'll find the others. I'll leave her loose postcards too, in my travel bag, just to reinforce those particular places in India. In case that's not enough, in case she doesn't see the trail in the images, I'll leave the name and address of the guest house in Varkala between the pages of a book to lead her directly to Five-toes, with whom I have talked about many different things, including my longing to go to Hampi.

Leaving clues:

I'll stand in front of flower-sellers, temple priests, shoe-guards, imprinting my face, my will, my personality on them, like trying to convince a character in a lucid dream that he or she or they or we or I will remember this when we wake up.

Time limit:

This time I won't wait until I die inside and soil myself and am eventually found by someone else. I'll lay the trail as soon as I leave Madurai (which will happen very soon) and when it's done I'll give her ten days, but not an hour more. Ten days, strong clues, pieces of myself to ponder. Eye-openers so that when we next meet, it will be eye to eye, not eye to eyelid. And if she doesn't come, I will move on, trail-less.

Practicalities:

I'll leave my passport so she knows I'm still in India, so reducing the search from one person in six and a half billion to one person in just over a billion. I'll pack a small rucksack with a change of clothes and the cash I'd normally use to pay the hotel bill, and leave town by bus. I'll go to Bangalore and imprint myself on the man who takes charge of visitors' shoes at the Bull Temple. I'll talk to him animatedly about where I am heading, ask him about his family. I'll do the same with several publicly placed individuals in Hampi and Mamallapuram.

Of course, this means I can't tell anyone – Dad, Grandma, my friends – where I am. And that's not good; I don't want to make people worry about me. This is the thing I hesitate over the most. The idea of them feeling scared for me makes my skin go rubbery. But I need my mother back, and this is the only way I can see of pulling her back to me so that we can step over the drowned baby memories and the guilt and the blame and start again. I'll make it up to everyone afterwards. This is the only way.

Saturday, 19 July 2008

I am sitting in front of one of India's most perfect sculptures of an elephant. Life-sized, she gleams in the sunshine and I can clearly trace the lines of love in the curve of her rump, the smile fanning from her eyes. The sculptor lived and breathed elephants as he worked, he understood their skeletal and muscular workings, he read their thoughts. This is stability of form, and as I look I realise something shocking but undeniably true: Kizzy, I have more memories of you as a dream elephant than as a person. You have always been a guilty memory or a love-charged lucid dream image, but for years you've been more dream than reality for me. The baby inside me is more dream than reality, too, but little by little, day by day, she is solidifying into a physical reality. I am starting to wonder what it will be like to hold her for the very first time. Will she smell faintly of strawberries?

263

A beggar with one and a half legs is staring at me from bottomless eyes. He looks as if he would like to ask me a question, or at least peer over my shoulder to see what I am writing. I can't stop, though. All this writing about the past is helping me to see more clearly. I can see the little girl I was, and I can see you, Kizzy. I can see the bumble bee, zooming through our garden on a warm evening, accidentally entering a bathroom window and leaving death in its wake. The droning whir of those wings made me forget myself to the point where I let you wink out of existence just inches from me.

You were sitting so solidly, Kizzy. What happened? Did you tip your little head back to follow the arc of the bee's flight and fall backwards?

Alida has always blamed me for not noticing, not helping you. Blamed me, resented me, pushed me out because of it. Loved me less, way, way less. So that my skin grew thin trying to absorb more love and I took to carrying a phial of vanilla essence around with me because it's the only way I can feel her mother love, even faintly. Sometimes I think it even crossed her mind that I pushed you under on purpose, that I'm guilty of fratricide, and when I think that it feels as if molten lava is forming behind my eyeballs.

It has to stop.

The trail is fail-safe because once Alida leaves Varkala, if she doesn't find the people in the know at one site, she will find them at another. All of them point directly to me. Over the past week, for better or for worse the trail has been laid. The emptiness inside my room at Hotel Guru will have long since been discovered and acted upon, a call placed to my mother, whose contact details are inside the back cover of my passport. It's up to her now whether she follows the trail or not.

Tomorrow I go into hiding and the ten days begin.

She has until Tuesday, 29 July to find me.

Chapter Thirty-Eight

The car trembled to life with alarming jerks and Alida waited a while for the engine to run more smoothly before she manoeuvred them out on to the street. The seatbelt rubbed uncomfortably against her bruised right shoulder and her neck was still stiff but she had insisted on driving.

'If I avoid it, I might develop a complex about driving in the future,' she explained. She was half expecting a flippant remark from Taos about how it might be safer for other road users if she did develop a driving complex, but he seemed distracted and simply nodded as he climbed into the passenger seat with the directions in his hand. When they were out of Mamallapuram, he spoke.

'Will you meet up with Ian?'

'I don't know. Probably, yes.' She screwed her eyes up against the brightness of the sun bouncing off the tarmac.

'I guess you won't want me hanging around when that happens.'

She glanced over at him in surprise. 'Why do you guess that? Taos, if we don't find Mia in the next few days, I'm going to carry on looking, you know.' She flexed her hands on the steering wheel. 'I'm not going to let Ian change things. No matter what, I'm going to keep looking for Mia in my own way. And if you want to keep travelling around with me, I'd love that.'

He relaxed visibly. 'I have no plans,' he said. 'I'm still

in the process of reinventing my life. Anything could happen.' He smiled at her, his big, beautiful smile which made his eyes look greener, the skin at their corners splitting into laughter lines. Alida glanced over at him and kept her eyes on his face for a moment, distracted by the power of his smile, but as soon as she returned her gaze to the road, she grew sombre.

'But you know, nothing is clear,' she said, pushing her hair out of her face with one hand and grimacing through the windscreen. 'It's the thirty-first of July, she's been missing for twenty days, and I can't see any more how this trail might finish, whether my hunch was right and Mia is waiting for me somewhere, or whether' – she shuddered – 'or whether Ian will find her in Madurai morgue.' She overtook a bicycle with a whole family clinging to it before continuing, her throat tight with emotion. 'I can't imagine what my life will be like if Mia is dead, you see. If she's dead, how will I go on?'

Taos turned around in his seat to face her. 'Don't talk like that,' he said roughly. 'You know you'll be able to carry on; you've done it before.'

'But that's just it, Taos,' she cried. 'I *cannot* do it again.' She bit down on the insides of her cheeks, struggling to calm down and focus on the road. 'The worst thing is, I know that I've wronged her in the past, that I blamed her for Kizzy's death even though it was my own stupid fault for leaving a baby unattended by an adult in a full bathtub. I understand now just how much I need to say to Mia to make things even remotely OK between us, but if she's dead, then I'll never be able to tell her.' Her face crumpled and she started to cry, her hands gripping the steering wheel tightly.

Taos laid his hand on her knee. 'Don't cry,' he said. 'You'll find her.' He squinted at the splattered bodies of flies and beetles which were increasingly appearing on the windscreen as they headed west. 'Maybe even if she isn't

266

alive any more, she'll somehow know that you've forgiven her?'

Alida wiped her eyes with a derisive snort, the comment snapping her out of her sadness. 'No,' she said. 'I don't buy that. If she's dead, it's too late. How can I explain myself to a corpse?' She glanced at Taos and saw from his face that he agreed with her.

'I just don't like to hear you talk that way,' he said, rubbing at his forehead. 'You told me you weren't the type to commit suicide.'

She glanced at him in shock. 'And I'm *not* the suicide type,' she insisted. 'All I'm saying is that it'll be hard – almost impossibly hard – to carry on if Mia's gone too.'

'You'll find her,' said Taos again. He looked weary and troubled. Alida stretched out her hand and found his for a brief moment. They relapsed into silence. The car was absorbing the sunshine like a solar panel and beaming heat at them from the seats and windows, and the dashboard was boiling to the touch. The directions to Mandipur Hill were clear but the route grew complicated towards the end. Once they had left the main road, they had to concentrate fully on navigation for the final few miles, as they found themselves on a network of mud tracks which passed through tiered rice fields cut into the hills.

'Past the third pigsty on the left,' Taos pretended to read from the list of directions.

'It is a bit like that, isn't it?' she agreed as the car jolted along, wheezing exhaust fumes.

Five minutes later, they spotted Sunshine General Stores and were at the foot of Mandipur Hill. Alida pulled into a stony yard beside the tiny store and they got out and stood looking at the hill. It resembled a series of lumps of clay that had fallen one on top of the other; it listed curiously to the right and seemed slightly top-heavy. A footpath wriggled up it through thick foliage, and at the top the sand-coloured roof of a building could be seen.

'It must have a sort of crater at the top of it,' observed

Taos, 'if all we can see of that building is its roof. What an odd-shaped hill.'

'Taos,' said Alida as she stared at the building. 'I'd like to go up there alone.'

'Are you sure?' he looked at her with a hint of anxiety.

Alida didn't take her eyes off the building. 'I'm sure.'

'OK, but if she's not there, come straight back down, won't you?'

Something in his tone made her glance at him sharply. 'You're not seriously worried that I might do something foolish, are you?'

'Well, from the way you were talking in the car...' He sighed. 'I just don't want you to be up there all alone in despair.'

She gave him a small, brave smile, her eyes flickering over his face. 'I promise I'll come back down,' she said, and she stood on tiptoe and kissed him. Taos wound his arms around her and as the kiss deepened they swayed together. For a moment Alida didn't want to go anywhere without him, couldn't imagine going anywhere without him. Taos tasted of sunshine, lemon grass and the banana cake they had shared before they got in the car. He was strong and alive and he understood her. When they stopped kissing, she hugged him to her, pressing her face into his neck. Then she remembered Ian's visit to the morgue.

'Is your phone on?' she asked him.

Taos nodded. 'Yes. God knows if we'll get a signal out here, though.' He pulled it out of his pocket and checked it. 'Oh, there is one. Fairly faint, though. Do you want to take it with you in case Ian calls?'

'No.' Alida felt panicked at the very thought. Her action and Ian's action seemed to be from two different worlds; she couldn't allow one to intrude upon the other. 'I want to check out the hill before he telephones,' she said. 'You keep it with you. I'm going up there now.' They disengaged themselves from each other and Alida smoothed the pink sarong she was wearing over her hips with damp palms.

'I'll be here,' Taos said.

'And I'll be back soon.' Alida crossed the road and made her way to the beginning of the path. As soon as she began to walk, she realised that reaching the top would take longer than she had thought. Although she wanted to rush and scramble and leap, she paced herself, concentrating on not slipping on the jutting stones. When she had been climbing for ten minutes, she heard the electronic shrill of a telephone. It could only be Taos's mobile; there was nobody else in sight. Alida stopped in panic. It rang three times, then there was silence. Taos must have answered it. She couldn't turn around. Tears blinded her.

'I can't,' she said aloud. 'I can't turn back now.'

Slowly, she continued to walk, her eyes and heart straining forwards. Her ears were straining back, though, listening out for a cry of despair, a desperate shout to signal Mia's death by strangulation. The wind was blowing into her face, blowing her tears out of the corners of her eyes; the sound would be flung back away from Taos. She continued to climb. If she had looked around, she would have seen Taos, his arms folded across his chest, the call over and done with, his eyes boring into the shape of her as she climbed up and away from him. He knew something that she didn't yet know, but she couldn't intuit whether that knowledge was dark or light. All her suspense could not make her turn around at this late stage. She had to see this action through.

The exertion of climbing in the heat was making Alida breathe heavily, and she was reminded again of that half-minute eighteen months ago in Hyde Park when she and Mia had stood together and seen the shape of their breath as it puffed out of them in pale clouds. These were the moments that counted in life, the moments that added up to a happy existence, precious shared minutes and half-minutes and seconds. Mia had talked about coloured breathing and the alive feeling it gave her. In this warm Indian air, Alida's breath was invisible, but she realised that she had never felt more alive. The world stood around her in detailed splendour, smells and colours and sensations rushing to touch her with fingers of juniper and ochre, while the sweat running loosely down her spine contrasted with the tight scratch of the grass on her toes and ankles. Raising her arm, Alida used the back of her wrist to wipe all traces of tears from her cheeks.

The top of the hill wasn't far now. Taos had been right; it dipped into a crater so that the roof of the building, although closer, was barely any more visible here than it had been from the bottom. She paused momentarily to catch her breath, hands on hips. If she looked back now, Taos would be an inch and a half tall; she could catch him between finger and thumb and blow him a kiss the size of his head. She didn't want to look back yet, though. After all, she would be looking back all the way down, watching his transformation from a distant figure with a pale oval for a face into a solid, lemon-grass-flavoured man to hold in her arms and share her happiness with – or her grief.

It could wait. Alida walked on.

Chapter Thirty-Nine

Monday, 28 July 2008
Am I crazy, how could she ever hope to find me all the way out here in the middle of nowhere, not even a village, just a hill in the middle of India? I finished laying the trail nine days ago and time is running out fast. Why didn't I lay an easier trail? Write on the back of those loose post-cards: 'Clue 1', 'Clue 2' ...?

Because I want to give her a way out, an excuse for not finding me. I don't want to have to hate her.

Even if I make her wait, I shouldn't make Dad wait any more. He's been a distracted, half-hearted father since he left and went to live with Maggie all those years ago, but he doesn't deserve to be made to worry. They might be starting to think something bad has happened to me by now. I'll phone him as soon as I leave this place so that he knows I'm safe, and I'll tell him I'm not coming home. I want to curl up in India, wrap it around me and the baby, let it cover us in anonymity.

I want to forget I have a mother.

Tuesday, 29 July 2008
It tastes as if a fruit fly just flew into my mouth and I acciden-tally crushed it between my teeth. Bitterness bordering on poison. I want to spit it out but there's nothing there. Why hasn't she come? I have been stretching my mind out to hers. I

have sat on my coral-coloured rug and visualised her approaching me. In my thoughts, I have shown her where I am. All I wanted was a sign from her. This elaborate treasure hunt, this call for action, this ridiculous dream that love might rise up and form a shimmering pink heart around the two of us, has got me nowhere. She is not able to love me and so I have to try to stop needing her love. Today is the tenth and final day.

I have become a time mathematician. I calculate hours and minutes. I estimate the moments when the clues were found. Hotel Guru would have discovered my absence after one day, or two, or three. Four at the very most. I work out the dates, tapping my forefinger across the blank spaces of my diary. I reshuffle the order in which the clues might have been discovered, and I recalculate. I left the main collage in my room, so she would definitely have seen it – the one with the Five Rathas postcard that very nearly shows exactly where I am, echoed as it is by the stone elephant trinket with Kizzy's eyes. If she knows me, she'll understand that the collages and the loose postcards are clues, they're my arrows, my trail. Surely, if her mind was even the tiniest bit open to me, she would realise that? But no matter how often I add and subtract elements of chance and factors contributing to delay, I arrive at the same conclusion: she should have already shown up here.

If she's looking for me at all.

So she can't be looking for me, which means... the game is over.

I just can't gather the strength to leave yet. Technically speaking, she has until midnight tonight.

Thursday, 31 July 2008

For the past eleven days, I have waited hermitlike in this room which feels like a pink mollusc shell, with its soft light and draperies. Today is the morning of the twelfth day. I've already waited beyond the generous ten-day mark. I could waste my whole life like this, adding one day

272

on to the next, giving her chance after chance. One day I'll write: 'Twelve years have passed since I laid the trail.' I could wait my whole life for her forgiveness, not knowing if it will ever come. When does enough truly and finally become enough? When I was younger, I used to hold my breath until I lost consciousness. I called it 'beating death'. I thought of it as 'breathing in colour', although in fact I wasn't breathing at all. I have been holding my breath, metaphorically speaking, ever since Kizzy died. I'm holding my breath now, waiting for Alida to come and show me that everything's finally going to be all right.

I sit up straight-backed and cross-legged on my bed. My eyes rest on my sarong, which has swirls of purple running through it like blueberry ice cream. I suck a deep breath into my lungs. It waits there in a fine pink mist.

Forty-five seconds or so pass.

My head feels warm. The colour of my breath slowly deepens to a velvet ruby. I pinch my nose between finger and thumb and the pressure mounts.

The feeling's starting – that feeling of double-aliveness, double-brightness, endless possibilities.

My breath is fluttering black around the edges like singed paper and it's beautiful.

But this can't be good for the baby so I release my nostrils and breathe out and it's like glass-blowing because the form of my breath on the air holds wobbly-firm and the colour stays right there in front of my face, dark red on the exhale turning to sharp green on the inhale. I'm breathing in colour. As I breathe out a two-tone marmalade orange, I realise that life is filled with endless moments of choice.

Gradually, the colours fade, and my breath becomes calm and invisible.

I used to hold my breath while I waited for life to change. I never knew when to let go, when to breathe out all that blackening air so that a new colour could appear, shining and flexible with possibilities.

The five-year-old me always knew she would find me. I used to lie there and imagine her flying towards me on a magic carpet, sweeping up my arrows with one long bright arm as she went, connected to me by a kind of unstoppable magic, by love. She knew what I was thinking and feeling, knew how to enter my bad dream and pull me from it.

But I'm not five any more.

If this was a lucid dream that I could shape with my own desires, she would be puffing and panting up the hill right now and I would fly down into her arms and lose myself in the joy and the wonder of seeing her.

But it isn't a lucid dream.

I'm here, now, in waking reality: Mia Salter with the baby in my womb beginning its slow press out into the future but my head and my heart twisting back and back to the past, twisting so hard that soon my heart will strangle its own beating and my head will snap off. Do I really believe that her forgiveness is the only thing that can release me from this contortion so that I can walk on?

The deepest, most silent flutter in my centre reminds me. I am an almost-mother.

With a sudden, rash leap, I snatch my bag from the nail on the wall and start to fill it with my possessions, scooping everything into its wide throat like fish being propelled into a whale's belly.

I can't afford to wait any longer.

Chapter Forty

Alida reached the top of the hill and saw that the dip was filled with trees and a lone, sprawling building with many windows. She stood looking at it while her breath calmed in her chest. Her sarong was sticking to the backs of her legs, and her face was damp with perspiration. Either Mia is here, she thought, or she's lying dead in the morgue under Ian's gaze. For a moment, she felt that she couldn't go on. She should have brought Taos with her. She couldn't do this alone. Please, life, she prayed, and her head seemed to float on her neck. Please, give me my daughter. In spite of her earlier resolution not to look back, her body turned and her eyes travelled down the bumpy green hill. There, standing at its base, was not Taos but the disc-headed man, his body wobbling in the heat like a mirage. Alida raised a hand and waved at him, and he waved back. His disc shone serenely; he was beautiful, willing her onwards. A smile traced Alida's lips as she turned from him and walked down the slope towards the building.

Signs of life fluttered from the windows in the form of towels and items of clothing. A door opened and a Chinese girl with dreadlocks sauntered out barefoot. Alida quickened her step, drawing Mia's photograph from her bag. She showed it to the girl, who shook her head doubtfully and talked in what Alida thought could be Mandarin.

I wish, she thought fleetingly, that I spoke all the

languages of this world. She looked into the girl's face, at the crease which appeared across the bridge of her nose as she stared at the picture, and she waited to be made to understand that Mia had never set foot in this place, that she was irreversibly, irrevocably gone. But then the girl shrugged and pointed a delicate hand up towards the back of the building, somewhere up there, at the top. And shrugged again, and smiled prettily, and sauntered on. Alida pushed the photograph back into her bag, entered the door the girl had come out of, and picked her way up some rickety stairs, her ears and eyes straining for any sign of Mia. All she could hear was a booming silence which rolled around her head, making her dizzy. If she's not here, if she's not here, she thought, but the sentence dropped away into nothingness.

At the very top of the steps was a door. It was ever so slightly ajar.

Alida hesitated, and then pushed it open.

Chapter Forty

Mia

The door opens and the world falls silent.

There's a pinprick of time, hot on my skin, where I understand that this woman with disaster-dark eyes, wearing my sarong, is my mother, now and always, and that she has come for me. The world turns to warm vanilla custard and I fling my arms wide and she embraces me with great force, as if she's agreeing with life, and now she is saying, 'Thank you,' through the salt thickness of tears which fall like stars and she repeats the words over and over so that they take on a vibrant orange sheen which expands in the air around us.

Author Note

The UK Synaesthesia Association describes synaesthesia as a "union of the senses". This is not an illness, but a sensory condition in which textures might be tasted on the tongue, or musical notes experienced as colours. In synaesthesia, the five senses, which most people experience as separate, are mingled in almost any combination, so that one sensation involuntarily conjures up others. Estimates as to how many people have synaesthesia vary. Leading synaesthesia researcher Dr Richard Cytowic has claimed that one in 25,000 people have the condition, but that some type of synaesthetic experience occurs in as many as one in twenty-three people.

I'm not a synaesthete, but certain shades of purple or yellow can stop me in my tracks, filling my mind completely with their richness, and I've always dreamed in an array of colours so dazzling that they seem to reach out and touch me. The idea of writing about a character with synaesthesia came to me when I had a lucid dream in which I experienced a fistful of sand as having an orange texture and taste: on a strong sensory level, the sand was orange before I'd even looked at it. This made me consider the different ways in which the world is perceived through the senses – some people seem to see brighter colours, while others have a sharper sense of smell. I started to ask myself questions: To what extent might perceptual differences transform an individual's experience of the world? And just how different might the world then be?

When I came across Cytowic's online articles on synaesthesia, I knew this would be a wonderful condition to work with. Synaesthesia blends perfectly with the imaginative world of writing; it forced me to experiment with my own sense perceptions and the Mia narratives became the most fun parts of the book to write. I would close my eyes and wait for a mingled sense perception to emerge, becoming Mia for that short space of time, entering her remarkable perceptual world as much as I was able to. I do hope that synaesthetes reading this book will be able to forgive any blunders I may have made in rendering the condition: in addition to careful research, I relied on my imaginative interpretation of the phenomenon. Synaesthesia can be very mild to very strong – some people barely notice it until the chance comment of another person makes them realise that not everyone has a coloured alphabet, for example. Mia's synaesthesia needed to be very strong, and this is how it is portrayed in the novel. I also set no limits on what could trigger the synaesthetic response: some synaesthetes predominantly experience coloured hearing, while shape-tasting is more rare. In common with some synaesthetes, Mia experiences any combination of sensory fusion.

Synaesthetes have widely differing perceptions, and it seemed to me as I read up on this that almost anything goes: the colour green could be experienced by one synaesthete as having a lemon sherbet taste, while in another, it might produce a feeling like raindrops hitting the skin. As a writer, this gave me a lovely freedom to explore what my own synaesthesia might be like, if I had the condition myself. As a non-synaesthete, writing from the point of view of a synaesthete is like writing poetry: the senses extend out in all directions as an attempt is made to grasp the reality of what is experienced.

In many ways, synaesthesia seems to provide a more vivid experience of the world, and my research tells me that most synaesthetes wouldn't wish to be without it. For those interested in learning more about this fascinating condition, I recommend Dr Richard Cytowic's *The Man Who Tasted Shapes*, and Patricia Lynne Duffy's *Blue Cats and Chartreuse Kittens*, as well as the UK Synaesthesia Association's website for further information: www.uksynaesthesia.com